DARK FLAME

Dark Flame: The Flame Series - Book 3

By Caris Roane

Formatting and cover by Bella Media Management.

ISBN-13: 978-1530231553

DARK FLAME

The Flame Series - Book 3

Caris Roane

Dear Reader,

Welcome to the third installment of the Flame Series called DARK FLAME!

Committed to the rule of law, Border Patrol Officer Robert Brannick falls hard for a beautiful fae woman who illegally seduces him in his dreams…

Brannick works with Juliet Tunney to help several human women escape the nightmare of Five Bridges. But something isn't right. Juliet acts as though she knows him really well, yet he's only met her once. Unless…the dreams he's been having about her aren't dreams at all. When a sensual dream surfaces in vivid images and sounds, he knows something's up with the beautiful fae woman from Revel Territory. And if what he suspects is true, Juliet has a lot to answer for.

Juliet fell hard for Brannick the night she first signed on to help out with his rescue operation. She even violated a serious Revel Territory law by invading his dreams. What she hadn't expected was how readily he took her up on her illegal dreamgliding offer. With her special fae abilities, she's been his secret lover for five months. Sworn to withhold the nature of their dream-relationship from Brannick's conscious mind, she faces the hard truth that she's in danger of losing him forever because she broke the law. Once the truth surfaces, will Brannick ever be able to forgive her?

I hope you're enjoying the Flame Series. I've had a wonderful time developing a world inspired by my love for bridges and of course, hunky warrior vampire types!

Enjoy!

Caris Roane

PS: For the latest releases and coolest contests, be sure to sign up for my newsletter!!! http://www.carisroane.com/contact-2/

CHAPTER ONE

Robert Brannick stared at Juliet, every suspicion lit on fire. She'd been the star of a recent dream and the hot-as-hell images kept streaming through his head like a porn movie he couldn't shut off.

Yet something about the dream wasn't right.

He just didn't know why.

He was in the garage of a private homeowner, moving boxes away from a secret tunnel entrance he'd built to smuggle abused human females out of Five Bridges. Tonight, Juliet had driven the van containing four of them, each rescued from Revel Territory sex clubs. With the vehicle in the garage and the door shut, the neighbors wouldn't be able to see what they were up to.

He steadily shifted boxes and plastic tubs out of the way.

Another image flashed.

Juliet's long curly hair splayed out on his red sheets.

Lips parted.

His body moving over hers, connected.

Her cries filled his bedroom.

He could see each freckle on her creamy skin and her hair smelled like strawberries.

So real, *like more than a dream.*

Doubt nagged at him about what had actually happened between them, as in something very fae and highly illegal.

He glanced at Juliet again, the star of his cockfest and a beautiful *alter* fae woman. He couldn't seem to move as he watched her.

She stood next to the van and wore a loose, light green dress, a gauzy thing that draped her curves. He'd seen those curves in his dream, beautiful, lush, full. His hands and mouth had been all over her. Would she look the same as what he'd pictured beneath the dress?

She glanced at him and turned her hand in question, probably because he was staring at her. She had large, dark blue eyes, even delicate features and all those faint freckles that in the dream he'd kissed over and over.

She was about to open the door, but when he remained silent and staring, she let go of the latch and turned in his direction.

"Everything okay?" Her voice had a soft, melodious sound. She was a feminine kind of woman, not like the vampire females he banged noisily in Crescent Territory. But then Juliet was an *alter* fae who lived in Revel, not vampire at all. In many ways, she was his opposite.

He tore his gaze away from her, resisting the urge to clear his throat, then put his feet in motion. He called out, "Everything's fine."

But he knew in his gut it wasn't. As soon as they got the women to safety, he'd have to confront her about what he suspected was going on.

He heard the van door slide open, then Juliet as she spoke quietly to the women inside. "I need all of you to refrain from talking. We're on a residential street and don't want to alert anyone in the area of our presence here. But please don't worry. You're in good hands and you'll be back in the human part of Phoenix within the hour.

"We work with excellent people as dedicated as we are to ending this nightmare in Revel Territory. And that man over there? Moving the boxes? That's Officer Brannick of the Crescent Territory Border Patrol. He's the one who's set up this whole operation."

Brannick scowled as he shifted a dusty, rolled up carpet out of the way. He didn't like to hear that kind of praise, though he understood Juliet's motivation. The women had been badly used by men for a long time. They would need to know he was someone they could trust.

He forced himself to focus on the task at hand and set the box on the growing pile off to the side. The owners of the house had agreed to let him run a tunnel up to their garage so that he could get abducted women out of Five Bridges. It was a dangerous set-up for everyone involved.

Brannick took great care to keep his operation on the down low. For that reason, he hadn't used this particular tunnel in two months, a policy that helped keep suspicious neighbors from reporting unusual activity.

The three cartels that ruled Five Bridges paid a lot of money for tips leading to the discovery of exactly this kind of covert operation.

The upper part of the door leading down to the underground tunnel was half visible now. He needed to let the sex dream go and pick up the pace. He shifted a couple more dusty bags and plastic tubs.

Juliet wasn't even supposed to be driving the van tonight. That was Mary's job. Juliet coordinated with a team of Revel Border Patrol officers who worked their off-hours to rescue abducted humans, mostly female. The women were used in the sex trade in Revel Territory while pumped full of the dark flame drug. Each bore the teal flame markings on their hands, necks and faces. Drug addiction was hard to disguise in Five Bridges.

So where was Mary? For as long as he'd worked with her, she'd never missed a run.

As Juliet continued to talk to the women, answering their hushed questions, he glanced at her again. She wore her long, curly hair pinned up but with a lot of curls hanging free. She looked messy in an artsy way, but then she didn't. She looked fresh and alive. Beautiful.

He'd played with those curls in his dream.

Shit, that dream again and how the woman would make, intense cries of passion…

Once more, he forced himself to look away and to keep shifting the boxes. He pulled a heavy one, but set it off to the side. It should be closer to the bottom. He didn't want the stack to fall over after they were gone. The door needed to be kept hidden at all costs.

He'd met Juliet five months ago, having arranged to look her over at the White Flame club in Elegance, to see if she might be a good fit for his operation. She'd come highly recommended by one of his extraction team, a hard-core Revel Border Patrol officer by the name of Keelen.

Maybe it was the vampire in him, or maybe the human part that had always been able to read people, but he'd trusted Juliet right away. He'd liked the way she held his gaze, spoke in a clear direct if soft manner, and set her chin when he asked about her commitment.

He'd liked her so much in fact that apparently he'd made her the star of his dreams.

The truth was, he hadn't seen Juliet since his meeting with her at the club. He'd spoken with her several times on the phone and he'd checked her out on the net. She was an up-and-coming civic leader in Revel Territory as an apprentice to Agnes Munroe, who served on the Revel Board of Sages.

Mary was the one who drove the van to the exit-point houses each week. But she hadn't shown up and when questioned, Juliet had said she didn't know why.

Brannick had been shocked as hell when Juliet had pulled into the garage. He was profoundly attracted to the fae woman, something that didn't make him happy at all. The moment he'd realized she was in the van and not Mary, his jaw had dropped and that dream had started playing over and over in his head.

The weird part, however, was that when she'd crossed the garage floor to greet him and shake his hand, he'd felt as though he was looking at a really good friend. If he believed in past lives, he'd say they'd known each other in one.

Or maybe, as he suspected, something else had been going on, something a powerful fae could have done with him.

Or to him.

Despite his drive toward the woman, he kept moving boxes. But that didn't keep him from looking in her direction about every third trip.

Right now, one of the women wept. She sat in the seat closest to the open door and Juliet was comforting her. The human woman had bruises on her face and up and down her bare arms. She was missing a couple of teeth and of course had the teal colored flames on her cheeks.

Juliet went to the front seat of the van and returned with a small box of tissues. She handed the woman one, who in turn blew her nose. Blood came out.

He watched Juliet rubbing the woman's shoulder as she spoke to her in a low voice. She kept handing her tissues and taking away the bloody ones. The woman leaned her head back and closed her eyes, her fingers pinched over the bridge.

There were only four women in the van, against the hundreds, maybe even thousands, who needed his help. He felt grim about the whole thing, about how impossible the odds were against any kind of success, long-term or not. As many humans as he rescued, more were abducted from the Southwest to fill the void.

He wouldn't give up though, despite the numbers. He reminded himself of something he'd heard recently, an old quote from a Chinese philosopher, 'The journey of a thousand miles begins with one step.' And this journey was at least a thousand miles, maybe more like ten thousand.

He frowned. He swore he'd heard the saying spoken to him in the past few days, but he couldn't recall who'd said it? He'd begun to wonder if living in Five Bridges for thirteen years as an *alter* vampire had started affecting his mind.

But as he turned back to his task, rage boiled all over again at the state of the world he lived in. Years ago, Five Bridges had devolved into a ghetto because of the drug and human trafficking that had made a cesspool of the place.

Sometimes his hatred of the flame drugs and their companion *alter* serums got to him. Thirteen years ago his family had been wiped out in one trip to the supermarket. He'd taken his family north from Phoenix to their cabin in Flagstaff to escape the summer heat. His wife had gone to the store for groceries and among the provisions was a six pack of corrupt soda.

He'd heard of this kind of thing happening, but he felt sure his family was safe in Flagstaff. Most of the *alter* serum crimes occurred in the Phoenix area, not in the more remote satellite towns of Arizona.

But over the past thirty years, Phoenix had become an increasingly difficult place to live as had all the major cities of the U.S. A large portion of north Phoenix had become the province of Five Bridges where each of the five *alter* species had been segregated in order to protect the human population.

The U.S. had its own border patrol guarding the entrance and exit points of the five main bridges leading into his world. Human visitors could come and go at their own risk, but only a few *alter* species could leave and then only on official business. Most of the workers at the Tribunal, the main governing body for Five Bridges, had passports that allowed them to travel to the human part of Phoenix on limited business. Everyone else had to stay put or risk on-the-spot execution in the human part of the world.

Unfortunately, the full panorama of the flame drugs had become a highly popular recreational substance. And the three powerful cartels worked hard to keep the supply moving. Humans came into Five Bridges every night by the hundreds, and on the weekends by the thousands, to score drugs and to take advantage of the dozens of sex clubs scattered throughout all five territories.

The world he lived in had become a freak show of drugs and a nightmare of trafficked women who got used up in the clubs. Very few escaped. Most died at the hands of their captors.

He glanced back at the van. The women had emerged and Juliet stood with her arm supporting the one with the bruises and bloody nose. They were a quiet, broken bunch and would need years of therapy to recover.

Brannick shifted the last of the boxes away from the entrance to the tunnel. Moving close to the door, he knocked quietly three times, until he heard the answering response of one rap, a pause, then two rapid knocks. He changed the signal often to alert him to treachery. If he'd heard anything other than the correct order and frequency of knocks, he would have piled the women back in the van and taken off.

He glanced at Juliet and held up his hand to her. She understood and turned to the women, a finger to her lips. Silence fell; no one breathed.

The signal might have been correct, but he wasn't taking any chances.

He drew his Glock, standard issue for the Crescent Border Patrol, then pulled the door open.

Lily stood there. She was the dispatch operator at the station and smiled as she glanced down at the barrel of his gun. "Good evening, Officer Brannick. Good thing you don't have an itchy trigger finger."

Brannick relaxed and holstered his gun. He trusted Lily with his life.

The feisty woman had short, white-blond hair and gold-green eyes. She was tall at six feet and had one of the toughest jobs in Crescent Territory. She had to balance her dislike of half the officers who were on the take with the other half who tried to do some good in Five Bridges.

Their chief, Easton, was as corrupt as they came. He'd been sleeping with the cartels for a long time. Yet somehow, Lily combined pragmatism with a certain amount of stealth and made it all work.

He drew in a deep breath and smiled in return. "How you doin', Lily? Are we secure below?"

"We are. We have a half-dozen female support staff in place ready to walk the women out. Our contacts are waiting at the other end with an emergency vehicle to transport them to the hospital in Deer Valley." Lily glanced at the group and frowned. "They're pretty beat up. Did they come from one of Roche's establishments?"

"Yep."

"He's a real bastard, that one."

"He's at least that."

Neal Roche ran one of the biggest sex and drug trades in Revel. He was hooked up tight with the cartels and was rumored to have a large, underground manufacturing set-up that produced dark flame. The powerful drug supposedly helped some of the more gifted fae in his employ to engage in an intoxicating form of sex during dreamgliding, something peculiar to Revel Territory

Roche also had a reputation for dropping off female corpses at the Graveyard every single night.

Brannick gestured for the women to come forward. They moved slowly, shuffling and in pain, a sight that made him wince.

He moved himself to the far side of the garage as the women drew close. They'd been handled so badly by men that he didn't want to add to their current distress. He waited as Juliet and Lily ushered them through the door, down the stairs and into the tunnel.

Juliet returned a few minutes later. She appeared at the threshold, her eyes brimming with tears. She crossed into the garage, then turned and closed the door firmly behind her.

He drew close and kept his voice low. "Hey, what's wrong?"

She shook her head and pressed the crook of her finger beneath each eye. "Nothing. I'm so happy for them and for a stupid moment, I felt sorry for myself."

"What? Why?"

She turned to face him more fully. "Honestly, once I saw the tunnel, all I wanted to do was keep walking. They'll be free, but I won't. I'm an *alter* fae. I'll never be free again."

A feeling of familiarity swamped him once more, as though they always talked like this, like she'd said similar things to him before. Yet he'd only met her once at the club.

The sound of a vehicle on the street drew his attention away from her. He turned to listen. The car stopped outside the house.

He glanced at Juliet. Her eyes were wide as she drew close. The tunnel house was owned by a vampire couple who wanted to help. They were both intelligent and wouldn't have arranged for any kind of delivery or service appointment at the same hour Brannick was working to get another group of humans into the tunnel.

His heart pounded in his chest. He could hear steps up the walk, a man's stride.

He followed the sounds, turning his body with each footstep. He drew his Glock, then extended his hearing. The doorbell rang and he listened hard. Carl, the owner, asked, "Can I help you?"

When he heard the stranger's voice, he cursed softly.

Juliet tapped his telepathy. *You recognize him, don't you?*

He glanced at her, surprised that she could communicate mind-to-mind. The woman had power.

He dipped his chin once. *He's corrupt. This isn't good.*

What's he saying? I can only hear a mumbling sound and you vampires have much sharper hearing than the rest of us.

He's asking about me. He's saying I told him I was headed over here. But Carl is playing it smart. He says he only met me once in a pool hall near some Chinese

Restaurant east of Rotten Row. He doesn't know why I'd say I was coming to his house. The officer is pressing him, but he's not getting anywhere, thank God.

He felt Juliet's hand on his arm. She was trembling.

He held her gaze. *Hold steady. We're still okay.*

She squeezed his arm. *I know.*

Our host is shutting the door. The officer is moving away.

The man's footsteps echoed all the way down the walk. A moment later, the vehicle roared to life and a few seconds later rumbled down the street.

"Oh, thank God." Juliet turned into him and as though he'd done it a thousand times, he surrounded her with both arms. She shook from head to foot. With his heart slamming around in his chest as well, he wasn't doing much better.

If things had gone south, he would have been forced to kill the man and the gunshots would have been reported. He was grateful it hadn't come to that.

Juliet pulled out of his arms. "Sorry, Brann. But that was a close one." She put a hand to her chest. "My heart is racing."

He stared at her. Wait a minute. Had she just called him 'Brann'? No one called him that. His wife had when they'd been married, but no one else and definitely no one in Five Bridges.

A sudden dizziness hit him hard. He stepped away from Juliet. He could barely keep himself upright and stumbled sideways.

He felt her hand on his shoulder. "Brann, what's wrong?"

There it was again. 'Brann.'

He squeezed his eyes shut. He couldn't think. He didn't know what was going on.

Then suddenly, the erotic dream from earlier exploded through his mind, only this time in full color, every sensual detail and smell and taste hitting him like a Tsunami. It hadn't been an ordinary dream after all.

Juliet was under him and he had his fangs buried in her neck, tasting blood that wasn't blood. The sounds of her moans pushed him on, drove him harder. He wanted her to come.

He'd said things to her, wicked things. Her hands moved over his back. 'Brann.'

She'd called him Brann in the dream.

A dream that was more than a dream.

Regaining his balance, he stared at her, his heart pounding in his chest all over again. The reality of what must have really happened struck him hard, like a hammer between the eyes.

"Juliet, what the fuck have you done to me?"

~ ~ ~

Juliet Tunney stared at Brannick for a long, difficult moment. Something had happened just now, but she didn't know what and she was afraid she'd say the wrong thing. So she remained silent, watching him carefully.

She could hardly breathe. She suspected it might have to do with their secret bedroom activities, but his dream-self had sworn her never to reveal the truth. The real-time Brannick wasn't supposed to know what they did together in her fae dreamglide.

Yet here they were, face-to-face, and it looked like he'd just remembered one or more of their shared dreamgliding experiences.

She decided the best course, given her gag order, was to pretend she didn't know what he was talking about. "I don't know what you mean, but you seem really upset. What's going on?"

He narrowed his green eyes. "I'm not sure, Juliet, but what I just saw flashing through my head in extraordinary detail makes me think it wasn't a dream, but something else. A dreamglide, in fact."

Juliet had feared this moment for a long time, when Brannick's subconscious mind would finally force the truth to the surface. However, it appeared he was only recalling one dream and not everything that had happened between them.

She shuddered just thinking about how Brannick would react once he knew the whole truth, especially how their affair had gotten started. She was guilty of breaking a law, a big one in both Revel Territory and Five Bridges. Once Brannick knew what she'd done, he could prosecute her.

She needed to buy herself some time.

She glanced at the closed tunnel door. "We need to get this job done, then get out of here."

Brannick glanced at the boxes then back to her. "You're right. But then we're going to talk."

"Of course." She'd have to stay calm and let him lead the conversation. She didn't need to tell him anything he couldn't remember.

He headed over to the scattered tubs, bags and boxes and started picking them up and moving them back into place.

She offered to help, but he said he'd prefer to arrange them according to weight and it would be faster without her assistance.

She didn't argue. If anything, she wanted distance from him right now.

She moved to the van. The sliding door was still open, so she reached inside and grabbed a bottle of water from the small cooler. Water would help. Staying hydrated in the desert, even for an *alter* fae, was important.

The van was sufficiently large and her ass just small enough that she could sit on a combination of the floor and the running board. Wearing a dress, she angled her knees away from Brannick.

She unscrewed the lid of her water bottle and took a sip, then repressed a heavy sigh. She'd been dreading this moment for months now and couldn't believe it had come. Although, she suspected it had happened because they were together physically for the first time since the dreamgliding sex had started up.

She'd been warned this could happen. Her sage teacher, Agnes, had told her all about dreamgliding, how it was done and how only fae of a certain level of power could engage in a dreamglide. Though it was also true that the dark flame drug could prompt dreamgliding even in humans.

She could kick herself for not having provided a secondary transport option for the women. Mary always drove which had prevented Juliet from ever seeing Brannick in real-time.

Up until tonight, Mary had been completely reliable. But life happened, especially in Five Bridges, and moving forward Juliet would engage a back-up driver.

She took her cell from the pocket of her dress and checked for a text from Mary, but nothing was there. So, where was she?

Juliet smiled. Mary was tall, blond and gorgeous and had been a model in her previous, human life. She always had men buzzing around her. Maybe one of them had finally caught her eye, and Mary had lost track of time.

The van would stay in the garage for at least a week, and Juliet would fly out with Brannick, just as Mary always did.

Juliet would have him take her to her canal home in Revel, using his vampire cloaking ability to shield them from any other species that might be out flying. It was an easy way to get home and at the same time avoid the requisite vehicle stops at either of the intervening main bridges and their security checkpoints.

As Brannick worked to stack up the boxes, Juliet wished the van faced a different direction so she didn't have to look at him. Like most of the male, border patrol officers, he had a body to die for. Watching him move around tore at every resolution she'd worked so hard to build over the past several months.

He wore a typical border patrol uniform of black leathers, a way-too-sexy tank top, and his Glock holstered on his belt, though he'd left off the short sword. The uniforms of Five Bridges were very different from the human part of Phoenix and enhanced the physiology of the *alter* species. The essential change in DNA added to the muscles and power of the men designed for law enforcement, a necessary component for any species grappling with drug-runners and killers every night.

Brannick was a gorgeous man and the mere thought of what they'd been doing in secret, had her trembling all over. She sipped some more water and tried to calm down, but she had it bad for the vampire. She wished it otherwise, but she'd gotten to know him over the five months they'd been seeing each other in the dream-world.

Five months ago, she'd offered to become part of Brannick's operation to rescue abducted human women out of the Revel sex clubs. The brief time she'd spent with him at the White Flame club while he interviewed her had been intoxicating.

She'd responded to him like a woman on a date and that alone had felt miraculous, besides being sexy as hell. She'd experienced a sudden powerful attraction to him the moment she laid eyes on him.

After she'd gone home, the solitary and very lonely nature of her existence had hit her hard.

So it was, in a moment of terrible weakness, she'd entered her fae-based dreamglide for the first time but with only one intention: To find Brannick.

She'd found him all right. All she'd done was picture him and whoosh, she was there, hovering her dreamglide above him while he lay asleep in bed.

She'd done a very bad thing when she'd penetrated his dreams and essentially hijacked him into her dreamglide without his permission. This boundary was considered sacred by both Revel Territory and Tribunal law.

Within the dreamglide, she'd kept him in a half-sleep state while she climbed into his bed and began seducing him. By the time she'd brought him to a dreamglide level of consciousness, he was fully aroused and she was on top of him.

She'd meant to explain the situation, especially to let him know he could send her packing if he wanted to. But he'd been shockingly ready to be with her and had taken her on a ride that to this day caused shivers and chills to chase all over her body.

The man knew his way around a woman.

Now she was here, uncertain what to tell real-time Brannick about everything they'd been doing for the past five months.

She tilted her water bottle back and let more of the liquid flow down her throat.

As she watched Brannick, she'd thought more than once that he would have made an exceptional subject. She'd been a photographer before the *alter* transformation and couldn't help but see Brannick as through a lens. And it wasn't just the perfection of his face and body, but something more, something Brannick exuded through the sheer strength of his personality. He was like staring at a massive and very beautiful wall of granite.

He wore his dark brown hair combed straight back and had the most beautiful green eyes, though they had a pinched look most of the time. She understood why, since she'd come to know him so well over the past few months. The man spent his nights trying to right the wrongs of his past. Guilt drove him relentlessly.

She'd screwed up, though, calling him 'Brann'. No wonder his conscious mind had started filling in the blanks.

It was a weird conundrum to face the man she'd been having sex with for the past several months and unable to tell him that's what they'd been doing. Or how it was done. Or even that he'd forbidden her not to say a word. Very bizarre.

But there was another reason why she didn't want Brann to consciously know the truth. She knew, with every cell of her body, that the moment she fessed up, he'd never come near her again. Brannick had demons that kept him locked up tight as a drum. He'd gone berserk when he became an *alter* vampire and lost his family to the *alter* serum.

She'd heard about his mania and how he'd become a one-man death squad, attacking anyone in the drug trade. He'd kept it up until the cartels had sent assassins to take out his parents and abduct his sister, Tracy. Only then had he stopped his vigilante killing spree.

Juliet had heard many versions of his sister's fate, but the one consistent element was that Brannick had been forced to watch while dark coven witches used her as a human sacrifice.

Juliet couldn't imagine how Brannick had survived both the loss of his wife and children, then the guilt because of the deaths of his remaining family.

She cut the man a lot of slack because of it.

She sighed. She really, really didn't want her time with Brannick to end. She wanted him in her dreamgliding bed until she was lying in the Tribunal's overburdened morgue, an inch away from cremation.

She released a heavy sigh.

"Feeling guilty?"

She'd been staring at the cement of the garage floor, lost in thought. Brannick now stood in front her having finished stacking the boxes.

Looking up at him, she shook her head. "I don't know what you mean." She'd play dumb as long as she could.

"You're dreamgliding me, aren't you?"

He didn't look nearly as upset as he had earlier, but she still wasn't going to tell him anything. "What got you all upset before?"

He planted his fists on his hips, his biceps flexing. His lips turned down. "So you're going to play it this way, dumb as shit?"

She sighed. "I'm under a strong obligation to keep my mouth shut."

His green eyes narrowed a little more. "I don't get it. Who has you under an obligation?"

"You do."

He snorted. "Oh, that's damn convenient." He turned away from her. She could see he wanted to let loose with a few obscenities. His lips were definitely mouthing the words.

Then he grew very still and frowned, though staring at nothing. "I remember that we talked and you asked me something. You asked me if I would finally give my permission, but I refused." He turned back to her. "Permission for what? Does this have to do with drugs?"

"No. Oh, God no." She waved a hand in the air. "No drugs, I promise you."

"Juliet … " His deep voice carried the exact tone he used in the dreamglide, affectionate and almost weightless. "Talk to me."

She rose slowly to her feet as another compressed sigh forced its way from her body. "I can't, Brann. You have to trust me in this."

"Can you at least tell me how long this has been going on?"

"You told me not to tell you anything," she said.

"As much as I can't imagine how some dreamlike part of me would insist on your silence, I'm giving my permission now, here, in real-time. So, how long have you been sexing me up in the dreamglide?"

It took her a moment to make the decision, but she finally decided she couldn't hold back. "Five months."

"Holy shit." He shook his head back and forth very slowly. His lips worked again, only this time she didn't think he was uttering obscenities. Maybe he was trying to frame the right words for what was going through his head right now.

He frowned even harder. "You want to know what I saw earlier? What came to me?"

She put her hands to her throat and smoothed her fingers down the length. She was trying to ease the knot that now felt like a noose. Given that every dreamglide she'd ever had with Brannick either began or ended with sex, she found it hard to breathe.

The Brannick in the dreamglide was all in, one-hundred-percent. He was an exceptional lover and an engaging companion. If Juliet had to guess, they'd probably spent as much time in conversation as they had tangled up in each other's arms.

But there was only one answer to give him in this situation. "Yes, I want to know. Please tell me what you saw."

He moved to stand just a couple of feet from her. "We made love, in my bed, and you said the color of my red comforter was called Alabama Crimson. Dreams usually don't have such specific details, do they?"

"Sometimes they do." And just like that, she was right back there, with him. They often made love in his bed, sometimes in hers, sometimes they ended up in all sorts of places. The dreamglide could be amazing.

But this time, yes, she'd been in his bed.

He searched her eyes as though trying to understand. She knew he was thinking the whole thing over.

He moved closer still and took her arms in his hands. "It's as though I'm two people right now, Juliet. One of them knows you extremely well, the other is a stranger."

He leaned close and ran his nose over her temple, drawing in his breath at the same time. "You feel so familiar to me, yet not, and you smell like strawberries."

"It's my shampoo. And Brann?"

"Yes."

"I'm sorry."

He drew back and met her gaze. "Well, I'm angry."

How many times had she stared into his haunted, green eyes? A hundred? A thousand?

She knew he was struggling with the nature of the situation. She also knew that this could be the last time she'd ever be close to him in real-time. For one thing, he could easily drop her from his operation and she'd never see him again.

So, she slid a hand around the nape of his neck and mirrored what he'd done to her. She swept her nose over his cheek. She smelled soap and the citrus fragrance of an aftershave, only everything was more vivid because it was real-time.

She also caught the scent of him, the sweat on his skin, his vampire masculinity. All was new, yet familiar at the same time. The dreamglide could communicate part of the sensory experience, but not all of it.

She pressed herself up against Brann and slowly met his lips with hers. When he didn't pull away, she kissed him harder.

The same.

But different.

Yet so much better.

Real. So real.

She trembled as his arms slid around her in response.

Maybe this wasn't a good idea. Maybe this would make things a thousand times worse. After all, Brannick would never forgive her for coming to him illegally as she had. He was a man of rules, procedures and control.

She started to draw back, but he followed with his lips and captured her mouth. She gave a cry as his tongue drove within, familiar, yet so much more.

She slung both arms around his neck.

Brann.

She hadn't meant to communicate telepathically, but she was overcome.

She was in his arms at long last, this time for real.

~~~
~~~

CHAPTER TWO

Brannick had served on the Crescent Border Patrol for years. He'd faced death squads in Rotten Row. He'd had witches put their sizzling fingers up to his temple ready to kill him. He'd been cut open with a dozen sword swipes from fae and dead-talker bad guys. He'd had drugged out shifters, in wolf form, tear chunks out of his arms, legs and once his abdomen.

He knew what pain was.

He knew how to battle the enemy.

He'd grown strong on all fronts because of the hellhole he lived in called Five Bridges.

What he didn't have either the will or the strength to do, was to let go of the woman in his arms.

His lips were pinned to hers, his tongue plunging in and out. She even tasted familiar, which seemed impossible. He ran his hands down her back and felt her tremble beneath his touch.

He could recall the dreamglide now in perfect detail, how just hours ago he'd been buried inside her, watching passion move in erotic waves over her creamy, freckled skin. He could hear her moans and see how he leaned down to kiss her cheek. He'd shifted his position and given her a solid rock of his hips to which her whole body had rolled with pleasure.

But it had only been a dream. No, that wasn't accurate. It had been a *dreamglide*, an alternate reality the powerful fae could create.

He drew back and met her gaze. Holding her right now, however, was real life or 'real-time' as the fae called the present.

Setting his memory of the shared dreamglide aside, he could feel the flesh of her body through her dress and the way her breasts rose and fell against his chest. She felt amazing beneath his touch, familiar yet not, but now oh-so-fucking-real.

"Brann, what are you thinking? Talk to me."

"That you feel the same but so different. Better. More physical. More … *real.*"

She nodded three times very fast, and her breathing was erratic. Her tongue touched her lips. Because of the dreamglide, he knew the signs of her arousal and how easily he could take her to bed because of the state she was in. She was clearly vulnerable to him, which turned him on.

Christ, he'd been her lover for five months now.

But what did any of it mean?

Slowly, he let his arms fall away, then took a step back. He needed distance on so many levels. In an essential way, he didn't approve of dreamgliding. In terms of his work, it was illegal to turn yourself over to a fae who could invade your dreams.

Some of the more gifted Revel dwellers, like Roche, could do intensive searches within a dreamglide and ferret out all sorts of high-profile, highly classified information. The streetlights throughout Five Bridges and each of the security checkpoints at the main bridges were all governed by computers. This kind of information could be extracted during a dreamglide state and sold to anybody willing to pay.

Not that Brannick suspected Juliet of doing anything like that. Not at all. He trusted her allegiance to his cause.

Something else occurred to him. "You say this began five months ago? You mean around the time we met at the White Flame club?"

She tilted her head slightly. "The first time was that same night."

Brannick knew he'd been a willing participant, and he knew why. The whole time he'd interviewed her, he'd been in a partial state of arousal.

He'd sat across from her in a booth. She'd sipped a mai-tai, while he'd worked on a scotch. He could even remember what she wore, a somewhat loose-fitting glittery black dress, not too different from the gauzy one she wore now, but made for clubbing. She didn't seem to like snug clothes. Still, he'd thought her sexy as hell.

Nothing about her had been flirtatious, either. She hadn't come to charm him, only to support the image of a couple on a date while he interviewed her. She'd kept the conversation serious and to the point. She wanted to help. Mary had been talking to her for weeks about joining the rescue operation and Juliet didn't care that she'd be risking her life. She'd seen too many bad things in Revel Territory not to get involved.

After he'd made his assessment and welcomed her to the team, the conversation had shifted to their current lives and work. She was apprenticed to a woman named Agnes, a sage fae of great power, who served on the Board of Sages, which governed Revel Territory. Roche was on the same board and stonewalled most of the improvement projects the several good fae tried to move forward. No surprise there.

In turn, he'd told her about his work as a border patrol officer, the level of violence he faced every night and that he'd learned to carry a kit in his car to stitch up minor wounds. She'd asked what he considered a minor cut, and he said he measured it in inches—anything longer than a certain number and he'd head to the clinic to have a professional do the job.

Then she'd surprised him by offering a double-entendre about anything else he measured in inches and did he seek a professional to take care of that problem as well.

He'd been shocked at first. The woman had seemed so self-contained and somewhat prim. She didn't even blush, though she did offer a smiling apology. "Sorry, I shouldn't have said that. I was married to a great guy. We used to joke all the time."

Of course, she'd looked away from Brannick at that point. Hurt had flashed in her eyes when she mentioned her husband, reminding him of the pain he'd suffered thirteen years ago when his wife had died. Jesus, sometimes, at the oddest moments and without warning, grief could come boiling to the surface.

Juliet had taken a big drink of her mai-tai and ordered a second. He'd done the same with his scotch. He should have left then and there, since he'd concluded his business with her, but dawn had still been a couple of hours away and he didn't want to leave. Looking back, he realized his conversation with Juliet had been the first normal one with a woman in years, maybe since he'd come to Five Bridges.

"What are you thinking about?" The warm, musical quality of her voice brought him back to the present.

"About our conversation at the club, the night I met you for the first time."

She inclined her head slowly, her lips parted. "I think about that sometimes as well. Of course my cheeks tend to warm up as I recall what I said to you. Do you remember?"

"Yeah. About what else I measured in inches."

She smiled. "I'm still embarrassed."

He caught her elbow in his hand. "I liked it. It felt so easy. But I was surprised because you didn't seem like the type."

"I guess I don't." Her smile grew crooked. "But I am."

He continued to stare at her. He knew he was frowning harder than ever, but he couldn't help it. He was trying to understand how he'd let this happen. He lived a controlled life, something necessary because of his simmering, ever-present rage about being an *alter* vampire.

Giving himself over to a dreamglider meant he'd had no control. So, why had he done it?

He searched her eyes, her face, looking for some kind of answer that she couldn't possibly provide. He felt like he'd double-crossed himself and was now vulnerable in a situation that could easily spin out of control.

Finally, he let her go, then shoved a hand through his hair. "We should get out of here."

"Yes, we should."

He moved toward the door that led into the house and knocked quietly. His host, Carl, opened the door grim-faced no doubt because of the earlier unexpected visitor.

Brannick had already made his decision about what needed to be done for the host couple.

Carl led them into the family room. He moved off to the side of the sliding glass door, joining his wife. He slid an arm around her shoulders, then shook his head. "Sorry, Brannick, but we can't do this anymore. It's meant a lot to me and my wife that we could help these women, but we won't jeopardize our lives, not like this."

Brannick lifted a hand. "Don't worry about it, Carl. I hold to my word that if there was ever the smallest sign that your house was suspect, we'd be out of here, and that's what's happened tonight.

"I'll have contractors here within the hour, sealing up the tunnel at your home's exit point. They'll build in the closet like we discussed, though they'll dirty it up so it looks like it's been there a while. We backfill the stairs with dirt and pack it in good. Even if someone tried to break through the closet, they wouldn't get far. How does that sound?"

His wife burst into tears. Carl held her close. "Sounds real good. What about the van? Will you still wait to remove it?"

"Procedure has taught us that the van should sit there for at least a month now. I'll have my human team take it away sometime during the day when most of the *alter* species will be asleep. How does that sound?"

"Good. Real good. And we're sorry about this."

"Not your fault and please don't give it a second thought."

Brannick pulled his phone from his pocket and made a call to one of his human contractors and arranged for the tunnel work. When he put his phone back, he said, "They'll get started right away, though you probably won't even know they're here and they'll work through the day. Tomorrow night, go ahead and move whatever you like into the closet. Just try to arrange everything to make it look as though it's been settling for a while."

"Thanks so much, Brannick." He compressed his lips. "Do you have any idea how we became suspect?"

He shrugged. "It's possible a neighbor saw the van pull in and called the Crescent station. That's all it would take. But don't worry. I've closed up tunnels dozens of times."

"Will you have to dig a new one?"

"Not entirely. We'll arrange for a replacement host, hopefully on a nearby street not far from the tunnel, then cut in from there. Again, the contractors are skilled at what they do." He clapped Carl on the shoulder. "Thank you for your service. As for this evening, four more women were delivered safely through our network and are by now headed to a local Phoenix hospital and will get the care they need."

"That's good, but I sure wish that officer hadn't shown up."

Brannick nodded then glanced toward the night sky. "I wish you both well, but right now Juliet and I need to get going."

Carl drew back the sliding glass door.

Brannick stepped through. When he moved onto a small patch of grass in the center of the yard, ready to take off, he realized Juliet hadn't followed him.

He glanced in the direction of the house and saw that she was holding Carl's wife in a warm embrace and speaking softly to her. When she drew back, the woman smiled then wiped her cheeks with her hands.

For a moment, as Juliet turned in Brannick's direction and started crossing the patio, he felt as though something grabbed his heart and squeezed hard. She was kind and thoughtful, a loving woman, the kind he wished he could have in his life, a woman like his wife had been.

He shifted to look up into the sky, anywhere but at Juliet. He didn't want to be feeling like this, like if given the chance, he could fall for her.

He'd made a promise to himself the night he'd watched the dark coven witches burn his sister alive that he'd never allow himself to care for anyone ever again. He couldn't risk it. Not in Five Bridges. Caring had fueled his rage, which had set him on a vigilante course that ended with the death of the rest of his family, including Tracy.

He'd spent thirteen years atoning for something that he could never make right. But he had no intention of getting involved at this late hour with Juliet, even if he had been engaged in a serious affair with her.

When she drew close, he held out his arm and his right boot. "Have you flown much?"

"A couple of times. But, yes, I'm a nervous flyer."

"I'll take it slow."

She stepped up onto his boot, then settled her arm across his shoulders. Oh, God, she smelled so good. She smelled *familiar.* He slid his arm around her waist and pulled her close.

She leaned into him in a way that told him exactly how comfortable she was with him physically, as though she'd always been flying with him. Of course, it was another reminder that they'd been having dreamglide sex.

His whole body felt flushed. He needed to take her back to Revel, drop her off and make sure that within the structure of his tunnel rescue network he never saw her again.

He also needed to make it clear that there would be no more dreamgliding. Not now. Not ever.

~ ~ ~

As Brannick rose slowly into the sky, Juliet felt his special vampire disguise flow in a soft whirl around her. Even this unique power had the feel of Brannick as she'd come to know him in their shared dreamglide.

She felt safe in his arms and much less nervous than if she'd flown with anyone else. She could even look around.

Brann, I didn't realize we were this far north. She probably shouldn't use his nickname. She'd have to work on that.

Only a half mile from the Loop 101.

As she took in the terrain of Crescent Territory, she clucked her tongue. *Most of Five Bridges really has the look of a warzone, doesn't it?*

Yes, it does. Want to have a good look?

You mean as in take in more of the land?

Yep.

Honestly, I'd love it. And she meant it.

He turned slightly to face due north, then slowly moved in the direction of what they called the U.S. Border, even though it was in the middle of Phoenix. The entire outer boundary of Five Bridges was locked down tight with more barbed wire than she'd ever thought to see in her entire life.

Searchlights also rimmed the border area, hunting for drug-runners who foolishly tried to make their way across the pitted landscape. The same lights tracked the skies constantly, hunting for those with the ability to levitate. The shoot-on-sight outside of Five Bridges was a real deterrent.

She still couldn't believe that she lived in a geographical area that used to be the north central part of Phoenix. But after the *alter* species had been segregated into a ghetto some time ago, the U.S. finally resolved a lot of governing issues by cordoning off large areas in the major cities across the country, complete with tens of thousands of linear feet of barbed wire. Formal U.S borders were created in order to keep the *alter* species from being part of the normal human population.

Can you take me up higher?

His husky masculine voice rolled through her mind. *You sure you're up for it?*

I am. I think because I'm with you.

Holding her secure, he rose swiftly, then stopped to hover in the air. *Before we move forward, I need to check the airspace.*

She understood why. Many species could levitate, and he would need to know who was out and about in Crescent right now.

He slowly spun in a circle, but the air was clear. She could see other species in the far distance, small dots moving across the night like unmarked aircraft. She had the odd thought that the Tribunal government should establish a law requiring identification lights on anyone levitating.

The thought made her smile, not just because it would be out-of-place to see flashing lights on Brannick's head or his boots. But the Tribunal could barely enforce its most basic laws so she'd love to see them try to regulate what happened during levitated flight. It was a cynical thought, of course, but then she'd lived in the province for four long difficult years. As for the U.S. Government, Five Bridges was a no-fly zone for human aircraft and easily seen from the air because of all the searchlights surrounding the area.

He drew close to Del Muerto Bridge, which connected Crescent to the dead-talkers of Shadow Territory. A lot of superstition ran rampant about Del Muerto Bridge, and as a result, it saw the least amount of traffic. Shadow Territory also described the land in this section of Five

Bridges pretty well. Shadow had the fewest street lights of any of the territories and a fairly low number of raunchy sex clubs. Humans who came to shadow were looking for a connection to loved ones who'd passed. Of course, this meant that a lot of businesses thrived by playing on the grief of unsuspecting visitors. Juliet had often thought there was absolutely nothing sacred in Five Bridges.

She felt a measure of relief when Brannick reached the border between her fae territory of Revel and the dead-talker land. Ventana Bridge was also one of the five main bridges that gave their province its name.

Brannick flew over the bridge and into Revel. He'd been to her home in their dreamglide world, but she had no idea how much he remembered. *Do you know where you're going?*

I gave up following landmarks a mile ago and have been using my instincts since. Everything is oddly familiar.

When he made a turn to head east, she huffed a sigh. *This is definitely the right direction.*

Wait a minute. I'm remembering something from one of the dreamglides. You live in the Lotus Tree development, don't you?

I do. But I may have told you where I lived the night we met at the White Flame.

Maybe. I don't know. But I definitely feel like I've been here before. He made his descent.

In many ways, it was like flying in a plane since the streetlights suddenly grew brighter and she could see the form of people moving on the sidewalks. The cars had stopped looking like something she could buy in a toy store.

He flew without hesitation, heading straight toward Lotus Bridge.

When it came into view, she asked him to fly north to where the main canal branched off to Lotus Stream. She'd often wanted to take a helicopter ride just to see this particular view.

Reaching the 'T' where the canal intersected with Lotus Stream, she asked him to drop even lower but to go slow. *I can't tell you how many times I've wanted to see this from a point of levitation. I think it's one of the prettiest places in all of Five Bridges.* She laughed. *Of course, that isn't saying much.*

No, it really isn't. We have a lot of work to do.

Brannick made a wide, slow turn, and his arm kept her secure the entire time. Her feet were perched on his right boot, which helped.

Brannick said, *I've never been to this part of Revel before, but my God it's beautiful.* He flew even lower, just ten feet above the mini-canal.

Along both sides was a park-like setting with a meandering sidewalk and dozens of trees fit for the coming summer desert heat. But there were green-belts as well, a lot of grass. Because it was spring, there were burgeoning flowerbeds scattered here and there.

Small footbridges, many of them made of stone, crisscrossed the canal with cottage-sized homes along either side.

A much larger stone bridge, over which vehicles could travel, kept traffic moving through the area. *Where does everyone park?*

How easily she could communicate with him telepathically. *We have long alleys here and the garages come off the alleys.*

This is fairly new construction.

The development was laid out ten years ago. My husband bought a home for me here when we divorced. She'd already told him everything in the dreamglide, but she doubted he remembered it.

That was big of him. I approve. It's a lot more than some have experienced.

I know.

He began to slow, another indication he knew where he was headed. He began his final descent toward one of the smaller stone footbridges. *This is Talisman Bridge, isn't it?*

Yes. She wondered why he was stopping here and not taking her to her canal home.

We've been here before, haven't we, in a dreamglide, I mean.

Oh, God, he was recalling another memory. *Yes, we have.*

Tears burned her eyes as he touched down on the stone path. No one was around, and they had the bridge to themselves.

When he released her, she stepped off his boot, slowly sliding her arm from around his neck.

She watched him. He frowned as he turned in another slow circle, taking in the entire area. "It's beautiful." He then shifted to face her. "You must love it here."

"I do. When I've finished with my night's work at the Board of Sages, I often come here, sometimes with my camera."

He frowned slightly. "That's right. You were a photographer before you became an *alter* fae."

She had to smile. During one dreamglide, he'd asked her a dozen questions about how she'd gotten interested in photography.

He rolled his eyes. "I take it we've talked about this before."

"I didn't mean to smile, but you were so curious. You don't remember our conversation?"

He shook his head. "No. Not about photography. Christ, this is bugging the shit out of me, that you hold this over my head."

She drew close. "Brann, never. I would never."

He scrubbed both hands through his hair, afterward pushing it straight back. She loved the look on him. "I didn't mean that you hold anything over my head, not exactly. I hate not knowing, when you know everything. It's an unfair advantage."

She took a moment before answering him. "You, especially, would feel that way."

"What the hell does that mean?"

"Only that you like control. You even dictated what you allowed yourself to know about our dreamglide relationship. But you can have complete access right now if you want it. I have a block in place, and I can remove it, something I learned as an apprentice sage."

She didn't tell him the rest, that she'd been compelled to learn the skills because Neal Roche had attempted to hijack her once in a dreamglide. She'd barely escaped. If he'd gained control of her, she would have been lost to him for a good long time, possibly forever.

Brannick frowned hard, a pit between his brows. "You can remove the block right now, and I can see everything?"

She dipped her chin.

"Have you been edging the block out of place? Is that why I've suddenly been remembering?"

"No, of course not. I would never violate our dreamglide agreement." She cringed slightly. She might not disrupt their current agreement, but she'd had no problem violating his dreamspace and seducing him within her dreamglide. In many ways, Roche had done the exact same thing to her. He just hadn't been as successful. If Brannick ever figured out exactly what had happened, she doubted he'd ever be able to forgive her.

In that sense, Brannick was a conundrum because during their first time together, his dreamglide self had engaged in their affair without the smallest hesitation. He'd also told her he didn't care that she'd seduced him.

"But I would never know if you broke an agreement, would I?" He ground his jaw.

She could tell the situation was getting to him, but that wasn't exactly her problem. He was the one who'd instigated the gag order.

What she found intriguing right now, however, was that he didn't automatically ask her to remove the block. Apparently, he didn't really want to know all that had happened between them.

In that sense, she was grateful. She was convinced he wouldn't be able to handle everything they'd been doing for the past five months. Not yet.

He paced away from her a few feet, his gaze skyward, then he spun in another circle. As a footbridge, Talisman was only about seven feet from rail to rail, though it spanned the thirty-foot wide canal stream.

She knew what he was doing. His training as a border patrol officer was always present, even in the dreamglides they shared. He was constantly checking his surroundings, which gave her a feeling of security.

"Let me understand. If you have a block in place, then why have I been remembering anything at all?"

She shrugged. "No one really knows, but it happens. Some say it has to do with the individual involved. You might be overcoming my block because you're an extremely powerful vampire. Another theory is that proximity will facilitate sudden memory surges."

"Memory surges?" He echoed the words softly. He drew close once more, his brow still severely pinched. "Like when you wore that red-flowered dress on this very bridge?"

A gasp left her throat. "You remember that?"

"I've seen little else since I touched down. I can even smell a fragrance that was in the air, very flowery."

"I wore perfume."

"How the hell can I remember a scent from a dreamglide?"

She smiled. "Because this is part of the *alter* fae world. You might as well ask how you can levitate the way you do. This is what it is to be fae. That's all."

He was still frowning. "I get your point."

She remembered the dreamglide moment he was referring to extremely well, one of her favorites, in fact. She'd wanted to dress up for him, so she'd donned the silk dress with white flowers on a red background. It showed a lot of cleavage and was cut longer in back at the hem. She'd even worn heels so that he had a much shorter distance to travel when he kissed her.

She moved to the side of the bridge. She'd been right here when he'd taken her in his arms. She placed her hand on the warm stone. It was early May and hot during the day. But at night, it was a beautiful balmy time of year in the Valley of the Sun.

All the trees and the water had helped to cool things down as well.

His voice was very low as he asked, "Are you thinking about what happened in the dreamglide?"

She nodded but shifted her gaze to look at the canal water. She saw the moon reflected in the breeze-swept ripples.

He came up next to her and slid his hand along her lower back. "As I recall, you stood here."

She didn't look at him. She was afraid to. "I did."

"You looked so beautiful. You'd dressed up for me."

"Yes." Her gaze skated to his face, then got stuck there. "The time we spent together in the dreamglide was like dating."

His hand was warm through her dress.

"And I kissed you, but not on the lips."

A shiver ran through her. She felt his interest like a soft jolt of electricity against her skin, and that wasn't fae at all, just very human. Her intuition told her he was actually thinking about repeating the process.

But should she let him when he was so angry about the situation?

He squeezed her waist then pushed the long curly strands of hair away from her neck. Leaning down, he kissed her neck, his lips warm and moist.

Juliet closed her eyes, her throat tightening. She'd loved her time with Brann in the dreamglide. But this was so much better.

For a moment she couldn't breathe.

She pressed a hand to her stomach. "We shouldn't be doing this."

He stopped kissing her and lifted up to meet her gaze. "Why not?" He moved to stand in front of her, leaning against the stone rail of the bridge. "You liked it well enough in the dreamglide."

She heard the edge to his voice and knew he was still angry. "I loved it in the dreamglide."

"Not right now, when I kissed your neck?"

She intended to be honest. "It was better just now, more real. Don't you think?"

He looked as though he struggled to make sense of what was going on, and she wasn't certain what to say to him. The man had just learned he'd been engaging in dreamglide sex with her for the past five months. "Ask me anything, Brann."

He hissed, then squeezed his eyes shut as though in pain. "Stop calling me that."

"'Brann' you mean?"

"Yes." When he opened his eyes, he looked haunted.

She sighed. "I'll try not to. But I've been calling you that all this time."

His brows tightened even more and his voice had an edge. "This is real-time now, real life. You haven't earned the right to call me by anything other than my full name."

"Fine. Whatever you say." She was angry now as well. The man she knew in the dreamglide was so open with her and wanted her calling him by his nickname. Yet, real-time Brannick could barely remember anything about their relationship.

"You're mad at me?" A cheek muscle twitched.

"Look at it from my point of view. All this time, you've welcomed me into your life."

He all but shouted. "But what happened between us wasn't real."

She was taken aback for a moment, then lowered her chin. "That's where you're wrong. Everything about the dreamglide is real, and the man in them had no problem connecting with me."

"Is that what you want? Connection?"

The question surprised her, and for a moment, she couldn't answer.

His lips curved down. "Oh, I get it. You're the supreme hypocrite. You liked the connection in the dreamglide because, though it might have a semblance of reality, you didn't really need to deal with me. Well, now it looks like you're going to have to."

Juliet huffed a derisive laugh, but not at Brannick. "You're right. I just never saw it until this moment. You were safe in the dreamglide."

"And I'm not now."

"How could you be? You're a vampire and this is Five Bridges. There's absolutely no hope for a relationship in this world."

"Now you're thinking clearly."

He didn't look all that pleased, however. He held her gaze, but she could see a new set of thoughts spinning within his mind. Finally, he said, "It may not have been real-time, but from what I'm getting, Jesus, it was beautiful."

"Yes. It was." She hated that tears started to her eyes. But her time with Brannick, real or not, had been extraordinary. Tonight, though, it was all coming to an end.

The muffled and very distant sound of gunshots pulled her out of the conversation. She shifted toward the southwest, leaning her stomach against the bridge. She waited to hear if more shots would follow.

Brannick moved next to her, resting his forearms on the stone rail. "Sounds like your border patrol caught runners in the desert."

"Probably. Roche has dozens in his employ. The Revel Border Patrol can't keep up. He uses a lot of decoys as well with jackets full of fake product."

"I've heard estimates that he has close to a hundred runners working for him."

"You've heard right. He's an arrogant man. I heard him boast about his runners in one of the board meetings. Of course he didn't actually use the word 'runner', but we all knew what he was talking about."

He glanced at her. "And he manufactures dark flame somewhere in Revel, though below ground."

"That's the word on the street." She held his gaze. "And dark flame is what you and I share in common above everything else."

"You mentioned your *alter* experience at the club. But I suppose you know the history of my transformation because I told you about it in the dreamglide."

"We've talked, yes. But long before that, I did a web search on you. There was a lot written about your tangle with the cartels and how they retaliated."

A haunted look entered his eye. He turned away from her, staring into the moonlit water below.

She decided to break up his memories by sharing some of her history with him. "I was abducted right after a photo shoot. I'd taken a couple to one of my favorite desert locations, and when we were done, they took off. I was just packing up when three men found me. They'd given me too high a dose of the dark flame drug and, coupled with the *alter* fae serum, I went into a coma. I was left for dead at a gas station then taken to a hospital. I didn't know anything about what had happened until I woke up and found that I was no longer human.

"Brann … Brannick, I wanted to die so badly. My husband had been with me throughout my three days in the hospital. The nurses said he never left my side." She'd told him all this during one of their dreamglides, but knew he wouldn't have the memory of it yet. "And you and your pregnant wife as well as your daughter, drank tainted soda."

He dipped his chin slowly, his lips compressing. "We'd made a toast, then drank together. How many times have I wished I'd tested it first? They'd still be alive, all three of them."

"I'm so sorry for your loss."

He held her gaze. “And I’m sorry for yours. Your husband sounds like he was a good man.”

“He was the best. He wept when he signed the divorce papers. I had always thought that I wouldn’t be one of those people who left their spouse after the *alter*. But when I came out of the coma, I understood how profound the *alter* change truly is. I could feel it in every part of my body. Even colors looked different through my new fae eyes, and I had this unexpected ability to read people that went way beyond anything I’d known as a human. I could feel my husband’s revulsion of what I’d become, his fear as well. I didn’t blame him, though. The wife he’d known was gone.

“He provided well for me after the divorce. I’ve been happy here in Lotus Tree.”

She was about to ask him if he’d like to see her house in real-time, when movement caught her eye.

She turned to look at the waterway toward the south. And there, flying above the water between the rows of majestic sissoo trees moving with the wind, were seven warrior fae and an eighth man. It took her two blinks to realize who the last man was.

“Oh, God. It’s Roche. But what is he doing out here?”

Brannick rose upright. “You sure it’s him?”

“I know it is. He has a fae signature that I can read at any distance. But why is he out here with his security detail?” Roche lived mostly underground, the mole-like creep that he was. “Brannick, am I seeing right? Do all those men have their swords drawn?”

“Yep. And they’re coming right toward us.”

CHAPTER THREE

Brannick cursed under his breath. "Juliet, get down and stay down." If he levitated, Roche and his men would chase him. But how did they know he was here or were they after Juliet?

A surprising but very strong instinct surged within him, letting him know that Roche was after Juliet. He knew why as well. Given her high level of fae ability and power, Roche would want her for his dreamglide sex club.

He thought about covering Juliet and himself with his vampire shield, but he wasn't sure if Roche had the power to see through it or not. Some of the most powerful fae could do that, and he didn't want to take the chance of getting trapped.

He drew his Glock, then supported it with his free hand. Every shot would have to count if either of them were going to survive.

He aimed at the fae warrior on the left and fired, then shifted immediately to the one on the right, pulling the trigger a second time. Both men spiraled toward the canal, dropping into the water.

The remaining five, along with Roche, flew closer.

He took a measured breath and fired to the left again, then the right, quick shots. The first warrior fell into the water, but he'd missed the other one who drew close to the bridge, sword raised.

Brannick fired into the man's chest, then levitated at the same time, diving forward to catch the warrior's sword as it flipped from his hand midair. Brannick heard him hit the water as well.

The three remaining warriors were farther back, guarding Roche. Yet still they flew toward the bridge.

He needed to lead them away from Juliet.

He levitated to the west bank. When he touched down, he turned and fired at the fifth man flying straight for him. The shot hit the fae's left arm, the force sending him spinning backward. He landed hard on the far bank near the sidewalk, but rose to his feet immediately. Brannick had only nicked him.

Juliet's voice entered his mind. *Fae warrior to the north and behind you.*

He took Juliet at her word, spun and drove his sword into the man's abdomen. The warrior fell backward as Brannick withdrew the blade.

Brannick turned and started to levitate, but the warrior whose arm he'd nicked caught him at the waist and brought him down hard on his back. Brannick still had his Glock in his hand, and he dragged it between their bodies and fired. The recoil slammed into Brannick's gut but the warrior fell limp.

He pushed him off and rose to his feet. He'd lost track of the other warrior.

Brannick, behind you!

He had just started to turn, when he felt a tremendous pressure on his back. He looked down and saw the point of a bloody sword emerge from his own abdomen. He couldn't feel his legs. He couldn't think.

His enemy jerked the sword from Brannick's body. He watched the blade disappear, then fell face down on the grass not far from the man he'd shot to death. He heard shouting near him, the sound of victory.

Where was Juliet? Was he leaving her to the enemy?

His mind began to swirl with black clouds. Juliet. He had to get to her, to help her.

But his consciousness faded, then he fell into a black hole.

What seemed like a second later, however, he emerged inside what he knew instinctively was his own dreamglide. He had no idea how he'd gotten there, or how the hell, as a vampire, this was even possible.

He was on the bridge with Juliet, yet not with her, but hovering nearby. She wasn't in his dreamglide with him, which meant he needed to figure out what kind of trouble she was in.

Roche was on the bridge not ten feet away from Juliet. But he kept looking around as though he couldn't see her.

Juliet, can you hear me?

Brannick, is that you? Wait a minute, where are you? I'm seeing your body through the stone balustrades of the bridge. You're lying face down in the grass. You look like you've passed out. How are you in my head?

I'm in a dreamglide, something I think I created by myself though I have no idea how I did it. And I'm right next to you. Can you come to me? Brannick couldn't fathom how much power it required to do exactly what he was doing. How could a vampire perform a fae skill?

He felt Juliet grow very quiet and a moment later, she drifted into his dreamglide. Within the half-dreaming, half-waking state, she rose to her feet and turned to stare at him.

She gripped his arms. *Then you're not dead?*

Close, but not yet.

Suddenly, memories of all their times together from the past five months rushed forward. The swell and sensation was so great, he almost fell, but righted himself at the last moment.

He and Juliet were lovers. No wonder the sight of her in Carl's garage had started leaking memories to his conscious mind.

His first inclination was to haul her into his arms, but he had a couple more important things to attend to.

Through the blur of the dreamglide, he could see Juliet below him in real-time. She sat on the bridge ten feet away from Roche, her legs pulled up, her knees pressed into one of the curved stone balusters.

It looked like Roche couldn't see her, but she'd done the smart thing curling up against the bridge rails.

Roche was a dangerous *alter* fae with red hair to his shoulders and small dark eyes. He had teal flames on his neck and cheeks. He might be lean because of drug use, but he was bulked with muscle as well.

Juliet, I'm not understanding something right now. It appears to me that Roche can't see you. Why is that? It didn't make sense.

I'm not sure.

Within the dreamglide, Brannick drew close to Juliet and slid his arm around her. He was very weak, a sure sign he was close to death. Still, if he could save Juliet right now, nothing else mattered. *Tell me what you did when I first started firing at Roche's men.*

I dropped down as you see me now on the bridge. I thought it would be wise to make myself as small as possible.

Very smart. But can you tell me what thoughts went through your head when you did this?

Juliet huffed a sigh. *I wanted to tell you to use your vampire shielding power, that it was my guess none of the men, not even Roche, would be able to see you, but everything happened so fast.*

Then that's it, he said. *And I can feel it now, an energy you have that is all about the vampire ability to create a shielding cloak.*

I feel it, too. Although, at first I thought I was just so full of adrenaline, I couldn't stop shaking. But now I know what I'm experiencing is vampire power. So how am I doing this?

I suppose the same way I took on your skill to create a dreamglide.

Brannick felt himself fading a little more. The dreamgliding would soon come to an end as his unconsciousness took over. *We need to figure out how to get your real-time self to safety. Can you get to your feet, in real-time I mean?*

Yes, but not until I leave the dreamglide.

Roche turned in a slow circle, still hunting for her.

Juliet, before you leave the dreamglide, listen. I'm right at death's door, but there's one person who might be able to help, the witch, Emma. Call the safe house in Elegance Territory that Vaughn and Emma operate together. Emma has powerful healing abilities, though Vaughn will need to help her as well. Apparently, he facilitates her power.

I will, Brann, but please stay with me 'til I make contact.

Of course. And one more thing. You need to find out if the shield includes the disguising of your voice. Roche might not be able to see you right now, but it's possible he could hear you.

Okay. What do I do?

When you leave the dreamglide, clear your throat softly. If he doesn't respond, do it louder. If he still doesn't appear to hear you, call out his name. You'll know by then.

As she dropped out of the dreamglide, Brannick heard her clear her throat, but Roche gave no indication he'd heard her. She followed the process Brannick had suggested, and when she spoke Roche's name in a clear strong voice and he still didn't respond, Juliet sat up and pulled her phone from the pocket of her dress. She then contacted Brannick telepathically, *What's the safe house number?*

She tapped each in as he spoke them. She reached the safe house but was being routed to Emma, which might take some time.

He watched Juliet as she waited. She kept her gaze pinned to Roche's position, but looked ready to bolt if he got too close.

Fortunately, Roche was still a good ten feet away, his gaze extended to the surrounding garden. He called out to his last remaining guard. "Keep checking. We all saw her. She has to be here somewhere." The fae warrior flew from one side of the bank to the other, scouring any bush large enough to hide her.

Finally, Juliet made contact. "Emma, it's Juliet Tunney in Revel. You don't know me, but Robert Brannick told me to call you. He's been mortally wounded, a sword through the back. We need your healing power at the Talisman Bridge in Revel Territory. Can you come to us? He said you'd need Vaughn with you as well."

Juliet appeared to be listening. Then after a long moment, she covered her face with her free hand and said, "Thank God. I'll be waiting for you next to Brannick."

He heard the sob in Juliet's voice as she ended the call.

She tucked the phone away and slowly rose to her feet. She kept a guarded pace as she began walking carefully in Roche's direction. She'd have to pass by him to get across the bridge to where Brannick's body lay.

Brannick stayed right with her in his dreamglide. *You're doing fine.*

I can smell Roche. He reeks of dark flame.

I know. Just keep going.

She gave Roche a wide berth, but as soon as she passed by him, she broke into a sprint and ran the remaining distance to Brannick.

Still within the dreamglide, but feeling weaker as each second passed, Brannick watched two Revel Border Patrol SUVs pull up. The doors flew open and four officers emerged. He knew a couple of the men, good men. One of the neighbors must have called in the sound of gunfire.

Brannick checked Roche's position. But he and his one surviving warrior were already in the air. Roche no doubt didn't want a confrontation with the border patrol, especially with men who opposed the drug trade as these officers did. Within a few seconds, they rose high into the night sky then disappeared from view.

Juliet knelt beside Brannick's body. He watched as blood seeped onto her light green dress. She leaned over and pressed both hands against the wound in his back, trying to staunch the flow.

One of the men he knew, Officer Keelen, knelt beside Brannick's body. Keelen was one of his main contacts in Revel, who worked his off hours to get human women out of the dangerous sex trade.

On the side opposite to Juliet, Keelen pressed two fingers to Brannick's neck. He called over his shoulder to his fellow officer. "He's gone."

Juliet spoke to him. "No, he's not."

But Keelen didn't respond to her in any way.

Brannick quickly realized the man couldn't see or hear her. *Juliet, you'll have to release the vampire shield. Keelen doesn't know you're here.*

Right. How do I do that?

Brannick thought for a minute, recalling his early days as a vampire when he'd had to practice building the shield then letting it go. But he didn't know how to communicate that to her.

The same odd, powerful instinct that had told him Roche was after Juliet now told him what Juliet needed to do, at least in this situation. *You have to let go of me.*

What? But Brann, I can't do that. I don't want to. I'm afraid if I do, you'll die.

He stared down at his body, at the severity of the wound, at the blood he could see pooled on the grass off to the side. His skin was very pale, unusual for him. Was he looking at his own death?

He also knew that the moment Juliet released him, the shield would peel away, he would leave the dreamglide, and she'd be visible to all four officers who had responded to the scene.

Juliet?

Yes?

It's okay to let me go, and I'll do everything in my power to stay alive. But I want you to know that I've loved my time with you. If I survive, please keep fighting for us. I have a lot of baggage, mostly I think because of losing my family and watching my sister die. But you mean everything to me. Will you do that?

He watched tears roll down her face. She still kept pressure on the wound. *I will. Stay alive. Please, Brann.*

I'll battle as hard as I can, I promise.

He felt her release him and at the same time, it was as though he fell backward into a dark empty void.

~ ~ ~

The moment Juliet felt the shield slide away from her, Keelen saw her and his hand went to his gun. Recognizing her instantly, he eased back. "Juliet, where the hell did you come from?"

Juliet didn't try to explain. "I've called for help, a witch with tremendous healing powers. Will you stay with me?" Keelen was a good man and had served as part of Brannick's rescue operation for a long time.

"Of course I will. We've called for more backup as well, but what the hell happened out here?" He glanced at the two dead fae warriors on the ground near Brannick, then toward the canal where no doubt the other bodies floated.

"Roche and his men attacked."

"Roche? Why? He rarely takes a battle to the streets. It doesn't make sense."

Juliet kept the pressure on the wound, but she had no idea if she was doing any good at all. As for Roche, she wasn't sure how to answer Keelen's question, but he might as well know the truth. "Roche has been after me for a long time, for my dreamglide abilities."

Keelen ground his teeth, then let loose with a long string of profanity. He apologized afterward, but Juliet had no problem with the words he'd chosen. Each fit the situation exactly.

He then tilted his head, trying to get a better look at Brannick. "And who's this? I sense that he's a vampire, but he's barely breathing." With Brannick's face turned away from Keelen, he couldn't possibly know who the injured man was.

She caught Keelen's gaze, and more tears ran down her cheeks. "It's Brannick."

"Holy fuck." More obscenities flew. He shook his head back and forth several times. "We can't lose him. He's made a difference in Revel. He's one of the few men I know who've even tried."

"I know." Her rib cage felt way too small, she couldn't seem to breathe, and the tears still fell.

Keelen suddenly shouted. "Incoming." She watched him kneel on one leg as another officer moved up next to him in support, weapon drawn. Keelen held his Glock in both hands pointing into the night sky.

She turned her head and saw the distant flyers. She reached out telepathically to the woman. *Emma, is that you?*

Yes, call off your dogs.

"Keelen, it's the help I summoned. Emma Delacey is a witch with a gift for healing, and she'll have a vampire with her."

"Okay, got it. Right, that's Vaughn. I know him, though I haven't seen him in some time." He whistled softly. "He's engaged to the witch, isn't he?"

"Yes, he is."

"And they run a safe house for abducted human teens."

"That they do."

Emma flew in quickly, a violet satchel over her shoulder. She put on speed at the end then landed next to Juliet. She took one look at Brannick and spoke to Vaughn over her shoulder. "I'll need your help, Babe. Juliet, please let go and move out of the way. You don't have to go far, but I've gotta have room to work. And it's urgent."

Juliet scooted backward on the grass. Both her hands and her dress were covered with Brannick's blood, but she didn't care.

The odd pair moved into position.

Without warning, power boiled from the couple. Once again, Juliet couldn't breathe but for a totally different reason this time. She'd never felt anything like it.

But hope rose as well. No wonder Brannick had told her to call them.

Vaughn remained behind Emma but kept his hands gently on her shoulders, or maybe they were just hovering. Their connection seemed profoundly intimate.

There were times in the dreamglide when she'd felt that way with Brannick, that they had a similar connection. Oh, God, she couldn't lose him.

She grew dizzy as she watched the couple work on Brannick. But to Juliet's eye, their movements appeared to change as though they now operated in slow-motion. When Vaughn spoke to Emma, his voice was in the bass range his words slurred. Emma's were as well.

Juliet knew she was in shock. Had to be. She wanted to touch Brann, to yell at him to live, to wake up, to kiss her again. But none of that would help, and might even hurt the process. So she stayed very still, her hands in her lap.

Emma looked worried as a sheen of sweat appeared on her forehead. She was lovely with long, thick wavy red hair that she wore with the front half pulled into a top knot. Energy rose off her body like a mirage of heat waves above a distant asphalt highway.

After a few minutes, Emma leaned back, her face pale and drawn. There was still no movement in Brannick.

Juliet swallowed hard. "Is he dead?" Speaking aloud somehow shook Juliet out of her slow-motion stupor.

Emma turned slightly in her direction. "Yes and no. He's hovering in a very distant place that I can't seem to reach." Her lips were compressed and she had tears in her eyes.

Vaughn held Emma's shoulders. He looked gut-shot himself as he stared down at Brannick's inert form. Juliet knew how much Vaughn meant to Brannick. They'd been friends and brothers-in-arms for a long time.

Vaughn's voice rolled through the space. "I've known him from the time I entered Five Bridges. He got me into the border patrol and saved my life. Jesus, he was with us a month ago when we rescued those girls in Savage and later at Loghry's mansion."

Juliet swallowed hard, sliding her gaze slowly back to Brannick's wound. Despite the level of healing that Emma and Vaughn had given Brannick, the cut still seeped, and his breaths were shallow and infrequent.

But Emma wasn't done. She reached for her satchel, drew out a jar and unscrewed the lid. She then pushed Brannick's bloody, black tank up above the wound. Pulling the salve out in a big glob, she spread it over the wound, then pressed it in with the palm of her hand. The ointment had a pale violet color and smelled like flowers.

Brannick still didn't move. The witch's concoction melted into his skin and appeared to stop the bleeding.

Emma turned to Juliet. "I've done all I can for him. You'll need to take him home, then coax him back to life. Is that something you can do?"

More tears rolled down Juliet's face. "I know him well, and I'll do everything I can."

Emma nodded. "You'll do."

When Juliet stood up, she wasn't sure what to do with her hands since they were caked with Brannick's blood.

She was about to rub them on her already soiled dress, when Emma stopped her. "Hold on. I've got something you can use."

Emma reached into her satchel and drew out a small tub of wipes. She stood up, plucked about half-a-dozen from the container then went to work on Juliet's hands as well as her own.

Juliet could have done it herself, but Emma's touch, still vibrating with her witch power, eased Juliet. Emma took her time getting every bit of blood off Juliet's fingers.

Juliet watched her perform this service as though she stood outside her body and observed Emma dispassionately from thirty feet away.

Emma then hugged her, an act that jerked Juliet back into herself. "You can do this, Juliet. I know it's hard, but you can do it."

The witch's kindness had an immediate effect, filling Juliet with something akin to hope and definitely with purpose.

At about the same time, an EMT vehicle arrived.

When Emma released her, she and Vaughn apologized for having to leave, but they needed to stick close to the safe house.

Juliet totally understood. Their operation had proved a big success for human teens who escaped their captors. But their efforts had become dangerous work as well and the facility was under a constant threat of attack. Vaughn headed up the heavily armed security team that protected the building.

The moment they left, Juliet had the EMTs put Brannick on a stretcher. Each territory had a small hospital, but medical care wouldn't do Brannick any good at this point. She would take him to her home just a couple hundred yards away. Then, God help her, she'd find some way to bring him back from the dead.

~ ~ ~

Brannick's eyes were open, though he knew they were closed. Weird. From his time dreamgliding with Juliet, he recognized her home. It had a retro feel because of the bamboo furniture. He lay on his side on her couch with his chest bound tight. It was hard to breathe, though he wasn't even sure he was taking any breaths at all. His heartrate had slowed to a few beats a minute.

On some level, he knew he was either dead already, or right on the verge.

He saw Juliet on the patio. She wore a long flowered skirt, backlit with dusky, late afternoon light that revealed the lovely shape of her legs. He could recall during one dreamglide that he'd run the palms of his hands over every curve. He'd kissed the same places, spending a lot of time on her inner thighs until her hips were rocking and she begged for relief. He'd loved working her sex, using his tongue and occasionally his fangs to give her pleasure.

She returned the favor as well. She was the kind of woman who enjoyed the male body and she'd shown it. She had a special fondness for his shoulders and had spent time sucking and biting them.

He'd loved his time in the dreamglide with Juliet.

He called to her now. *Juliet?*

Though he tried to reach her several times, she didn't respond, but remained on the patio, oblivious.

He realized by the time of day, that he'd been unconscious all through the night after the battle at the canal and through the next day as well. That was a long time to be lingering between life and death.

Juliet sat down on a patio chair and laid out some birdseed on the tile not far from her feet, and waited. After a minute or so, the increasingly brave sparrows that had lined up on the rail, flew down to feed.

Why can't you hear me, Juliet?

Another woman's voice floated through his head, a very familiar voice. *Because this isn't her dreamglide. In fact, it's not a dreamglide at all.*

He shifted slightly, surprised that he could feel the pain of his wound. The ghost of his dead wife, Olivia, sat curled up in the nearby tall, wicker chair. She held one arm balanced on the side. She seemed at peace.

You look beautiful. Radiant.

Olivia smiled. *I suppose I would.*

She had blond hair that she wore in a twist, and she even had on her favorite pair of turquoise and silver earrings. They were large and dangly with three oval stones each. Her eyes were a lovely blue enhanced by the stones. One brow was raised slightly higher than the other. She'd always looked somewhat amused no matter the subject.

He asked the logical question. *What are you doing here?*

She shrugged and smiled some more. *Thought you might need me.*

Can you heal me?

She shook her head. *Sorry, I don't have those kinds of powers. Wish I did, and I also wish I'd survived the* alter *serum. When I passed, along with our children, I knew your solitude wouldn't be good for you. Robert, you were always the kind of man who needed a family. You need one now.*

He snorted, or at least that was the sound he was trying for. *Not in this rathole.*

You mean Five Bridges?

Of course. His gaze shifted involuntarily to Juliet. She stood up from her seat and snapped her fingers. The birds all scattered into the air. He wondered why she'd disturbed them until a yellow-striped cat jumped up on the narrow railing, lithe and ready for a quick meal. He stopped and stared at her then jumped into the patio.

Juliet smiled as she spoke to the cat. "You've ruined my biggest afternoon pleasure." The cat meowed in response and rubbed up against a nearby plant stand.

Brann smiled as Juliet sat down once more then patted her lap. "Fine. Then come over here and I'll give you a pet."

Brannick sighed. He knew Juliet had a relationship with her neighbor's cat. The feline was already purring as it leaped into her lap, took a complete circuit in order to find the best curling-up position, then settled in.

If cats could smile, this one did as he stared up at her. She looked down at him with an equal amount of affection and pushed her hand over his head, forcing his ears back. She ran her fingers in a slow sweep all the way down to the cat's tail.

She petted the cat the way she made love to Brannick, as though there was no greater pleasure.

You love that about her, don't you?

Olivia's voice startled him. He should have felt embarrassed that he was enjoying the qualities of one woman while chatting with another who had once been his wife.

But he wasn't really doing that, was he? Another indication consciousness had little to do with his present condition.

He fixed his attention on Olivia, wondering why she was here. She had a considering expression on her face as though she was trying to understand him. *Why haven't you remarried, Brann? It's been thirteen long years.*

I've already told you, because of Five Bridges.

Is it that bad?

It is. Corruption and murder, the trafficking of young women, drug-running and the cartels here are intent on expansion. That's why you and the children died. Remember?

Of course. She wore tight black pants and ballet flats, a clinging blue top. Her clothes had always hugged her body, the opposite of Juliet.

He wondered if he was delirious. *Where is this place that I can talk to you, yet still be here on Juliet's sofa?*

Right at the edge of paradise where you're hovering. Apparently, you can't decide to leave this world permanently, though you're trying like crazy to do so. What's hounding you toward death?

He shifted his gaze once more to Juliet. *I couldn't bear to lose her.*

Is that the reason you're trying to leave your body? You're afraid of hurting again should Juliet, or anyone else you care about, die on you?

Was that what he was doing? He didn't feel at all like he was trying to leave. But he could tell he wasn't making an effort to stay, either.

The next moment, Olivia moved off the tall, wicker chair and knelt in front of Brannick. She took his face in her hands. How was that possible?

Brann, you've never let me and the kids go. That's why I'm here. You've kept all of us on the edge of paradise, and I need you to move on so we can, too.

Olivia and the kids.

A feeling like fire burned hot in his chest, searing his heart. Grief flooded him, a profound agony a thousand times worse than his current sword cut, or any other battle wound he'd suffered over the years.

But how could he make a ghost understand his suffering? Olivia had perished with one child dying in her belly and the other already cold as ice and gone from the world. He'd been left behind to bear the weight of their lost lives, something Olivia had never experienced. So, how could she understand?

I did let you go, Olivia, to the degree I could.

You'd be married again already if you'd been able to pass through your grief.

He felt a spike of annoyance shoot through his head. *Easy for you to say.*

Her lips twisted in an amused smile. She leaned close and kissed his forehead, a strange ghostly sensation without real substance, yet real anyway. *Let us go, Brann. I'm getting our children all grown up here in paradise and when your life has truly come to an end, when you've accomplished all that you need to in Five Bridges, we'll be waiting to welcome you home.*

He was going to argue, but just like that, Olivia was gone. The fire in his chest slowly died down, yet continued to deliver a constant familiar ache. He still missed his family. But had her visit been real? Was he really stuck at the edge of a place she called paradise, keeping his family from moving on?

Or was this just the delirium from a mortal wound?

His gaze once more shifted to Juliet. The cat had disappeared, and she now stood facing the canal and the eastern skies. The sun had set, and he could see stars above the homes opposite Juliet's place. Her arms were crossed over her chest.

As had happened earlier, the awareness of how they were lovers in the dreamglide filled his mind. He couldn't believe he'd kept the two parts of himself so thoroughly separate. He had a split mind in the same way he couldn't seem to figure out whether to stay or to go.

He'd been lying to himself for five months, and he hated this reality. He felt like a coward, and the last thing he would ever be was a man who ran from a tough situation.

He knew his grief over the loss of his family held him in a tight, crushing grip. But it had also served to keep him focused on what was important in his life as an *alter* vampire. Anything that prevented him from doing his duty as a border patrol officer had to go. He was committed to being a force for law and order within Crescent Territory.

So, how had he ended up in Revel? How had he become a powerful fae woman's lover in a forbidden dreamglide environment?

And what was he supposed to do now?

~ ~ ~

Juliet stood on her patio, watching the last of the sunlight disappear from the emerging night sky. Because the back of her home faced east, she often spent this hour reflecting on her life. Agnes had taught her well.

The fae world tended to lean toward the philosophical, which of course made men or women like Roche an inexplicable anomaly in their territory.

The part of the canal over which her house looked was narrow but had strips of trees and grass and intermittent footbridges. In most ways, it resembled the main canal and surrounding landscape she and Brannick had flown through earlier.

She was at peace, or at least as much as she could be. For whatever reason, Brannick's proximity to death had taken her back to her own near-death during her *alter* transformation.

She'd been in the hospital for most of the body-wracking experience, while the part of her becoming fae had flowed back and forth with her human self. It hadn't been so much a battle of one form oppressively taking over the other weaker human part, but rather a merging. In that sense, it had been a simple adjustment, and she didn't mind being a fae woman at all.

As a sage apprentice with a wise sage mentor of great spirit and strength, Juliet read and composed essays on the nature of life as an *alter* being. She had a blog that had over ten thousand human followers and about five hundred fae plus a few dozen more comprised of the other *alter* species. Her thoughts on life in Five Bridges tended to the theoretical and not the personal which meant she'd never once alluded to her dreamgliding with Brannick.

Until this moment, her *alter* life had been entirely intellectual, hidden, surface-based and in many ways a complete lie. She used a vampire in her dream-world to get her needs met. But she refused to date or to engage in any way that would be considered normal and healthy in real-time. Essentially, she was full of shit.

She could blog all she wanted about the beauty and majesty of life, but she wasn't really living.

She turned back and stared at Brannick. His eyes were half-open and unseeing. She knew he wasn't fully present. Emma had been right when she'd said he was hovering in some dark space between life and death. She knew he wasn't gone, but he wasn't with her, either.

He'd been in her home through the daylight hours and she'd gone to him at least a dozen times to try to 'coax' him back from the edge, just as Emma had told her to. But he'd been unresponsive.

A few minutes ago, when she'd had her neighbor's yellow cat on her lap, she'd felt a shift in the energy in her living room. She'd hoped Brannick had started returning to his corporeal self.

But the energy had vanished a few minutes ago, and Juliet was back to waiting, but with hope dimming yet again.

She knew she had to make another effort to reach him, but she'd been putting it off.

Tears welled in her eyes. She didn't want Brannick to die. She feared if she pressed him again, he'd take the last step and disappear from her life completely. Only then had she come to understand that despite the hidden quality of their relationship, he'd come to mean a great deal to her. She refused to call it love. She wouldn't go that far. But he had eased her loneliness.

She knew that courage came in many forms. She wasn't a powerful witch like Emma, who had taken out a monster of a wizard just a month ago. Emma was the kind of woman Juliet admired tremendously.

But Juliet had her own brand of courage as one who helped women escape Roche's domination. The powerful fae still didn't seem to know what she was up to, though she suspected the attack on the bridge could be a hint that he'd caught wind of her activities.

She released a sigh then turned away from the soothing canal waters and the balmy evening breeze.

Moving back into the house, she decided it was time to make another push to bring Brannick back from wherever the hell he'd gone.

What she knew in her spirit was that Brannick belonged here, in Five Bridges. He was needed.

She'd long since pushed the bamboo and glass coffee table out of the way to give herself access to him. He lay supported on his side by a pillow in front and one behind him, his lower half covered with a soft blanket. She knelt close to him and shifted the front facing pillow out of the way. Fresh blood stained the white bandage wrapped around his chest.

Her heart sank. Bleeding indicated he wasn't healing himself. All *alter* species could self-heal to some degree. The more powerful the man or woman, the better the healing. Brannick should have been well on his way to restored health by now.

She placed a hand on his hip and another on his shoulder. She closed her eyes and entered her dreamglide world. She loved the initial entry moment, because she felt free, something she rarely experienced in her night-to-night fae life. Her normal existence felt bound up as if by ropes. She lived with a certain amount of tension every day, especially from the time Roche had tried to hijack her in a dreamglide.

But for this moment, as she entered the half-world most often associated with sleep and dreams, she was at peace.

Within the dreamglide she rose up from the side of the couch and watched Brannick closely. His breathing became regular though he didn't open his eyes. At least in the dreamglide his eyelids were fully closed. In real-time they were half-open, an indication of his proximity to death.

Brann? Would he be able to respond?

Juliet? Her name returned very faintly, though in real-time Brannick was still out cold.

Juliet's heart rate soared. The intuitive fae part of her knew he wasn't dead. But hearing his telepathic voice was a powerful confirmation that she had a chance right now to bring him back.

But how?

CHAPTER FOUR

Brannick's head hurt. That was his first thought as Juliet's voice penetrated his mind.

He lay in a dense, dark gray air. He couldn't see anything except wisps of smoky mist that clung to him, entwining around his arms and legs, pulling him toward the ground. A terrible fatigue had settled into every bone. He wanted to sleep, to fall into a slumber so deep he'd never wake up again.

Brann? Can you hear me? I need you to come back to me.

He wanted to respond, but couldn't. He remembered that his wife had visited him. She kept encouraging him to do something, but he couldn't remember what.

He forced himself to think, to figure out where he was and what had happened to him.

He'd been severely wounded, that much he knew. He could recall the blade point of a sword protruding from his abdomen, then disappearing. He'd felt nothing and passed out.

But, where was he now?

The dark mist tightened around him, pulling each limb hard. He had to get up. Had to fight this thing, but what was attacking him?

Some of the fog began to dispel, and he recognized Juliet's living room, but not the real thing. He could see that the edges were blurry, a sure sign of a dreamglide and one he was very familiar with.

Then he understood. He'd somehow pulled himself into a dreamglide again, like he had when he'd first gotten sliced through. He saw it as a good sign, yet the pull on his body was a formidable force.

The dreamglide hovered off to the side of the room a few feet away from Juliet. Through the blurred portion, he could see that his body remained inert on the couch and that Juliet knelt beside him, her head bent. She had a hand on his hip and one on his shoulder. She looked like she was praying. Maybe she was.

Lifting his arm, he saw that he was not quite fully formed, another indication of his divided mind.

Yep, still at the edge of paradise.

Another entity moved into the room, a very male presence. It wasn't formed at all, just a dark mass that had a familiar stench, like someone addicted to dark flame.

In real-time, Juliet removed her hands from his body and slowly stood up. She turned, her eyes wide with horror. At first, he thought she would shift in Brannick's direction, that she was reacting to him.

Instead, she faced the intruder. *Get out of here, Roche. You're not wanted.*

Roche. Shit.

Brannick knew he needed to be with Juliet, to stand beside her against the fae monster who wanted her in his sex shop. But he was so damn weak.

During his dreamglide time with Juliet, she'd told him that Roche had attempted more than once to pull her unwillingly into his dreamglide or at other times to invade hers. If he ever succeeded, he'd essentially be able to take over her mind and Juliet would belong to him. More than one gifted female fae had disappeared into his underground lair never to been seen again.

He watched as Roche, in his black, cloud-like form, began to envelop Juliet.

Panic struck hard. Though he might have his own reasons for sticking close to death, he wanted Juliet safe. And right now she was in danger and needed his help.

Within his dreamglide, he began to forge his inner strength, to pull himself out of his lethargy.

From deep within, he summoned his essential energy, both human and vampire. Somehow, he'd find a way to support her and keep Roche from taking over her mind.

As he dropped out of the dreamglide, he began the slow rise to consciousness.

~ ~ ~

Juliet stood protectively in front of Brannick, her heart hammering in her chest.

As Roche's smoky dreamglide enveloped her, fear set in, and she found it hard to breathe. Would this be the one time Roche could break through her blocks and pull her into his world for good?

Roche's telepathic voice pierced her mind. *Come to me, Juliet. Even I can see Brannick doesn't want to live. Let him go and come to me.*

Despite her hatred of Roche, she felt a powerful call on her soul to be with him, to finally give in to his will.

At the same time she knew that the way Roche's words flowed into each other meant he was heavily drugged right now. He'd probably doubled up on dark flame.

Not good.

The dark flame drug had the unique ability to enhance the fae dreamglider, and Roche had pulled out all the stops on this one. The problem was if he sustained his assault, her lesser ability and power would cause her to succumb.

But Agnes had drilled her on one point specifically; her out-of-control emotions, including her fear of Roche, would feed the invading spirit.

She needed to grow very calm if she had any hope of fighting him off.

She closed her eyes and took slow breaths. She focused, as Agnes had taught her, on her own spirit.

Again, Roche's mind pressed in on hers, every word painfully seductive. *Come to me, Juliet. I'll give you pleasure as you've never known. I'll show you ways to enhance your dreamgliding until it's the only place you'll ever want to be. I'll even let you keep Brannick with you as your pet, if you like.*

Every word he spoke, chipped away at her resolution. She found herself longing to be with him, to surrender to his will.

She reached toward Brannick. *If you can hear me, Brann, I need your help.*

She felt something from behind her, a small stream of energy that wasn't Roche. It was faint, but it was there. As it moved toward her, she drew the power within her. The moment the electrical pulses made contact, she felt a vampire connection.

Her heart leaped.

Brannick.

She blocked Roche's telepathy and reached out to Brannick. *Are you alive?*

Barely, but I'm here. Take hold of what I am as an alter *vampire. Use it. Use me. I'm here.*

She'd felt something similar on the bridge, when she'd created a cloak around herself. For whatever reason, she had a powerful connection to Brannick, even though he was deathly ill.

She invited the stream of energy to flow upward, to fill her chest, then flow into her mind. Once there, it cascaded over every other part of her, all the way to her hands and down her legs to her feet until she hummed with vampire power.

What the hell is this? Roche's words floated through her head. *I can't see you anymore. I can't feel you. Where did you go?*

Juliet didn't respond. Instead she began side-stepping away from the smoky dreamglide Roche inhabited until she was completely disengaged from him.

Once separated, the dreamglide vanished as though it had never been there. Roche was gone.

She almost started celebrating, but the fae part of her sensed another danger. She knew Roche had assembled a force in real-time that was now headed toward her canal home.

She and Brannick were both in trouble.

Returning to the couch, she discovered that Brannick's eyes were open, but they kept rolling back in his head. He'd finally come back from the brink, but he wasn't in any kind of shape to battle a powerful group of fae warriors.

She had to think, and she had to figure this out fast or they'd both be dead.

She could feel Roche now in real-time. He and his force weren't far from the Lotus Tree development.

Using her new ability to invoke a vampire shield, she surrounded herself and Brannick as tight as she could.

She almost spoke aloud to him, but knew it would be wiser to refrain from making any kind of sound.

She switched to telepathy. *Brann, we're in physical danger. I've got to get you off the couch. Now. Roche has seen your location in the dreamglide and he's coming to destroy us both.*

Juliet, I'm damn weak. You'll have to lift me up from the couch. Try using pure physical strength, but focus on being more vampire than fae. Do you understand?

The suggestion stunned her at first. But if she could create a cloak, why not take on Brannick's pure vampire physical brawn as well? *I'll try.*

She focused all her energy on enhancing her physical strength. And with a thought, there it was.

With Roche and his men so near, she didn't have time to test it out. She simply bent her knees, slid her arm under his back and tugged his arm over her shoulder. She lifted him up and kept lifting until he was on his feet. She couldn't believe how strong she was. Brannick was six-five and all heavy muscle.

Though he sagged against her and was barely conscious, he could still shuffle his way alongside her toward the arched doorway leading to the bedrooms. She kept him moving, one foot after the other.

But she could feel him slipping away again, which meant she wouldn't be able to get him all the way to the master bedroom as she'd hoped. As soon as she reached the door of the smaller second bedroom, she hurried him inside. The moment he lost consciousness, he became a dead weight. She didn't have quite enough strength to hold him up and fell with him to the carpeted floor at the foot of the bed.

At least they were out of the main room of the house and with luck, combined with her still-functioning vampire shield, maybe Roche's men wouldn't find them.

She lay facing Brannick. His eyes were closed, his face pale, but he was alive. She drew close and surrounded his back with her arm. *I've got you. Don't move. Don't make a sound. Roche and his men are coming into the house.*

Sounds of men shouting and their feet slamming against her wood floors sent jolts of fear through her mind. She forced herself to stay relaxed and not to panic. She kept her breathing steady.

A masculine voice at the door called out, "There's no one in this room."

More pounding feet toward the master bedroom.

Another man shouted. "The door to the back patio is wide open. They're gone."

Juliet smiled. She always kept the patio doors open during early May. She loved the flow of air and the balmy sweet smell of the spring flowers she'd planted at night in her garden. How odd to think this one small habit might have just saved both their lives.

A moment later, she heard distant footsteps, and by extending her fae senses, she could tell Roche's force was gone.

She remained where she was but fished her phone out of the pocket of her long skirt, then called Vaughn. She knew he couldn't leave the safe house. But when she explained what had happened, he sent over a squad of four of his security force, each of them former Elegance border patrol officers, who would stand guard over her house.

She pulled the comforter off the bed, and covered them both. Even though he was unconscious, she knew this was where she needed to be.

She only lowered the vampire shield long enough to talk to the warlock in charge. Once she gave her orders, she restored the shield.

Occasionally, she heard the men talk to each other or move through the house checking to make sure everything was secure. She probably could have joined them, but her faeness told her to stick close to Brannick.

Hours later, when dawn grew near, the warlocks closed all the shutters and sealed up the house. They would stay in her canal home through the day.

Sensing the house was secure, she finally fell asleep.

~ ~ ~

Brannick woke up from a series of dreams that may not have been dreams. He lay on his side in one of Juliet's back bedrooms and on the floor, and she was with him. He spooned her, his arm draped over her waist, but he couldn't quite remember how he'd gotten here.

He ached head-to-toe, but that's when it dawned on him. He wasn't dead.

He hadn't died after all.

Somehow, he'd come back from the edge of paradise. But who had called it that?

He squeezed his eyes shut and settled his head on his arm. His vampire healing had kicked in at last. He had a terrible pain from below his sternum, through to his back, and it was hard to breathe because of it.

But he was alive.

Something had given him a push back to the living, back from paradise.

His eyes popped open.

His wife.

He'd been with his wife in Juliet's home. She'd looked so beautiful, even if she'd only been a ghost.

Without warning, tears slid from his eyes. She'd looked exactly like he remembered her, except in her ghost form, she hadn't been pregnant. When she'd died, she'd been seven months along.

He huffed a sigh and lived with the pain of his loss for a few minutes, remembering Olivia and their four-year-old, Kelly. Eventually, his wife's most recent visit replaced his sadness. He even smiled.

She'd spoken about taking care of both their children, getting them grown up. Was that what happened after death or had he made it all up within his unconscious mind in order to make it back to Juliet?

Yet, somehow he knew it was all true. Life was a mystery, death an even greater one.

He checked his internal clock, the part of him created through the *alter* transformation that kept his sun-sensitive vampire nature safe. The black-out shutters were in place, which meant dawn had come and gone, but he was surprised to find it was past noon.

He thought back, trying to recall how he'd gotten to Juliet's second bedroom. He remembered dropping out of his dreamglide and somehow forcing himself to a place of consciousness to help Juliet. Roche had arrived ready to hijack her into some kind of weird-ass smoky dreamglide.

Yep, the bastard had tremendous fae abilities.

As weak as Brannick had been, he'd sent Juliet a stream of vampire power in order to help her fight off Roche. With it, she'd rebuilt her vampire shield, which had sent Roche packing.

But it was later, after each of them had left the dreamglide that she'd taken on his physical strength and supported him into the smaller, second bedroom. The shield had kept them hidden from Roche's men.

He'd passed out again. But Juliet had stayed with him.

He pulled her close now. She murmured something unintelligible in her sleep, then drifted off again. She'd saved his life in more than one way last night. Perhaps more significantly, she'd been the reason why he'd come back from death.

She'd needed him. Roche would have had her otherwise.

The battle with Roche and afterward the near-death experience had changed something inside Brannick. He'd been angry with Juliet when he'd first learned she'd been dreamgliding him. Yet he knew now he'd been a willing participant. More than that, he'd essentially been her lover for five months.

He had a hard time wrapping his head around this reality, even though the vivid memories which had surfaced told him the truth. He also felt a profound affection for the woman, but in real-time he barely knew her.

He leaned close and sniffed Juliet's strawberry-scented hair. She was so familiar, yet in many ways still a stranger.

He didn't know what to make of the situation. Maybe when he was fully healed he would understand better how to move forward with her.

For now, he needed to heal.

With that, he drifted off again.

When he awoke, he was on the floor alone, though he was covered by the bed's comforter. Checking his internal clock once more and seeing that the sky was dark, he was stunned to find he'd slept through another entire day.

He heard masculine voices coming from the living room. He listened for a moment, then smiled. He recognized Vaughn at once, as well as another man, Fergus, who was the alpha of the Gordion pack in Savage.

He put a hand to his chest. The pain was gone. He was completely healed.

He could also smell bacon frying, an aroma that somehow lifted him straight to his feet. He was damn hungry.

He had another problem, though. Except for the bandage around his chest, he was buck naked. He unwrapped the stained cloth and tossed it in the small waste basket by the dresser.

On the bed lay a clean pair of leathers, black socks and a black tank. Even his heavy, leather boots had been cleaned up.

Next to the nightstand was his tan and black leather bag, no doubt stocked with more clothes and hopefully his shaving gear. Vaughn would have brought this from Brannick's Crescent home.

Beneath his pants, he found his Glock and holster.

He stood there for a long moment, holding his gun, smoothing his fingers down the barrel. He'd taken out some bad guys the night before. But he knew it was a drop in the bucket compared to the force Roche had at his disposal.

Roche would be back, no question about that. But if the opportunity arose tonight, he'd do what he could to take the fae out permanently.

He wanted a shower first and didn't care who saw him in the raw. Because of the red-flowered dress dreamglide memory, he also knew the layout of Juliet's house. He gathered up his things and headed to the master bedroom and attached bath.

But no one was around.

He shaved first, then took a long shower. The hot water was exactly what he needed. Tonight he'd get a fresh start.

He dried off, then unfolded his leathers and slid them on. The tank followed. He was pretty sure Juliet was the one who called Vaughn and Fergus. Smart move. She knew her house needed a security detail.

Once he had his boots on and his belt threaded, he clipped on the holster. Sliding his Glock in place, he felt prepared for whatever the night would throw at him.

He left the bedroom and found Vaughn and Fergus sitting on stools at the kitchen island, eating bacon and scrambled eggs. Juliet's house was on the small side and their big bodies took up the entire length of the counter.

A few steps more and Juliet came into view. Most of her light brown curls were caught up on top of her head with some hanging haphazardly down her back.

The sight of her tightened his chest and for a moment made it hard to breathe. He'd always thought her beautiful, but maybe having ridden so close to death made her even more so. Her dark blue eyes were rimmed with thick black lashes. Her nose was straight except for a sexy dip near the bridge. She had strong cheekbones and full lips. She looked like she could pose for a fashion magazine and then some.

There was no question he was drawn to her. Yet, he also felt a strong need to be cautious. He didn't want a relationship with any woman, but he already felt connected to Juliet in ways he didn't get.

At almost the same moment, lovemaking images once more flowed through his head, reminding him how intimate they'd been in the dreamglide.

She turned toward him with a coffee pot in hand, her brows raised. "You're awake." Her gaze fell to his chest, the point of injury. "Feeling better?"

His hand went to his chest. "Like new. Thank you."

Her lips curved. "That door swings both ways. I owe you so much, Brannick. Roche would have had me if you hadn't helped me escape the pull of his dreamglide."

She poured coffee into a heavy, red mug and handed it to him.

He stood blocking the entrance to the small kitchen, his gaze glued to her as she moved around. She was cooking up another batch of scrambled eggs and had a plate ready. She wore a dark navy, sleeveless dress, loose like the others she wore, but this one seemed fuller around the skirt and went to mid-calf. She had on a pair of white sandals. She looked damn sexy.

He took a sip.

"You look a helluva lot better than two nights ago." Vaughn had his cup to his lips.

Brannick turned toward him, frowning slightly. "You were at the canal? After the battle?"

"Emma and I came out to help. We did what we could. Though, I'll admit, neither of us thought you'd pull through. Emma said something about you having slipped all the way to death's door."

He nodded, remembering Olivia talking to him and saying the same thing. "I did. I was right there. But Juliet pulled me back."

Vaughn scrubbed the side of his head, shorn close with tattoos showing through. He had black hair, gray eyes and was built like a tank. "Glad you made it."

Fergus lifted his coffee mug. "Here, here." He had a rough wolf's voice, something common in Savage Territory.

Brannick thanked him for helping out as well.

"My pleasure." The wolf's gaze, however, slid back to Juliet and he tracked her more than Brannick liked.

He knew enough about shifter ways to understand it wasn't personal; wolves, especially alphas, were constantly on the hunt for the right female. Despite Brannick's understanding of the situation, he took a step farther into the kitchen and caught Fergus's eye.

Brannick lifted a brow.

Fergus eyed him with a wicked glint in his eye, then took a sip of coffee. Shifter rules were different. A woman was free game unless spoken for.

Brannick stared hard at Fergus. "Keep your paws off, Fergus. Juliet's mine. And don't think I won't fight you in one of your sand pits, if it comes to that." Savage Territory had a number of pits they used for fighting, usually dominance battles among the males. As an alpha, Fergus had seen his fair share. Brannick had witnessed a couple and thought it possible he'd never survive a contest with Fergus. But like hell he wouldn't put up a fight.

Fergus had a mane of dark hair with a braid on one side. He was a handsome bastard and exuded a quality – some said a wolf musk – that had women following him in droves.

A plate with a fork appeared in front of Brannick. Juliet wore a crooked smile, her eyes full of laughter. "Eat. Now. You're still looking a little pale. And if you're going to battle Fergus, you'll need a little more muscle on your vampire bones."

Both Vaughn and Fergus chuckled. Juliet hadn't tried to refute his verbal claim on her. She knew wolves as well, since Revel bordered Savage Territory.

Her nearness, however, had awakened a couple of other needs, one of them very vampire, the other typically male. Despite his serious reservations about getting involved with Juliet, he almost set the plate down, crossed to her and pulled her into his arms. If they'd been alone, he would have. His drive toward her seemed to be increasing at light speed.

But she was right about his need for food, and the aroma of the bacon called to him.

He stood at the counter, at a right angle to Vaughn, and dug in.

After he'd finished half his meal, he glanced at Juliet. She leaned her hip against the far counter. Her arms were crossed over her chest, though she still held her mug in her hand. She looked amused.

What's so funny?

She shrugged. *I know we're* alter *species and all that, but every man I've ever known seems to chow down in the same way, like his life depends on it.*

Brannick shrugged, but smiled. *It's a primal need.*

Like other things he could think of.

Of course the real question was whether he should engage with her at all. His instincts told him she would be a willing partner, even in real-time and despite his professed reservations about what they'd been doing in the dream-world.

As he finished his meal, four security guards flew in, two warlocks from Elegance and two shifters from Savage. Vaughn explained that he and Fergus had decided to split the team with warriors from each territory.

Brannick greeted each one and thanked them for being willing to help out. He didn't take their involvement lightly. Roche was a demon with a small army he could put to use at any time.

Vaughn took off shortly afterward, needing to be back at the safe house, but Fergus remained. He spoke in his rough voice. "Vaughn asked me to stay for the duration, so I will."

Simple as that.

Brannick told the remaining men in detail about the dreamglide attack, then added that Roche was after Juliet to join his stable.

Even Fergus let loose with a sound somewhere between a growl and a disgusted grunt. Brannick couldn't have agreed more.

When Juliet moved closer to the group, Brannick watched as Fergus changed places with the warlock next to him, making sure Fergus was positioned farther away from Juliet.

Brannick approved. Fergus had a wildness about him, more than usual. He thought the shifter might be entering the mating phase of his annual cycle. For an alpha wolf that was a tough time, requiring tremendous self-control, especially around women who met his mating criteria. Clearly, Juliet was one of those.

Brannick glanced at Juliet and watched as she twisted a long curl around her finger. He became aware suddenly that he'd seen her do this dozens of times. Without warning, another dreamglide memory surfaced from their five months together, arriving in brilliant hues and sounds like the other two before this one.

Jesus H. Christ.

In this dreamglide episode, he'd taken her into the air and she was completely naked. He'd made love to her high in the night sky. She'd been uninhibited and had cried out the most erotic things, about his size and how his cock felt buried inside her.

The images, as before, rolled through his head like a movie he couldn't shut off.

Juliet turned toward him, blinking slowly. A crease appeared between her brows. She moved toward him and caught his arm. *What is it?*

He was acutely aware of the men standing close by, but he couldn't tear himself away from Juliet. They really had been lovers. *I'm remembering the time we had sex in the air. You were so … willing.* He thought that was a polite way of saying, game for anything, and she had been. *Holy fuck, Juliet.*

A blush crept up both her cheeks.

Fergus intruded. "What's going on? Is it Roche?"

Brannick turned back to the shifter and shook his head. "No, we're okay." But they weren't. Not by a long shot. Not if the memories kept surfacing like this. The images had worked him up, and he wanted to get her alone.

Juliet's blush deepened. She excused herself and left the room.

Brannick turned to Fergus. "Things are complicated right now between me and Juliet. We're sharing powers, the way Vaughn and Emma do and I'm on constant alert in case Roche should try to attack her again in the dreamglide. But I need to go talk to her right now. Will you take charge of the detail?"

Fergus sniffed the air and appeared as though he was examining carefully what he smelled. "I'll see to the men. You go to Juliet. Call me if you need anything."

Still, Brannick hesitated. He didn't feel good about abandoning the men right now.

Fergus turned to the two warlocks. "I want you both on the front door." Pivoting to the shifters, he issued a second set of orders. "One of you stay in the back patio, the other in the alley behind the garage. I'll be here, on the canal entrance side." He then turned to Brannick. "Go. She needs you." He lowered his chin, his eyes darkening. "And take your time. Whatever this is between you and Juliet, she needs you right now as much as you need her."

A silent understanding passed between the men.

He found Juliet in a study opposite the second bedroom. The small space held a large desk and barely enough square footage for the two of them to inhabit at the same time.

He'd meant to reassure her that he had no expectations and to apologize if he'd made her uncomfortable with his abrupt recounting of the in-the-sky sex.

But the moment he moved into the room, she swept a hand in the direction of the hallway. "Shut the door and lock it."

Aw, hell. So much for keeping his distance.

His whole body lit on fire. He whipped around, closed the door with a not-too-polite 'bang', and locked it.

By the time he turned back to Juliet, she'd stripped off her dress so that she stood in her navy lacy thong and a bra that pushed her breasts up into an inviting line of cleavage. Both sights made it difficult for him to unzip his pants.

She drew close and planted a hand on his chest. "Get your boots off, too. I'll need you to maneuver. I'm thinking from behind with my body splayed out on the desk."

For a quiet, artistic fae woman, she could be commanding during sex, and the vampire in him loved it.

As he worked to get his boots off, Juliet moved stuff off the desk, then turned to face him.

With his boots gone, she slowly slid her thong down her thighs and over her feet. When she rose, his gaze went straight to her light brown landing strip. His mouth actually watered as he removed his tank top.

He started toward her, but she held up a hand. "Wait."

He froze. She slid her hands behind her back and undid her bra. He watched the cups fall away from her full breasts.

He dropped to his knees and in the same motion cupped a breast and drew the already beaded nipple into his mouth. Fergus had understood what needed to happen here.

Looking up at her while suckling, he slid into telepathy. *Thank you for this.*

Her eyes flared. *Same here. The minute you walked into the kitchen, I started aching between my legs.* She had both hands on his head, caressing him.

He rose up and took her in his arms, letting her feel his cock against her abdomen. He plundered her mouth as he had while making love to her in the night sky. He hadn't been gentle with her, and from the moans she was making, it sounded like she wanted some of the same right now.

He drew back, arching his hips into her. She held onto him, digging her nails into his back.

He was rock hard. "So you want to be face down on the desk?"

"Yeah, I do."

He flipped her around, and she fell forward, arms outstretched, as she gripped both sides of the wood surface for leverage.

His cock was already twitching. When she spread her legs wide for him, he had to look away, because damn if he didn't almost come. "I need to feed as well. You good with that?"

"Yes. God, yes. I need the real thing. I've needed it for such a long time." Her hips shifted from side-to-side.

He put his hand on her sex. The woman was streaming and ready. He used her juices to lube his cock, then bent down to ease himself inside.

She moaned heavily as he pushed his way in. She was tight, almost too tight. "Am I hurting you?"

"No." She sounded breathless. "You can't imagine how good this feels to me. Dreamgliding was awesome and as close to the real thing as anything can get. But this is so raw. Fuck me, Brann. Do it now and do it hard."

He took her at her word and began to thrust, slowly at first. He was a tall man, so he had to bend his knees given the low height of the desk. But it all worked.

His balls were damn tight. It would take so little to come.

He pushed the long curly tendrils of hair away from her neck. "Arch a little for me so I can get the right angle."

She tilted her head forward.

"That's it. You ever been bitten before?"

"Only in the dreamglide. I've longed for this. Longed to feed you, Brann. Can't explain it."

"I need your blood." His fangs thrummed in his mouth, then descended. He licked her neck until he could feel the erotic pulse of her vein, then slowed the movement of his hips to focus.

His jaw trembled as he drew back, angled, then struck. His fangs hit the right depth and blood flowed onto his tongue. He surrounded the wound with his mouth and began to suck, heavy pulls on her neck.

The moment he began to drink, his vampire thrall became a seductive flow of energy that eased over Juliet. She groaned heavily in response. *I can't believe how all of this feels. Your thrall is like nothing I could have anticipated. I mean, I felt it in the dreamglide, but not like this. Oh, my God.* She shoved her hips back against his.

He sped up the thrusts of his hips, which brought a series of sharp cries from her mouth. She'd never be able to escape his hold on her because of the thrall, but her body was free to respond to his.

As he drank, he slowed down his thrusts so that he could move the full length of his cock deep inside her body.

He drew back, lost in the combination of sensations, the lushness of her hips, the tightness of her well, the way her sex gripped and released as he pushed in, then pulled out.

Between moans, she uttered small cries of pleasure. Each sound she made had his balls tightening a little more, getting ready to explode with pleasure.

He slid a hand beneath her breasts and squeezed. His palm covered both and he could feel her erect nipples. *I'm not going to last long, Juliet. You feel too good.*

Go faster then, because I'm about to come apart.

He increased his speed and felt her accompanying tension as he continued to suck at her throat.

"Oh, God. I'm coming, Brann." A long, lusty cry left her throat.

He went even faster, which sent another cry out of her mouth.

He was ready. He released her neck and swept his tongue over the wounds to seal them, then leaned back. He grabbed her hips with both hands and plunged into her.

"Brann, you'll make me come again."

"Then do it for me, baby. Let me feel your tight sex grabbing onto my cock."

When she cried out a second time, his release arrived, a hot stream through his cock, coming in pulses that felt like he was at the center of the universe giving rise to the fucking world.

He shouted as the fiery pleasure kept exploding through him.

The woman beneath him rolled, arched and writhed.

"Again, Brann." She panted.

He kept up the pace, something he could easily do as an *alter* vampire, even though he'd already come.

But what surprised him was that his balls filled up once more. "Holy fuck, Juliet, I'm going to give it to you again."

"Yes. Brann, I'm hot with need. Go vampire fast, the way you could in the dreamglide."

He was right back there, high in the night sky, holding her tight in his arms and fucking her brains out. "I'm seeing you as you were, shouting at the stars."

"I love that you're remembering more."

He sped up, the way no normal human male could and in this moment he loved his *alter* body and what he could do with it.

"I'm coming again." Her melodious voice sounded even better caught up in ecstasy.

His balls fired up once more, and because he'd already come, the sensitive passageway lit up like he'd never had an orgasm before. He roared his pleasure, the sound of his voice like a freight train inside the small study.

And it kept coming, a stream of pure pleasure, taking his mind on a trip around the entire planet. What sex he could recall from dreamgliding with Juliet had been extraordinary, but this was even better.

When at last he was satisfied, he began to slow.

Once more he slid his hand beneath her chest, fondling her peaked nipples, each of them tight from the orgasm. He kissed her neck where he'd suckled down her blood.

Gratitude was what he felt, a profound sense that the woman had given him everything right now. God, she'd fed him breakfast, offered up her vein, and let him fill her with his come.

"If I died in the next half minute, I'd die a happy man."

She chuckled. "Well, don't, please, because I need more of that. I thought I was satisfied in the dreamglide because you always made sure I finished. But this was something else." She sighed heavily.

He kept kissing her throat, her cheek, the back of her neck.

She giggled. "Do you think there's a possibility all these men *didn't* hear us?"

"Sorry, not a chance in hell. A few of those cries of yours pierced my eardrums and I think my roars were probably heard in hell."

"No, not in hell. Heaven, Brann. All pure heaven and then some." She sighed again, which helped him know he was probably leaning on her too heavily. He was a big man with thick, powerful muscles. He weighed a lot.

He drew back. "This might get messy."

He watched her slap her hand on the desk, then reach for the right-hand drawer. She pulled it open, then plucked a hand towel from its depths. "Thought we might need this. Actually, I was desperately hoping we would, and I was right." She chuckled again.

He laughed with her. He drew himself out then caught their combined fluids with the towel. He loved the sight and smell of this visceral result of their lovemaking.

He pressed the towel up against her body.

"If you want a shower, use the pocket door. I had it put in the same year I bought this place. I like more than once entrance to a bathroom."

He picked up his clothes and boots. "Join me?"

She parted her lips, maybe to decline, then her shoulders relaxed and she smiled. "I'd love to."

CHAPTER FIVE

Juliet grabbed her clothes and followed Brannick into the master bath. She hadn't had this kind of adventure in mind when she'd had the pocket door put in, but she was grateful for thinking ahead. She knew one of the guards was posted on the patio outside the master bedroom and really didn't want to see him right now.

Brannick got the water running right away. She wrapped her hair up in a towel and joined him. Of course, sharing the small space with such a big man led to another round that just couldn't be helped. He was one solid mass of muscle as she slung her arms around his neck. He kissed her fiercely as though it might be the last time. It wasn't long before he lifted her leg high on his hip and entered her.

She still couldn't believe this was happening, that she was finally having real-time sex with Brannick. She came while kissing him, his hips pistoning so fast it was like a vibration inside her body. She held Brannick's hand over her mouth as ecstasy arrived in a hot wave, her cries muffled against his palm.

He held his own roars down to a soft series of shouts. He clung to her afterward, holding her tight against his body.

Heaven.

When his breathing had finally settled down, he drew back and kissed her, thanking her profusely. She returned with her own repeated expressions of gratitude and wondered if two people had ever said 'thank you' so much after sex.

He washed her afterward, a gentle act that reminded her again of all that he was as a man and a lover. Brannick had an amazingly tender side. For such a big man, his touch could feel like a soft sweep of feathers.

Once she finally left the shower, she dried off then wrapped herself up in a towel. She brushed out her hair, restyling all her long curls in the messy configuration that worked best for her. Most of it was pinned to the top of her head and left to cascade with a few loose strands dangling down her back and a couple over her shoulders. With her curly hair, she'd given up having a more controlled look a long time ago.

While she finished up, Brannick put his clothes on. Afterward, he settled a hip on the marble sink and watched her. His dark hair, wet from the shower and combed straight back, accented the clean, handsome planes of his face. She put on a little mascara, made use of an eyebrow pencil, because her brows were just a little too thin, then touched some pink gloss to her lips.

"You're beautiful." His rich voice rolled through her, sending a shiver all the way to her toes. He reached over and touched her throat. "Are you feeling okay? Your skin is still red, though the puncture wounds have sealed."

She caught his hand and met his gaze. "I feel wonderful."

Still, he frowned. "Not dizzy? I took quite a bit."

She stood up a little straighter and weaved around on her feet, testing herself, then looked up at the ceiling.

She was smiling as she glanced back at him. "Not even a little. But you know the worst part of what we just did?"

She didn't miss the dart of concern that shot through his eyes. "What?"

She felt guilty about teasing him. "That I want to do it again so bad I can hardly stand it. How is that possible? You just took me to the heavens and back, and I want more. Guess I'm greedy."

He smiled, and his shoulders lost some of their tension.

With his hip still on the sink and one boot planted on the floor, he grabbed her around the waist and drew her close, settling her between his legs. "I know what you mean. I'd love to take you to bed and keep you there for a long time."

He kissed her, and she forgot all about her make-up and hair. She relaxed against him, sliding her arms around his neck and holding him tight.

Things heated up again so that when a loud rap sounded on the door, it took a moment to remember where she was.

She drew back, but didn't take her arms from around his neck. "What is it?"

Fergus's rough voice returned. "Sorry to bother you, Juliet, but your phone was ringing and Roche's name came up on the screen. Wanted you to know."

She drew back from Brannick, her chest tightening. She called out once more. "Roche texted me?"

"'Fraid so. Something about a woman named Mary."

She put a hand to her mouth and met Brannick's gaze. He eased her away from him, then lifted up off the sink, his brow growing pinched once more.

She called out to Fergus. "We'll be right there."

"I'll be on the canal patio."

She dropped the towel, but didn't look at Brannick. She put her thong and bra back on, then slid her dress over her head so fast, she displaced half her curls. She took a moment to straighten the worst of the lot, slid into her sandals then headed to the door.

Brannick followed her, a hand at the small of her back. Once in the living room, he waved Fergus in from the patio.

She found her phone on the kitchen counter. With trembling hands, she picked it up. In all the difficulty with keeping Brannick alive, she'd forgotten to follow up on Mary's whereabouts. Although, it had never once occurred to her that Roche might have abducted her.

She held the phone so Brannick and Fergus could see everything.

She slid the cell face a couple of times, until Roche's text came up, and there it was. *I have Mary. You have three hours to turn yourself over to me at the Fae Cathedral or your friend dies.*

She glanced at Brannick, who scowled heavily. "So this is why Mary didn't show up to drive the van. Ask how long she's been with him."

She texted back. *How long have you had her?*

Waiting for a response felt like an eternity.

Then, finally, *Ever since I found out she's been helping you steal my women and tunnel-run them out of Five Bridges. Be at the Fae Cathedral and come alone.*

She glanced at the phone again. "What should we do?"

"Well, you can't go to him. I won't let you."

She opened her mouth to protest, then realized immediately he was reacting to the situation, not offering a solution. She opted for stating her own thoughts. "I have no intention of turning myself over to that bastard, but I have to tell him something."

"Look, he's the one who said 'three hours'. Tell him you'll be at the entrance to the cathedral within his timeframe. That'll give us a chance to put a plan together."

And there it was, the response she needed.

She glanced at her clock. It was already nine. She typed again. *I'll be there before midnight. Alone.* She didn't mind lying to a liar.

Fergus nodded his approval, then resumed his post on the patio overlooking the canal. He levitated several feet in the air, disappearing from view. Even a few feet higher would give him a much better view of the entire canal. The more powerful wolves could levitate as well as transform into four-footed creatures.

While holding her phone in her left hand, she absently rubbed the top of the case with her index finger. She had to think. She couldn't turn herself over to Roche. He'd use her to service his wealthy clients while in the dreamglide. She'd die before she became enslaved to Roche.

Brannick blew the air from his cheeks. "I've never been to the Fae Cathedral. Have you?"

Juliet turned to face him. "Once. It's a large club that has three different venues within the main building. But it also houses the entrance to a massive underground development called the Village. Off to the left side of the foyer is a large, descending ramp built like a corkscrew, the kind used in big parking garages. People who live in the Village use the ramp to come and go, though no cars are allowed. I think the main form of transport is electric golf carts.

"The ramp is heavily guarded as well. It's a residents-only development. I've never gone past the large foyer, however. Never wanted to. And I don't know anyone who lives in the Village."

"So this is all below the Fae Cathedral?"

"It is." She thought for a moment. "Rumors have it that Roche runs his drug organization from the southern end, if I remember correctly."

Brannick slid his fingers through his hair. "Basically, we need to get down that ramp without being seen."

"We could use your vampire shield and sneak in to bring Mary out. That could work, couldn't it?"

"Yes, absolutely." She watched his gaze skate around.

"What are you thinking?" she asked.

He stared at her hard. "That before we can put a decent plan together, I need to know more about your fae world."

Juliet knew her territory was the least understood of all five, mostly because their lives were lived almost in secret. At least a quarter of the population lived in underground housing. There was more than one development like the Village.

There were also hundreds, heavily addicted to any one of the flame drugs, who did their own excavating and lived in filthy dug-outs. They were known as mud dwellers, because these places flooded when the summer monsoons arrived. Every year, dozens of *alter* fae drowned in the poorly constructed living areas.

In that sense, her territory had a huge disparity between places of beauty like Lotus Tree and those areas where the mud dwellers lived.

She knew she'd shared some of these details about Revel with Brannick during their time together in the dreamglide. But since he didn't have a full recollection of their many conversations, she answered all of his questions.

She then elaborated on being apprenticed to Agnes, which meant she'd become an expert in dreamgliding.

"Why is it called that, 'gliding' I mean."

"Because the more control a fae gains over this process, the more he or she can make a dream move or glide from place to place."

"So your ability to be in different places while in a dreamglide is an advanced ability."

"It is."

"A portion of your people also have telekinetic abilities. I've seen some of your fae border patrol officers draw weapons out of their opponents' hands."

"That's true, but it can be tricky. A gun can discharge during telekinesis. Only the most powerful even attempt it."

Brannick dipped his chin. "What else about your people?"

She couldn't help but smile a little. He'd asked the same question in the dreamglide, in exactly the same way.

"It's often hard to explain to an outsider what it is to be fae. We have a connection to the dream world, which is clear to everyone because of the horrendous abuse in the illegal sex clubs, like the kind Roche runs. But we also have similarities to the dead-talkers in that we seem to have a much more mystical take on life. I have a blog in fact with a number of followers."

He shifted his gaze away from her. "Wait. I'm remembering that from one of the dreamglides. You showed it to me on your tablet. You'd written about the journey of life being a marathon and learning to take the long view. In fact, you quoted a Chinese philosopher—"

"Right. 'The journey of a thousand miles starts with one step.' I did."

He pressed the heel of his palm against his forehead, then turned back to her. "It's weird when a memory resurfaces. I get a fuzzy sensation in my mind, and suddenly a memory arrives." He took her arm in his hand. "We were here in your bed. We'd been together. Christ, Juliet, did we talk that much?"

"Yes." She couldn't breathe for moment. His memories were really starting to open up and not just about the sex.

Unfortunately, with every surfacing memory, he would grow closer and closer to the truth about what she'd done to him, how she'd seduced him to be with her. There'd be a time of reckoning, and the more she was with him, the more she started dreading what now appeared to be the inevitable.

Once he knew what she'd done, she doubted he would ever forgive her. Or even if he could, he'd use the knowledge as an excuse to shut her out of his life for good. Brannick was a man who believed in the rule of law.

He gave her arm a gentle squeeze. "Hey, are you okay?"

She forced herself to blink a couple of times. "I'm fine. But I think all of this is overwhelming. For one thing, you keep remembering different dreamglides and each one gives rise to an entire host of memories. And for another, I've never spent this much time with you. It just feels so odd."

"It is strange." A rueful smile touched his lips, and he moved a little closer to her. "But it's been great, hasn't it?"

She took in a long stream of air and released it slowly. "More than I can say."

~ ~ ~

Brannick glanced over his shoulder, and seeing that Fergus was making an elevated sweep up the canal in the direction of the main bridge, he took Juliet in his arms. The memories that had started to surface showed him how comfortable he'd been with her in the dreamglide. Because of it, he couldn't help but feel a powerful attachment to her in real-time.

She seemed so familiar to him now. And yes, they'd talked a lot, and everything she'd just shared with him about the Fae Cathedral and the Village, she'd already told him in a dreamglide.

Still, part of his mind shouted a warning. He'd never planned on pursuing a relationship with any woman in Five Bridges. He would be wise to let her go.

Yet, he'd been Juliet's lover in the dreamglide for five months. And right now he wanted to know what would it be like in real-time?

"Brann, we don't have to do this. We don't have to do anything."

"I know. But I want to." He let his concerns slide away as he settled his lips on hers. He felt her entire body melt against his, a perfect fit. God, she felt good in his arms as the recently remembered dreamglide memories now merged with the real thing.

After a moment, he drew back, kissed the freckles on her right cheek, then the left. He'd definitely done this before.

"I love your freckles." He kissed the curls dangling near her forehead. He caught the strawberry scent of her shampoo. But did he know it from the White Flame club where he'd originally met her? Or had this been in the dreamglide as well?

He couldn't help himself; he kissed her again.

Her voice entered his mind. *Oh, Brann, you feel so good.*

You do, too. But this is a bizarre experience, holding you and kissing you while knowing I've done this hundreds of times before.

It's amazing.

Reluctantly, he drew back. "But we have work to do."

"We do." Juliet turned away from him and actually shook out her hands and fingers. She then glanced at him and smiled. "You get to me so quickly, you know."

He loved that she'd said that to him. He loved her dark blue eyes, her freckles and her mischievous smile. He wanted to take her back to her small office and bend her over her desk again.

But other things were much more important. "We have Mary to think about now."

"Yes, we do," she said.

With difficulty, he let her go. She lowered her chin and blinked a couple of times, then turned away from him.

Fergus landed once more on the patio and dipped his chin to Brannick. He immediately turned toward the canal.

Brannick felt a strong pull within his chest as he watched the wolf, a sensation similar to the way the dreamgliding memories arrived. Only this wasn't a dream, but it definitely felt very fae.

As he stared at the shifter, he realized he was once again experiencing an instinct more in keeping with the *alter* fae community than with his vampire self. He turned back to Juliet. "Fergus should come with us."

A frown deepened between her arched brows. "The wolf?"

"You sound surprised."

"It's just that he can't create an invisibility shield like you can. He's not a vampire."

Brannick glanced at Fergus again, but he felt the same pull as before.

Fergus was a powerful man and ally. His mane of hair went all the way to the middle of his back. The wolves, especially the alphas, grew their hair out long and wore braids to hold it away from the face. Although, he'd seen some with leather straps across their foreheads.

His *alter* instincts continued to warm up but with a fae tone rather than the cold, direct manner of his vampire nature. "Juliet, I can't explain why, but Fergus needs to be with us as we hunt for Mary."

Juliet caught his arm with her hand. "I'm feeling it too, though I'm pretty sure the weight of my conviction is coming from you. You seem to be reacting more like a fae than a vampire."

He held her gaze tight to his. Something similar had happened between Vaughn and Emma, this odd transference of powers. He'd watched Emma levitate when she'd never done so before, and she'd had Vaughn's complete skillset while doing it.

Now here he was with Juliet. She'd used a vampire shield while on the bridge and had later taken on some of his physical strength to bring him to the second bedroom.

"You know what amazed me? I can recall how you carried me to the other room. I still find it hard to believe, even though I told you to do it."

He watched her lips curve. "Would you like me to show you how strong I am?"

"I would."

She moved over to stand next to him. "Drape your arm over my shoulder."

When he did, she caught his forearm from behind and locked it in place. "Now, slowly ease your weight onto me."

He didn't want to hurt her. The muscles he carried could do damage to such a willowy female. But as he began to relax and transfer his weight to her, damn if she didn't hold steady.

Even she seemed surprised. "I can do this better than before. I mean, I doubt I'd ever be able to pick you up and carry you around, but can you feel the strength I can take on?"

"I can."

He removed his arm from around her shoulders and stared at her for a long, difficult moment. He felt uneasy suddenly. He knew what had happened to Vaughn and Emma. The couple was engaged, for Christ's sake. A witch and a vampire.

He didn't approve of the species mixing like this. Life was hard enough in Five Bridges without becoming the brunt of anti-species hate.

He also thought the level of intimacy that kept expanding between them was a big mistake. "This isn't right."

Juliet searched his eyes. "I get it, Brannick."

"You do?" He wasn't sure he believed her.

She turned her gaze away from him as though remembering. "This feels like a kind of forced connection, something neither of us wants. Though it is reminding me of decisions I made when I set up house in Lotus Tree. I haven't dated once during the four years I've lived in Five Bridges. I haven't wanted to. Life here, in the world of the flame drugs, requires a different focus. Staying alive, for one thing. And helping others as needed, like Mary right now. Anything else is exactly as you've said. It isn't right. Maybe that's why dreamgliding worked for both of us. It wasn't real. Not like this."

He was grateful she understood and that they seemed to be on the same page. But it didn't help much; her sincerity made her even more appealing. "I'm with you."

She settled her hands on her hips. "All right then. So, you and I aren't going to take this seriously, whatever this is." She waved her hand back-and-forth between them. "Agreed?"

"Yes."

She nodded briskly. "Good." She glanced at Fergus and saw one of the warlocks land on the patio. "What are your new fae instincts telling you about the rest of our security detail? Should they come with us?"

He shook his head. "I don't think so. You mentioned earlier that I could use my vampire cloak and disguise us while we moved, but an entire group could become problematic. Three of us, if needed, yes. Besides, I think they should stay here and continue to guard your home. I don't want Roche anywhere near this property, whether you're present or not."

"I like the sound of that, especially since Roche is cozy with the dark covens in Elegance Territory. If he ever got his hands on any of my personal property, he might be able to have a witch conjure a dangerous spell against me."

Brannick cringed at the thought. "I hadn't even considered the possibility of a spellcaster being involved. Then we're agreed, the rest of the security detail will remain in place."

"Yes."

"All right. Now, how about we have a chat with Fergus, then get over to the Fae Cathedral?"

~ ~ ~

Juliet inclined her head in agreement and gestured for Fergus to come in from the patio.

As Fergus drew close, he moved to stand on the other side of Brannick. She felt a strong wave of heat emanate from Fergus, very sexual in nature. She hadn't been around a lot of shifters, but she'd heard about the alpha cycle that tended to force the men into a heavy mate-hunting period. Even she felt drawn to him, as though whatever natural musk he exuded called to all women.

Brannick turned toward her, scowling. *What the hell is going on?*

She felt her eyes go wide. Busted. *Sorry. It's something about Fergus. He's very wolf right now.*

Well, dial it down because your sudden interest in him is like a fire creeping over my skin.

She stared at Brannick, aware of just how little it would take for him to start brawling with the wolf.

She drew close and took Brannick's hand. Some things, especially with a hot wolf hanging around, needed to be said aloud. "You're my man, Brannick. For as long as this mission holds. I'm with you." She avoided eye-contact with Fergus.

Brannick's nostrils flared. She saw more than one emotion pass quickly over his face: Lust, pride, and of course fear of what they were sharing together. "You're with me."

He glanced at Fergus, who slowly dipped his chin in acknowledgment.

Brannick then explained to Fergus their current plan, but he didn't let go of Juliet's hand.

She knew it was important to sustain the connection for a few more minutes, to cement their relationship in front of the wolf, but the intimate connection with Brannick started having a powerful effect. Her knees suddenly weakened and desire tore through her. Had her statement of belonging to Brann somehow triggered something inside her? Whatever it was, it felt very *alter* in nature, not something a normal human would experience.

The fae weren't big on traditional marriage, but those couples who grew committed to a relationship shared a powerful connection that enhanced an aura around each of them, especially when they were close. Her fae sage advisor, Agnes, had that kind of relationship with the man in her life. It had been unsettling at first to witness the faint silvery light that pulsed when they were near each other.

Agnes had also told her that the stronger the fae connection, the more powerful the sexual urge became, even at times overwhelming.

Right now, as she held Brannick's hand, her need to be with him physically had her chest in a stranglehold. She could hardly breathe, and she ached all over again between her legs.

Fergus folded his arms across his chest and took a step back. Then another.

Juliet stared at the floor. Her skin was so hot, she felt as though she was on fire.

"I'll give you two a minute." Fergus whirled around and headed back out onto the patio.

Brannick turned to her, and his eyes widened. "Juliet, what the fuck is going on? You're all silvery. Wait a minute. I know what this is. Juliet?"

She lifted her gaze to him and at the same time, tugged her hand from what had become a tight grasp. He stared at his own hand. "Shit. I'm glowing as well. This is so fucked up. We're not connected you and me. We can't be."

She held her hands to her face. She was trembling with pure sexual need. All Brannick had to do was push her up against the wall, press his hips to hers and she'd come apart.

She knew Brannick was upset, but she was having the worst time calming herself down. She finally forced herself to move into the kitchen. She opened the freezer and pulled out a handful of ice cubes. Taking them back to the sink, she held them up to her neck and closed her eyes. She focused on the birds in her patio earlier and the yellow cat that kept disturbing their feeding.

Thinking about birds helped. A lot.

Brannick's resonant voice, edged with anger, poured into the kitchen space. "Is this how it's going to be? Are you going to keep trying to seduce me?"

"I promise that's not what's going on here. Just give me a minute."

She took deep breaths and moved the ice cubes over her throat and up and down her arms.

"The glow is receding." Brannick sounded calmer as well.

When the intensity of the experience passed, she stood upright. "Brannick, I don't want this kind of connection any more than you do. Let's just go get Mary, then you can go home. We'll never have to see each other after this."

The furrow between Brannick's brows grew more pronounced.

She dropped the half-melted cubes into the sink, then walked back into the living area. "I'm going to change into some pants, then we can go."

She passed by Brannick and headed to the master bedroom. She had no intention of levitating while wearing a dress.

She put on a dark blue top and a pair of matching slacks. Adding a pair of brown leather flats she made her way back to the patio. Brannick was already there talking with Fergus.

When she arrived, Fergus inclined his head to her, but quickly looked away.

Brannick asked Fergus if he'd talked to the rest of the security detail. He nodded, then tossed his chin toward the south.

Juliet followed the line of his gaze. One of the warlocks assigned to the alley levitated in their direction.

"He'll be taking over for me," Fergus muttered.

As soon as he arrived, Brannick offered Juliet his booted foot, but she shook her head. She wanted to say something more to him, even to apologize for how much her faeness had encroached on his life.

Instead, she slowly rose into the air. "I meant to tell you sooner. In the same way Emma took on Vaughn's ability to fly, seems like I've got yours."

"So I see." Brannick's voice sounded subdued. She wasn't surprised. This thing between them kept taking hard, uncomfortable turns.

Though Juliet was worried about what was going on, she set aside her concerns and focused on Mary.

She rose into the air, slowly at first, getting used to her new vampire-based levitating skill. Some of the more powerful fae could levitate on their own, but she'd never been able to, though she'd tried countless times. Of all the magical *alter* abilities to possess, this one felt like freedom to her, like maybe she could truly find a new life in Five Bridges, even if she and Brannick parted ways. She could sense the ability belonged to her now, no matter what happened in her relationship with Brannick.

She entered Brann's mind. *Follow me. I'll take us to the front entrance of the Fae Cathedral. Also, I can shield myself now.*

With that, she covered herself in Brannick's vampire disguise and began moving swiftly toward the southeast. She heard Fergus call out, "Where'd she go?"

She also heard Brannick's explanation and that he'd shield Fergus.

It was better this way. Brannick and Fergus could work together, and she could go solo.

She didn't glance back at the men. Instead, she plowed forward. If her heart was weighed down with a desperate feeling of disappointment, she ignored it. She'd finally allowed herself to put a name to her relationship with Brann, but even thinking the word, brought tears to her eyes.

Oh, God, she couldn't be falling in love with him.

Dammit, why hadn't she seen this as a possibility when she'd first seduced Brannick into a dreamglide with her?

Or maybe she'd known from the moment she sat across from him at the White Flame that here was a man she could love.

~ ~ ~

Brannick's gaze was stuck to Juliet's ass. Was it the way she was levitating that had him fixated on the subtle sway of her hips or was it the searing attraction that kept hitting him like a punch to the gut?

For a hot moment he was right back in her small study, the round swells of each cheek waving in front of him, begging for his cock to pierce her from behind. And what kind of bizarre fae thing had created a silvery glow around each of them?

When she'd gone into the kitchen and covered her neck with as much ice as she could hold in both hands, it had taken every ounce of strength he possessed not to follow her. He'd wanted to strip her naked and release more of his seed deep between his legs, to mark her as only a man could show his claim on a woman.

Now he was flying behind her and feeling his leathers shrink.

But he knew the Fae Cathedral wasn't far and that he'd need to start thinking about something else or he'd embarrass himself once he landed.

The early night air was balmy as Juliet began her descent and he and Fergus followed. Fifty yards out, he saw the absurd stone spire at the center of a massive, round building. Additional rectangular buildings stretched toward the north and south, anchoring the otherwise dome-like shape. When he saw cars going in and coming out, he knew he was looking at the Village parking garages.

Whatever religious connotations the name and structure possessed were belied by the dozens of chasing gold lights on the front of the building that showcased the name, 'Fae Cathedral'.

Juliet landed thirty feet to the north on the sidewalk, away from the dozen or so males milling around the front. Cars drove up and down the street. The Fae Cathedral was definitely a Five Bridges hot spot.

Brannick dropped down beside her. Fergus landed on Brannick's far side.

No one looked in their direction, which told Brannick what he already knew; his vampire cloak was working.

Juliet turned toward him, but didn't make eye-contact. Not a bad thing. Focus right now was critical.

Telepathy? she asked.

Good idea. He glanced at Fergus. The shifter had lifted his nose to the street. He was about to contact Fergus telepathically when more of his encroaching fae instincts told him he had the ability to shape a group conversation.

He let Juliet know what he was doing, then opened up their shared telepathy to Fergus. *Hey. We're talking as three going in. You good with that?*

Fergus's nostrils flared as he glanced first at Brannick and then at Juliet. His lips turned down. *Guess I'll have to be.*

Juliet didn't seem bothered at all by Fergus's reluctance to engage with her. But then she would have sensed what Brannick knew to be true; Fergus was working hard to avoid any kind of contact with her.

We'll go in single file. Fergus, take up the rear.

He started marching before either could argue. But he felt their compliance.

Some of the group out front, all fae males, mostly addicts, called out to each other in loud voices. Each occasionally sniffed like they'd been snorting cocaine and made no effort to hide the tattoo-like flames that rose up their necks and onto their faces. The colors of the flames varied, which meant a number of drugs, including dark flame, were in play. He saw red for blood flame and a violet color for the amethyst flame drug. It gave each a severe look and since most of the addicts were emaciated, he had an impression of skeletons and Halloween.

He threaded his way, hearing both Juliet and Fergus side-step the erratic movements of the loiterers.

The entrance had a large bank of automatic double doors.

Once inside, he had the impression of an old movie theater. The walls were wood paneled, and the floor was covered with a thick black and maroon carpeting.

A long reception desk, also paneled but with ornately carved wood, served the clientele with a large display of pamphlets. Two young woman, wearing heavy make-up and low cut halters, sat behind the desk on swivel stools. Each smiled at the guests as they came and went and answered questions for any who approached.

To the left was the broad descending pathway, curving in the corkscrew pattern Juliet had mentioned earlier. Two cement posts broke up the entrance to keep vehicles from attempting to go into the subterranean region. Three burly fae warrior-types blocked the entrance, and anyone wanting to use the path had to present some kind of identification before they were allowed to pass.

Off to the right, guests moved in and out of three very different doors. When they went in or came out, depending on the venue, sometimes he heard music, other times laughter.

Fergus moved up next to him. *How far away from you can I move and still remain cloaked?*

In the same space, thirty feet.

He was on the move as he said, *I'll check for Roche in the far room.*

As Juliet headed to the middle one, Brannick took the remaining door. When a patron opened it wide, he glanced in. He didn't dare go inside, because of the shared disguise with Fergus. He needed physical proximity in order to sustain the cloak.

A band was playing alternative rock. Customers sat around a large number of small tables. It all looked harmless enough. Roche wasn't inside.

Both Juliet and Fergus returned to him. He shared what he'd seen.

Juliet shrugged. *Just as I remembered. A lot of drunks in there, and a gifted fae doing kinetic tricks. But no Roche.*

He glanced at Fergus who grimaced. *It's a goddamn restaurant and no, that bastard is not inside. So, where do we go from here?*

Brannick glanced back at the guarded pathway leading to the Village. *We know it's rumored Roche's drug organization operates from the Village. And we know he has at least one sex club that caters to wealthy clients. My instincts tell me he's keeping Mary imprisoned somewhere close to his interests.*

He glanced at Juliet. *How about you? What are you getting from this environment?*

He liked the stern set of her face. She was all business and her vampire cloak was tight as a drum. *I've focused my energies on Mary, but I'm not sensing her anywhere in the vicinity above ground. I say we go below.*

Fergus?

The wolf nodded his agreement. *Roche wouldn't keep her in a place so easy to get to. I say we head down as well.*

Brannick weaved his way through the increasing number of people entering the foyer. Juliet followed, and as before, Fergus guarded the rear.

Just as he reached the nearest guard, however, a strange communal awareness hit him, a very fae sensation. He glanced at Juliet. She'd turned toward the automatic doors, which suddenly opened up for a number of tough-looking security types.

To his surprise, Juliet took his hand and squeezed hard.

A moment later, Roche walked through.

Oh, shit.

At least ten more security men followed, maybe eighteen in all. Each bore a sword, a holstered handgun and AR-15s slung over their shoulders.

The predominantly fae crowd instinctively moved out of the way.

To Brannick's shock, Roche headed straight for him, though he quickly realized his object was the descending path that led to the underground Village.

The guards stepped aside for the entire crew.

Brannick held himself very still as Roche drew near. He could feel Juliet do the same.

Roche carried himself like a man who ran a small empire, keeping his dark feral eyes forward as he moved.

When the last of his men trailed through, Fergus's voice entered the group conversation. *Shit, that was close.* Even in Brannick's head, the wolf's rough voice made him sound like he was chewing on sawdust.

Juliet looked up at Brannick. *Should we follow after them?*

Brannick's lips twisted. *I think we should. Maybe Roche can do us a favor and show us where he's keeping Mary.*

As soon as the last of the detail crossed the threshold, Brannick slid in behind him. He then shunted off to the side to give Juliet and Fergus room to move in fast before one of the entrance guards unwittingly bumped into either of them.

Once inside, Brannick saw that the corkscrew led off in three different directions, which probably helped accommodate the constant flow of traffic.

He was about to follow after Roche and his men, but Juliet held him back.

What is it?

Juliet shook her head. *I can sense Mary, though faintly. Give me a sec. We might need to take a different route.*

You got it.

It didn't take her long. She pointed toward the far passage. *She's down there.*

Lead the way.

To his continuing surprise, Juliet levitated and flew swiftly, careful to avoid anyone walking up the corkscrew.

He joined her, moving fast as well. He knew Fergus would have no problem keeping up.

He liked that she'd gone a different direction entirely from Roche and his men.

But even as this thought went through his head, he knew it was only a matter of time before Roche figured out they were somewhere in his domain.

CHAPTER SIX

Juliet had never been to this part of Revel Territory, the subterranean world where hundreds of fae, possibly even thousands, lived and rarely left.

The ramp she levitated down was a broad spiral with tiled, curved walls all in a flowing mosaic of colors that ran the entire spectrum then repeated. It was so beautiful. She got lost in it for a moment and was surprised when the ramp opened onto a vast court with trees, planters filled with flowers and shrubs, and a host of food stalls. Dozens of fae milled about.

She moved off to the side. Brannick and Fergus joined her.

She was completely awestruck by what lay before her. There were even vendors selling all kinds of things, watches and jewelry, specialty t-shirts, hair extensions, and even some hardback books.

What the hell?

Juliet stared at Brannick. *I know, right?*

Fergus added, *It looks like an airport food court or something at a mall. I wasn't expecting this.*

Light poured down from dozens of massive fixtures, some mounted on the walls, others on the rock ceiling. No wonder the plants thrived.

Brannick drew closer to her. *Your people have created something amazing here. Why hasn't the rest of the province heard about this place?*

You have to remember, we're a secretive bunch. And even though I knew it existed, I never imagined it would look so modern and cared for. I suppose I always pictured huts or something. I don't know.

Fergus glanced up at the ceiling. *A lot of ducts and venting as well.* He groaned softly. *Am I smelling barbecue?*

Brannick added his own grunt of interest. *You are and maybe some pulled pork. Yeah, definitely.*

Juliet glanced at both men. She was about to remind them that they weren't here to eat, when it occurred to her she no longer sensed Mary's presence.

Shit. She'd uttered the word telepathically, forgetting for a moment she was linked with Brannick and Fergus.

Both men turned their heads in her direction.

What? Brannick frowned. *What's going on?*

I'm not feeling Mary anymore. I was the entire way down then I got sidetracked by the view. Now, nothing.

Brannick looked around. He took Juliet by the elbow and began guiding her in the direction of a poorly trafficked area of the court. *Come this way. Fergus, stick close. We're going to have to get creative.*

Juliet ended up with the two men behind a row of planters, her back against a wood paneled wall. She had no idea what he was thinking. But as she met his intense green eyes, his brow lined from endless concern, she could feel the faeness in him. He might be a vampire in essentials, but he was part fae now and the change felt permanent.

Brannick, what's on your mind?

I think you need to dreamglide her. We're not going to find her otherwise. Either Roche is blocking her or all these people are having an effect.

Fergus's nostrils flared. *You think she's asleep right now?*

Brannick shifted his gaze to the wolf. *More like drugged out.* He sounded so certain. *But even if she wasn't, Juliet could dreamglide to her location. Right?*

When he settled his gaze on her again, Juliet nodded.

He asked, *Are you willing to try to find her this way? In the dreamglide?*

Of course I am. There's only one problem.

Roche?

Exactly.

Fergus bristled at the sound of the man's name. *What about him? Why will he be a problem if Juliet invokes her dreamglide?*

Brannick turned to look at Fergus, his gaze intense. *Roche found Juliet in her dreamglide recently. He's got some kind of fix on her now, and he'll probably be alerted when she reenters it.*

Fergus's nostrils flared again, and he released a soft wolf-like grunt. *That bastard has way too much power.* He glanced at Juliet. *So, how do you do this thing?*

Juliet squared her shoulders. *First, I'll need physical support for the time I'm out.* She fixed her gaze on Brannick. He'd essentially need to hold her while she fell into a half-sleep. *It would probably be best if you held me, but I could sit on the floor, my back to the wall if that would work better for you.*

Brannick shook his head. *No, I'm going to hold you in my arms. If we need to move in a hurry, I'll be ready.*

Brannick, I know this isn't what you want. The closeness, I mean. Tears suddenly burned her eyes.

Hey, listen to me. Right now all that matters is finding Mary and getting her out of whatever hellhole Roche has her in. I don't think it's too much of a sacrifice to have my arms around you while you locate her.

Juliet would have expected nothing less from Brannick. He was a complicated man in many ways, but not in his essential character. He might have started out his adult life as a businessman, but he was a protective warrior at heart, and she warmed to him all over again.

Fergus asked, *So how does the dreamgliding work?*

She told him what to expect, especially the kinds of reactions he'd witness as she sank into her meditation.

Fergus lowered his chin. *I understand.* His expression grew grim as he took two steps away from her. She could smell the rise in his musk.

Brannick moved closer to her, even sliding his arm around her shoulders. The alpha was definitely approaching his mate-hunting cycle. She'd heard the wolves could become ruthless in their pursuit of a woman they deemed worthy of mating.

Brannick suggested she step up onto his boot and hold onto him as though they'd be flying together. That way, when she fell into the dreamglide state, he'd already be holding her and he could cradle her in his arms through the duration.

Juliet experienced an odd combination of dread and excitement. There was no place she'd rather be than in Brannick's arms, but once she entered the dreamglide, she feared encountering Roche. He was a male fae of tremendous power and probably wouldn't have to lose even a small level of consciousness to reach her in the dreamglide.

This reality also made her wonder if Brannick's recently acquired fae abilities would include something similar. As she stepped onto his booted foot, a sudden shiver of excitement traveled the length of her.

You okay?

Sliding her arm across his massive shoulders and around his neck, she tilted her head. *An errant thought.*

She was so close to him. The heat of his body through her thin blouse felt like heaven. When his arm gripped her waist in his familiar, strong hold, she couldn't help herself as she relaxed against him. She recalled all their lovemaking and knew it was just a matter of time before Brannick did as well.

Despite Fergus's presence, she reached up and cupped his face with her hand. Her gaze fell to his lips. How many times had he kissed her in the dreamglide? A thousand? Ten thousand?

A lot.

Ready when you are, Juliet. Even telepathically, his voice sounded resonant and had a husky edge she knew extremely well.

She looked away from him, leaning her head against his shoulder. She closed her eyes and began her descent. From years of practice, it didn't take long to arrive in the dreamglide. At the same time, she felt herself falling physically. As Brannick had promised, he caught her up in his powerful arms and now cradled her.

But the moment she entered the dreamglide, Brannick's voice was suddenly in her head. *Juliet, hold up. I'm getting something. I can feel that I'm supposed to be with you. I'm going to sit on the floor and join you. Fergus will stand guard.*

Okay.

Because the dreamglide for the present occupied the same space behind the row of planters, she watched Brannick sit down against the wall and arrange her body to lean against him. Fergus moved to stand at Brannick's feet his Glock in his hand.

The moment he closed his eyes, however, he appeared right next to her in the dreamglide.

She actually jumped. *You're here?*

I am.

Juliet had never been more stunned. What was happening between herself and Brannick that he could be in a place only the most powerful fae could achieve?

When he turned toward her, however, she realized this wasn't the Brannick in a half-conscious state sitting on the floor. Instead, this was the man who had been her lover for months.

He held out his arms to her. *Come to me, Juliet. I'm sorry my conscious self is being such a pain. I'm doing my best to work through my shit, but right now I'm here, nothing held back.*

She gave a cry and within the dreamglide leaped into his arms. He held her tight, then kissed her, a thorough, familiar exploration of her mouth that had her writhing against him, her arms encircling his neck.

He kissed her chin and her neck, suckling lightly on her throat. Her heart swelled about twice its size. *Brann, I've missed this. And you really don't like me to call you by that name.*

He kept kissing her throat and her neck. *I'm an idiot, what can I say.*

She had so many questions, though. She drew back, but couldn't quite bring herself to let go of him.

Now that he was in the dreamglide with her, they could talk, really talk, voices and all. His face took on a familiar affectionate expression, and he smiled as he looked at her hair. "I love your curls. Have I told you that?"

"Yes, many times."

He played with one of the tendrils close to her face, then met her gaze. "Again, I'm sorry my conscious self is so resistant."

"I think I get it. The dreamglide is a safe place for me as much as it is for you. The real world isn't. But your ability to be here with me so easily is stunning. How are you here?"

"It's the sharing of powers and something more. I bring my vampire strength to everything that's fae."

He glanced around and released his hold on her. She could feel his sudden tension. "What is it, Brann?"

"Roche. I can feel him moving at the edge of our dreamglide. He knows we're in the Village now, so we need to get a move on. The thing is, I'm not sure I can create the dreamglide. I can be here, right now, with you, but what we do is up to you, at least for now."

"I think I understand." She let her fae energy flow. "I'll focus on Mary."

Brannick nodded as she created an image of Mary within her mind. The fae female wasn't hard to locate. She called to her and because Mary had a lot of ability as well, she quickly entered Juliet's dreamglide.

Mary, wearing a loose, beige smock, hugged her. "You found me. Oh, thank God."

Mary released her then offered her hand to Brannick. "And you've come as well, Officer Brannick. Thank you so much, though I won't pretend I can understand how you're here."

Mary was tall and quite beautiful, a blond with light brown eyes. She could have been a model in her human form; instead, she'd been a veterinarian. Even in Five Bridges, she'd had a thriving practice. She also owned several cats and birds, most of them rescues. She didn't care for *alter* wolves, though. As a part-human, part-animal form, she thought them disgusting.

Brannick said, "Roche tried to trade you for Juliet. We're here to get you out."

Mary's lips compressed. "He's every vile thing that's wrong with Five Bridges, and I loathe him."

What Juliet noticed right away were the dark teal flame marks on her throat and cheeks as well as the dull light in her eyes. "You won't be able to rescue me," Mary added. "I'm in a heavily guarded jail cell. Roche has dozens of security personnel."

Brannick merely smiled. "Tell you what, why don't you show us in the dreamglide, then we'll go from there."

Mary agreed. Her lips parted as though she found it hard to breathe. Her cheeks were drawn as well.

Juliet caught her arm. "Roche really shot you up with dark flame, didn't he?"

"Yes, but it's also made it easy for me to respond to your search." She glanced around. "You dreamglide really well, Juliet. I had no idea you had such clarity of detail. You've been holding out on me."

Juliet had never shared her secret about Brannick, and she had no intention of doing so now.

But at that moment, Juliet felt an entity moving near the dreamglide. She knew at once exactly who it was. "Roche is here. Mary, listen. We've got to get going and I mean fast. Can you pilot my dreamglide back to your cell?"

Mary frowned for amount. "Okay. I get it. That way, when you leave the dreamglide and you're back here in the food court, you'll know the way to Roche's sex shop."

"You've got it." Juliet was grateful that Mary understood right away.

Mary faced the southern avenue. Juliet watched her shoulders grow very relaxed as she summoned her own dreamgliding power. A moment later, the dreamglide began to move and quickly picked up speed.

The underground world might have had more than one exit, but the corkscrew paths at the Fae Cathedral were the only ones Juliet knew about. Once they had Mary, they'd probably need to leave by the same path.

The street, though wide at the outset, narrowed in stages until it was the width of a car. The beauty of the courtyard had long since ended and most of the walls were rough-hewn rock with connected alleys and passageways and a few dim lights. At a main intersection, where a golf-cart lay overturned, Mary turned left.

The quality of air changed as well and the redolence of the teal-colored dark flame became more prominent. Even though they were still within the dreamglide, it was possible for fragrances or darker odors to permeate the space. In real-time, these scents would be much more profound.

"Can you smell the dark flame?" Mary glanced at Juliet, then shifted her gaze immediately back to the passageway. The dreamglide kept flowing, the edges of the space blurred.

"Yes," Juliet said.

"Even if he hadn't used a hypodermic on me, I think breathing the air would have made me addicted. One of the guards let it fall that Roche's laboratory is in the vicinity." She made a right, then a quick left.

The whole time the dreamglide moved, Juliet could feel Roche hovering around the edges, looking for a way in. She focused on the blocks that had kept Roche away for so long. But instead of engaging only her fae abilities, she drew on what had become a high level of integrated vampire power. She could feel the blocks solidifying, one after the other. She could also sense Roche's frustration and knew the moment he gave up.

She hoped this was good news. But given Roche's fae skill level, she wasn't letting her guard down.

Finally, Mary began to slow, then drew to a stop. "You can take the reins, now, Juliet, because right around this corner is the back entrance to Roche's sex club. I've stopped you here because once we turn the corner, you'll see the guards, the whole set up. You need to be prepared. I wasn't ready for what you're about to see, either. It's very distressing."

~ ~ ~

Brannick felt a profound urgency to get on with things. His fae instincts told him time was critical. But when he started hearing a lot of screams coming from a different part of the underground building, he froze. "What the hell is that?"

"Roche showed me around when he first brought me here. Unfortunately, dreamglide sex combined with real-time often involves violence. The women Roche uses for his high-class clientele have strong dreamgliding skills. But he murders the women who don't perform and of course sometimes they don't survive the sex itself. This is a brutal place."

Brannick's jaw tightened. "Bastard."

"He is at least that."

Brannick reached for Juliet's hand. He was surprised by her initial resistance. But when he glanced at her, the restraint in her expression disappeared. He thought he understood. He knew he was two different men with her, but he treasured his time in the dreamglide. It had come to mean everything to him, the reason he'd started feeling hopeful, like maybe he could have a life in Five Bridges.

The problem was, his conscious self was dug in and so far had only allowed a couple of memories to break through his refusal to engage with Juliet. She'd no doubt experienced his real-time distrust, and she'd responded accordingly.

But she drew close now and even held his arm as together Mary guided the dreamglide to the back entrance.

The double doors were wide open and four powerful, muscled fae warriors sat at a table playing cards. They were blurred so that Brannick knew the men weren't actively inside the dreamglide, but rather part of the real-time setting.

Mary led them to the left then to the right and down what proved to be a double row of cells. Though she didn't need to, she spoke in a quiet voice. "The dreamgliders, all women, live in cells like prisoners. Each is fed once a day, but injected with dark flame in the morning and at night. I'm the fifth on the right and sound asleep."

Brannick saw that each woman wore the beige shift that Mary had on.

Mary answered his question, before he asked it. "No, they don't perform their services in these sacks. When on duty, they're sent to be cleaned up, hair styled, nails manicured. They're then dressed in a costume the client has requested. After being used for the night, they return through the same process only in reverse, stripped naked, scrubbed in a shower, hair washed, nail polish removed and shot up with dark flame.

"Most hardly care because of the drugs. But I've watched them pass by. Every other woman returns cut and bruised. It's a horrible, perverse situation."

Brannick glanced into several of the cells. The women were either sitting on the side of a cot, staring into space, or passed out cold. Each had a toilet and a sink.

He still held Juliet's hand. Her soft voice broke through his horror of Roche's set-up. "Mary, I see you now."

It was no wonder Juliet had been able to bring her into the dreamglide; she was in a profound sleep and hardly breathing. She must have been recently injected because the teal flames were bright on her bare arms and throat, even on her cheeks. In an odd way, it was beautiful.

"So, what's the plan, Brannick? Are you and Juliet going to bust me out, or what?"

He shifted to look at Mary in the dreamglide. "That's the plan. We have Fergus with us as well?"

"Who's Fergus?"

"An alpha shifter from Savage. A border patrol officer."

Her nostrils flared. "Just keep him away from me."

Brannick stared at her, then remembered. Her sister had been killed in a shifter den during a dominance fight. She wasn't a fan of the wolf population of Five Bridges.

"Fergus is a good man."

Mary met his gaze, her eyes full of pain. But her shoulders fell. "Do what you must. The important thing is to get me out of here."

Juliet squeezed Brannick's hand and shifted to telepathy, though he could feel her include Mary in a group communication. *Mary, you can leave now. We'll take it from here.*

Mary offered a faint smile then faded away to nothing. Even Brannick knew when she'd left.

Juliet stayed with telepathy. *Roche is here. He's suspicious. Stay very still.*

Got it.

Roche appeared at the top of the aisle, shoving his thick, red hair back with one hand as he looked down the row of cells. He was blurred, which meant he was part of the real-time environment and an excellent sign.

Brann, as soon as Roche leaves my line of sight, I'm going to end the dreamglide, which will put us back at the court.

Ready when you are.

~ ~ ~

Juliet wouldn't do anything until Roche was gone. So, she waited. She wasn't sure what kind of temporal disturbance the cessation of a dreamglide could cause. But if it shifted the airwaves, Roche, as a powerful fae, would be able to detect it.

Once he'd disappeared the direction he'd come, she squeezed Brannick's hand, then let go of him.

When she woke up, she was in Brannick's arms. She felt dizzy from the sudden shift and took a moment to orient herself.

She glanced up at Brannick. He looked down at her, meeting her gaze, but he looked deadly serious. *Jesus, Juliet I remember the entire dreamglide, especially how I treated you and what I said to you about my own issues.*

He slowly released her and rose to his feet, lifting her at the same time.

Standing next to him, she asked, *Did all your memories come back?*

He shook his head. *No. I'm only remembering how I felt when I first saw you in the dreamglide. I'm experiencing the rush of seeing a woman who had been my lover for months. Jesus.*

Juliet stepped away from him. He reached for her, but his hand fell away. *I owe you an apology. I didn't know how conflicted I was about you or how much I was a full participant in our lovemaking. But enough of that.*

He seemed to give himself a shake as he shifted his attention to Fergus. Juliet felt him expand his telepathy to include the shifter.

Sorry. We needed to exchange a few words.

No problem. How we doin' with Roche?

Well, he's got one helluva a setup, but I think we can get Mary out.

Juliet listened as Brannick relayed the route to Fergus and described the setup at the back entrance, the guards and the row of cells.

Brannick turned to her. *Before we charge in there and disrupt the guards, is there anything else about Roche that you can tell us? Anything that might impact the mission?*

Juliet thought for a moment, but shrugged. *I honestly don't know much about what he does or how he does it, only that he's dangerous. Just never underestimate his overall power. And I should warn you, he has a connection to the dark witch covens in Elegance.*

Brannick settled his hand gently on her shoulder. *Okay. Good to know. Can you continue to use my vampire shield the way you are right now?*

Yes. No problem.

Okay. Here's how this will go. You unlock Mary's cell, and I'll keep Fergus shielded while we distract the guards.

She loved that he'd touched her. For a moment, he felt more like his dreamglide self. Was it possible his two selves were merging a little more? *It's an excellent plan, and I can hold a shield. If I need to cover Mary, I can do that as well.*

His lips curved. *Then let's get Mary out of there.*

Juliet levitated at the same time as both the vampire and the shifter. She was struck all over again how they were three separate species yet they shared the same mind and intent. The Five Bridges Tribunal had kept each territory separate for decades through the use of ditches, bridges and tons of barbed wire. She knew the reason for it, since the species tended to annihilate each other.

Yet here they were, having joined together to save one fae woman.

She flew swiftly, stunned once more that she not only had the ability to levitate, but the same skill set Brann possessed. And it rocked.

She loved the freedom of flying, as well as the joy of whisking by people, invisible to them.

More than once she glanced back to see them looking around for the source of what must have felt like a surprising movement of air.

She smiled as she flew, whipping left and right without hesitation at each juncture. She also saw that Brann knew the way as though it had been imprinted on his mind as well. Maybe the dreamgliding had done that.

She was in sync with him and began to slow at exactly the same split-second that Brann issued the order. As a group, they eased back when approaching the backdoor to Roche's high-class sex shop.

Within ten yards of the doorway, he dropped out of levitation and walked instead. He made hand signals to Fergus, specific moves that all border patrol officers knew.

She could tell Brann was communicating with Fergus and laying out a strategy.

She stood back from them and saw that the set-up was very simple. A metal box, about the size of a home fuse box, held the keys. It was even partially open so that she could see inside. She alerted Brann that she was going to check on the number of the cell, then be right back.

He nodded to her. *We'll wait to attack until you return, but get behind us in case this goes south and we need to leave in a hurry.*

Understood.

Concerned that her sandals might make a noise on the floor, she levitated once more. She moved carefully in the direction of the guards, but not one of them looked at her.

Seeing that she was free to move, she levitated faster and arced around the guard to the left, then sped down to Mary's cell. She hunted for a number and found it in the upper right corner.

She hurried back and returned to the position in the hall that Brannick had requested.

Brannick once more lifted his hand and the next moment, each drew his Glock, then switched the guns around to hold the sidearms by the barrel. Brannick came up behind the man with his back to the door and Fergus took the guard Juliet had flown around.

She watched Brannick and Fergus make eye-contact with each other then afterward slam the butts of their guns down on the backs of the men's heads. The man at the table flopped forward. The guard standing crumpled to his feet.

The other two guards froze, since they had no way of knowing what had just happened to the other two.

In an orchestrated and very quick manner, Brannick moved to the man closest to the key box and Fergus to the other fae warrior, who were both rising to their feet. They repeated the strikes of the weapons, and the other two guards fell to the floor.

Brannick gestured for Juliet to come in.

She levitated to the key box and fished out the correct key, then flew down the corridor. She took her time unlocking the door, intending to keep the noise down to a minimum just in case for some reason she could be heard.

Fergus was right behind her and as soon as the door was open, he moved in and picked Mary up in his arms.

That's when things went haywire, though Juliet didn't at first have a clue what was happening.

The moment Fergus held Mary against his chest, he lifted his head back and howled. With the woman pressed against his chest, his mating cycle must have kicked into high gear. The sound reverberated down the line of cells.

Brann, I don't know what to do. I think you'd better take care of this.

I'm on it. Come out of the cell.

Juliet tossed the key on the bed, slipped past Fergus and entered the hallway. Brannick immediately went inside, then caught Fergus's face in his hands.

Fergus became as rigid as a pole, though his mane of hair shook in an odd way. At first she thought he was fighting Brannick. Then she realized Fergus was forcing himself to regain his self-control.

Juliet glanced at Mary's inert form, her head pressed against Fergus's shoulder. The shifter's long hair brushed Mary's cheek where the drug's teal flame marked her face.

Juliet wanted to help but didn't know what to do. She kept glancing toward the head of the aisle. Fortunately no other guards had shown up yet, but she knew it wouldn't be long.

When Fergus's shaking didn't stop, Juliet felt compelled to return to the cell and put both her hands on his face as well.

He drew a sharp intake of breath and slid his gaze to her, his eyes wide. He blinked several times in a row, then dipped his chin. Just like that, the trembling ceased.

When he started to look back down at Mary, Brannick caught his chin and held it upright. He engaged in group telepathy once more. *No, Fergus. Don't look at her. We've got to get out of here. Your roar was heard everywhere.*

Fergus scowled heavily. *Shit. I lost control.*

Don't think about that now. Let's just get the women to safety.

Juliet moved out of the cell once more, and Brannick followed her. Fergus emerged with Mary cradled in his arms.

Juliet could feel the profound shield that Brannick held over all three of them now, while she kept her own disguise in place as well.

Roche's voice intruded. "I can smell you, Juliet. You're here, aren't you? You must have Mary as well since the door to her cell is wide open."

She turned around. Roche stood at the top of the row of cells with a formidable force arrayed on each side of him, at least a dozen fae warriors.

As he lifted an AR-15, Juliet followed her instincts and moved like she never had before. She didn't even have time to warn Brannick, because she knew it was now or never.

She levitated and flew fast, then took herself to a horizontal position close to the ceiling though only two feet above Roche.

When she drew close, she used a maneuver built into her because she shared Brannick's memories. She turned herself on her back, brought her feet up tight and as she got within inches of Roche's smiling face, she kicked him hard. He flew against the wall behind him, and dropped his rifle at the same time. His warriors backed away.

She didn't stay in place long. Instead, she remained levitating high above the men and stretched out horizontal once more. This time, she flew past the recovering guards and into the hall. She couldn't do anything to help Brannick or the others and could only hope they'd follow her lead. For that reason she continued to fly, though she dropped into a vertical position halfway down the narrow street.

Brannick's voice entered in her head. *We're right behind you, Juliet, so keep flying as fast as you are. Damn, but that was an incredible move. You looked like you'd been doing this your entire life.*

With the passageway empty in front her for fifty feet, she glanced back. Brannick, along with Fergus holding Mary in his arms, were flying swiftly and gaining on her.

She focused her attention dead on and flew even faster. She knew

Roche would be behind them, and that he wouldn't give up without a fight.

She had to do something.

Brann, I'm contacting Officer Keelen for back-up.

Do it.

She centered all her attention and fae ability on Keelen. It took a tremendous amount of energy because they were well underground. She focused as hard as she could. *Keelen. It's Juliet Tunney. Can you hear me?*

Nothing returned, so she tried again.

And again.

Finally, she heard his voice, though very weak, within her mind. *Juliet? Where the hell are you? You sound like you're in a cave.*

Something like that. She explained about the rescue and that Roche was on their heels. *I need back-up at the Fae Cathedral. I'm afraid that once we try to leave the building through the front entrance, he'll have us. We're shielded because of Brannick's vampire ability, but as you know, Roche has an army. If he figures out a way to trap us, we're dead.*

I'll get some troops over there right away. Maybe we can create a diversion that will help get your team out of there.

She puffed air from her cheeks. *I knew I could count on you.*

She cut off communication, then aimed her telepathy at both Brannick and Fergus, letting them know what was going on.

Within another minute she arrived back at the court but rose high into the air. Fergus and Brannick joined her. She could feel Roche now. He was in a rage as he headed in their direction, and he wasn't far behind.

A few seconds later, he and his squad flew into the courtyard though they stayed near the floor. Those shoppers nearby scattered for cover at the sight of thirteen powerful fae men with sidearms and rifles raised.

Brannick levitated next to her and took her hand. *You did good. How long will it be before Keelen gets here?*

Let me find out. She contacted Keelen, and he let her know he had five squad cars on the way. The first would be arriving within the next minute. The last, in three.

She told Brannick. But at the same time, Roche and his security force headed up the wide spiral pathway leading to the lobby of the cathedral.

She felt the tension in Brannick's hand. Invisible or not, with such a large force in a relatively small lobby, something could go wrong. She had Keelen to think of as well. If shooting started in order to provide them cover, some of the Revel officers could get hurt or worse.

This isn't simple, is it, Brann? I mean, even if we're shielded, something could wrong.

Yes, it could. But I have an idea.

She looked up at him. *What? Tell me.*

Let's go back the way we came, back to where Roche kept Mary in the cell. The clients don't come in through the Fae Cathedral lobby, so where do they enter? If we can locate it, we can leave. Roche won't even think to go that direction and Keelen and his force can keep Roche busy.

That sounds perfect.

Brannick addressed Fergus, *What do you think, wolf?*

Let's get the hell out of here.

Juliet didn't hesitate a second, but swept back down the avenue, heading south and moving faster and faster. The route was as familiar now as her own face in a mirror. While she flew, she contacted Keelen and told him what they were up to. Keelen said he'd do everything he could to keep Roche busy while they got away.

Juliet didn't slow until she approached the back entrance to Roche's sex club. The smell of the dark flame drug once more hit her full in the face.

She rose high, avoiding the guards. She began flying through what proved to be a series of large entertainment rooms. Scantily clad attendants worked the hallways, providing drinks or more syringes of the powerful dark flame drug, sometimes food.

She had to shut down the sound of the occasional painful groan or cry. She knew women were being hurt here, but she couldn't do anything for them. Not yet.

Brannick was right. As she worked her way steadily forward, she discovered a spiral path similar to the one at the Cathedral entrance. She immediately levitated up and up, with Brannick and Fergus on her heels.

At the top of the path, however, two fae warriors guarded a door. Fortunately, they gave no evidence of seeing her.

She drew to a stop. *Hold up,* she called to the group.

Brannick and Fergus moved in behind her, each silent. She could feel them both grow very still.

Let's wait for a minute and see what happens, she said.

Smart move, Brannick responded.

A moment later, she heard a buzzer, the door opened and two human men in business suits were allowed through.

The slow movement of the door prompted Juliet to rush forward. She used her acquired vampire strength to hold it open for the team. Brannick flew through followed swiftly by Fergus and a still comatose Mary.

Juliet slipped through right after them and the door continued its progress as though nothing had happened.

There was only one guard in the lobby of the sex club. A receptionist sat on a tall stool behind a desk, waiting for the next client. They both looked bored.

When Brannick opened the door to the street, she saw the guard turn in their direction. So, she put on some speed and whisked through behind the rest of her group.

The guard stepped onto the front pathway, sidearm drawn. He looked around carefully, but seeing nothing, he went back inside.

The moment Juliet looked around at the street, she knew exactly where she was in relationship to the Fae Cathedral. The entrance to Roche's sex club was near a fairly new gated community, though partitioned off by yet another set of gates to the south.

It was to Roche's credit that he'd been able to keep the location secret all this time.

She contacted Keelen and told him where they were, and how they'd succeeded in getting Mary out the back way. She could feel the tension leave the officer.

Thank God you're all right. Roche came out shouting about a minute ago that his lawyers were on the way and how we were illegally blocking the street and interfering with business traffic to the Fae Cathedral. So, what would you like us to do? Should we keep Roche rattled a little longer?

Juliet thought for a moment, then smiled. *Tell him the call that sent you there turned out to be a prank. But if you want to see his pale skin fire up, just tell him I said hello.*

She heard Keelen chuckle. *It'll be my pleasure. Take care of yourself, Juliet. And I'm glad Brannick made it.*

Me, too, and thanks.

A moment later, she was airborne and heading north with Brannick. Fergus stuck close to remain hidden within Brannick's vampire cloak, clearly not taking any chances. Mary would probably remain unconscious for several more hours.

A few minutes later, Juliet descended toward the canal side of her home. She'd long since released her shield and knew Brannick had already contacted the guards, letting them know four of them would be arriving shortly.

Fergus flew in first and by the time Juliet walked into her living room, he'd already settled Mary on the couch. She was still out cold.

He backed out swiftly, however, returning to the patio. Brannick went with him.

Juliet would call for medical support shortly, but first she wanted to thank Fergus for helping out before he took off.

Fergus had his arms crossed tight over his chest as he stared back into the house. He seemed distressed.

Juliet glanced at Brannick, lifting her brows in question.

He shook his head, not as though he didn't know what was going on but rather that he understood exactly.

She decided to go ahead and express her thanks. "Fergus, I can't tell you how much I appreciate that you were with us tonight."

He angled his body more in her direction. "You shouldn't thank me. I almost got us all killed." He then stared at her for a hard moment. "You were unbelievable by the way. Roche would have started firing if you hadn't acted as fast as you did. How did you know to fly at him like that?"

She thought for a moment, then glanced at Brannick. "I've gained some vampire skills lately." She chuckled as she slid her gaze back to Fergus. "I also hate that man more than anything else on this earth. It seemed like such a natural thing to head straight for him and kick him in the face."

Fergus frowned harder. "You're sharing Brannick's gifts, the way Emma shared Vaughn's. Maybe you've got some of Brannick's drive as well. But I apologize for putting us all in jeopardy." He glanced past her to the living room once more, to Mary lying on the sofa. "I don't know what the hell happened. Once I had her in my arms, my throat opened up."

He looked away, his gaze moving sharply to Brannick's. "I'm a danger to this mission so long as I'm near the woman. I'm heading back to Savage. Do you want me to send a replacement?"

Brannick shook his head. "I think we're good. I'll let you know if we need more troop support."

Fergus's lips turned down. "Listen. If you need me, I'm right back here. Okay? Don't hesitate."

Brannick lowered his chin. "Trust me. If Roche comes at us again, you're my first call."

Fergus glanced toward the open patio door. "Keep close watch, Juliet. I have a bad feeling about Mary right now."

"Hey, I've got this. Go home. We'll take good care of her."

Fergus, though clearly reluctant to go, said his good-byes, levitated high in the air, turned south and was gone.

CHAPTER SEVEN

As Brannick watched the wolf leave, a dozen thoughts ran through his head. Why had Fergus reacted to Mary like he did? He'd never heard of an alpha losing that much control. Was it Mary? Or the wolf's cycle?

But these questions spurred other ones as he turned toward Juliet.

She frowned. "What? You look really distressed."

He gestured for her to enter the house and spoke quietly. "Have you noticed these bizarre things that keep happening? First Connor and Iris and the way their powers moved back and forth. The same with Vaughn and Emma. And now you and me? None of this makes a lot of sense."

Juliet shrugged. "I don't know what to tell you except I think it rocks. I might not have said that before bringing Mary home, but I'll say it now. I could never have battled Roche before, not on any level, yet tonight was a different story. I took his ass to the floor." She shadow boxed, kicking her feet out a few times as well.

He couldn't help but smile at the woman with her curly hair in a wild mass, her dark blue eyes glittering.

The pleasure she took in her part of the rescue eased something inside Brannick. He recalled the moment with stunning clarity. She'd moved so fast in Roche's direction, her vampire disguise holding steady, that Roche couldn't have stopped her if he'd wanted to.

Brannick had immediately spoken with Fergus telepathically because he saw what she intended. They'd moved in behind her and gotten quickly past the guards, also flying horizontal to make sure they didn't clip any of the security detail as they flew out.

Now he was here, staring at an amazing woman. He was taken back as well to the moment he'd come out of the dreamglide and back to his real-time self. Though he could recall his time with Juliet, nothing else had come forward.

He'd hoped that all the memories of being her lover would coalesce in his conscious mind, but they hadn't. Yet he could feel now the level of intimacy they'd shared and why she'd so easily called him 'Brann' two nights ago in Carl's garage.

Juliet caught his arm in her hand. "Hey, what's going on right now?"

He opened his mouth to speak, but nothing came out. He didn't know what to say. What he did know was how much he was drawn to her, more than ever since rescuing Mary.

He might not have the words, but he knew what to do.

He took her in his arms and kissed her.

As she'd done so many times before she relaxed against him, a sensation that felt so familiar. As she parted her lips, he deepened the kiss. He wanted to take her to bed. Hell, he needed to make love to her right now.

But she drew back and slid her hands up his chest. "Just to be clear, I really want to be with you again. But we need to get Mary to a safe place. I'm thinking I should call Agnes. She'll know what to do."

He felt like a bastard being all over her when Mary was still in danger. "Of course. Where are you thinking she should go?"

"I'm not sure." Her cellphone still sat on the kitchen counter. She picked it up and scrolled for a number.

He watched her talk to Agnes in her soft yet animated way, the warm cadence of her voice pouring over him, making him hungry for her.

When she'd told Agnes everything, she turned to Brannick. "Agnes wants all three of us to join her in her compound. She says we'll be safe there and she'll be able to take care of Mary. I'm in agreement. Is that okay with you?"

"Of course." It sounded like a good plan, but he had no idea how secure Agnes's place was.

Juliet's eyes widened as she turned suddenly in Mary's direction.

Brannick could feel Juliet's sudden tension though he didn't know the reason for it.

He took a step toward her. "What is it? What's happening?"

"I don't know. I thought I felt something from Mary." She gave herself a shake. "Okay, not sure what that was all about, but Agnes said Mary will need drug rehab immediately. She keeps a nurse on staff in her compound and they're getting set up for her."

Brannick needed to know more. "And you're sure Mary will be safe there. What if Roche comes for her?"

"Agnes has a fortress. She often takes in refugees and right now that's exactly what Mary is. Roche won't bother her there."

"Not even in the dreamglide?"

"Not with Agnes around."

But once again, Juliet turned almost startled, toward Mary.

"Okay, what the hell is going on?"

Juliet took Brann's arm. "I think she's trying to tell me something. Not sure. I need to meet her in the dreamglide. Support me?"

"You got it." He held his arm out for her and she repeated the sequence in the Village courtyard. He felt her first fall into a meditative state, then she went limp. He caught her up in his arms and held her.

For a long moment, he looked down at her, at the faint freckles on her cheeks, at the curved and quite kissable bridge of her nose, the arch of her brows. Her lips were way too inviting. He was tempted to kiss her, but that's when he felt her calling to him from the dreamglide. She needed him to join her right now.

He alerted the guard on the patio to tell the entire team to be extra vigilant right now.

He took Juliet into the master bedroom and stretched out on the bed with her, holding her tight. He closed his eyes and relaxed, focusing on Juliet.

With a swift falling sensation, he landed in her dreamglide. The moment he arrived in what was a duplicate version of Juliet's living room, near her sofa, he could feel exactly why she'd called for him.

Roche.

Only he wasn't after Juliet. He was trying to take possession of Mary.

Within the dreamy fae environment, Mary was sitting up on the couch, looking dazed and scared. Both hands gripped the front of the sofa cushion.

That's when Brannick realized he wasn't in Juliet's dreamglide at all, but in Mary's, and Roche was working hard to break through.

He glanced at Juliet. "What do you need me to do?"

She headed to the perimeter of the space. He could feel her building up a protective field for Mary.

"I have to reinforce Mary's block. It's not nearly strong enough to withstand Roche and he probably got to her the first time because of it. But Roche is very close, can you feel him?"

Brannick took a moment and turned in a complete circle. "I can."

"Good, but if he busts in here even in a dreamglide, you'll need to battle him. Okay?"

"Hell, yeah." He drew his Glock and held it with his left hand supporting his right from beneath. "Just one question: If someone dies in a dreamglide, do they really die?"

She stared at him for a hard moment then dipped her chin. "Yes. We bleed, we get bruised, cut and hurt and those things stay with us. That's one reason you heard so many screams in Roche's club."

He nodded, feeling angry all over again. "He needs to leave this earth."

"Yes. He does."

Brannick once more pivoted in a slow circle. He stayed focused on Roche, while Juliet continued to strengthen the protective block all around Mary's dreamglide.

She'd gotten three-quarters finished with her task when a sudden flow of air alerted Brannick to the patio edge of the dreamglide.

Just like that, Roche walked through, his red hair flowing away from his feral, smiling face.

Brannick shifted his Glock in Roche's direction then fired. But Roche was a split-second faster and melted back into the blur of the dreamglide and vanished.

"Juliet, is he gone?" Brannick asked.

"For now, yes." She kept building. "Did you hit him?"

"No. He was too quick. Are you almost done? Because I suspect he's coming to your house next, in real-time. We need to get out of here."

"Only a few seconds more."

When she'd reached her starting point, even he could feel Juliet's shielding wall solidify.

Within the dreamglide, Mary rose from her couch and looked around. "I can feel how much better it is. But he'll come back. I know he will."

Juliet explained about all three of them moving to Agnes's compound.

Tears filled Mary's eyes. She crossed her arms over her stomach and a sob escaped her voice. "I never thought I'd survive this. I was sure Roche would take me again. But Juliet, how did you hear me call to you?"

Juliet went to her and embraced her. "I just did. Please don't worry. Brannick and I will get you to safety now. But we've gotta move fast."

Mary thanked them then once more reclined on the sofa.

Juliet smiled one last time at Mary, then took Brannick's hand. He felt a gentle squeeze of her fingers then suddenly woke up on the bed with her.

She didn't stay in a reclining position, not for a second, but leaped off the bed and quickly packed a bag for herself. "Go get Mary. I'll bring your bag as well."

Brannick headed into the living room but before he picked up Mary, he took a good look around. He wasn't taking any chances.

By the time he scooped Mary up, Juliet returned from the bedroom, their bags in her hands. He noted with approval that she'd already brought her new vampire cloaking power around her. If Roche was in the air, he wouldn't be able to see her.

He moved to the patio and let the guard know to expect trouble. "Get Officer Keelen over here right now in case Roche shows up."

"Yes, Sir."

Juliet launched into the air and flew swiftly in a northwesterly direction. Brannick drew Mary tight against his chest, shielded them both, then punched airspace.

By the time he caught up with Juliet, she was already making her descent. She also began easing off her vampire shield, a wise move given that several guards ranged in front of Agnes's compound.

All five heavily armed warriors lifted their weapons as she touched down. Brannick, however, chose to keep his shield tight and remained hovering in the air ten feet up.

Juliet spoke quickly. "Agnes is expecting me."

"Your name?" The officer in charge had a tough look about him, short black hair, square jaw and a grim expression.

"Juliet Tunney. I have a vampire with me, from the Crescent Border Patrol, Officer Robert Brannick. He's carrying the victim, Mary, in his arms."

The man looked her up and down more than once. "The names all check out." In a louder voice he called out, "Officer Brannick, show yourself, but remove your shield slowly or we will fire."

Juliet turned toward him. Her eyes held a concerned expression. She must have feared he wouldn't obey.

But Brannick respected the man right away and did as he'd been ordered. He released his cloak carefully, making himself visible in stages to all the men. At the same time, he eased down to the sidewalk.

Each guard grew stiff with tension at the sight of him, firearms held with both hands.

He understood why. Every known safe house in Five Bridges suffered intermittent and deadly attacks by the enemy. Vampires frequently worked as hired guns.

The men hired to guard these houses served heroically.

The lead guard glanced at Mary. "You may pass, all three of you."

The guards lined up on either side of the wide walkway. Brannick noticed none of them holstered their guns.

When the door opened, an older woman with wavy black hair drew the door wide and beckoned them to come inside.

The guard closed the door and Agnes smiled at Juliet. "It's wonderful to see you."

When Agnes opened her arms, Juliet moved in and accepted the warm embrace.

Agnes continued, "I've been so worried about you. I've felt uneasy every night for the past week. And now I see why."

Agnes wasn't nearly as tall as Juliet and had to look up at least a foot to meet Brannick's gaze. Juliet made the introduction.

The older sage fae had intense gray eyes and stared into Brannick's for a long moment. Her eyes narrowed and she settled her hand on his arm. "You're an *alter* vampire, but you're more than that now. Why? Or is this the thing I've been hearing about. Something to do with two other Crescent Border Patrol officers. What are their names?"

"James Connor and Nathan Vaughn."

"Yes, and each is engaged to a witch. They share powers now, don't they?"

"They do."

Agnes's penetrating questions forced Brannick to turn toward Juliet. Framed in relationship to Vaughn and Connor, he realized he was on the same track as these men.

Juliet returned his gaze, but lifted her chin. "We don't have to make the same decisions, Brannick. Your friends each had a very different experience from ours."

Not so different, in Brannick's opinion. But he didn't speak the words out loud.

Agnes shifted the subject as she placed her hand on Mary's forehead then traced the teal-colored flames on her cheek. "She'll be out for several more hours, but I can feel that her dreamglide blocks have been strengthened. Was this your work, Juliet?"

"Yes. Roche was coming for her in the dreamglide."

Agnes once more met Brannick's gaze. "You were involved as well."

"I fired at him when he broke through, but he escaped unharmed."

"Glad you were there." Agnes looked to be about fifty, which meant that was the age she'd been when she entered Five Bridges. The flame serum slowed the aging process so that long-life was attained by everyone enduring the transformation. But the serum didn't reverse age.

Agnes turned down the hall and waved them forward. "Come with me. My team is expecting Mary. She'll have medical attention as well as a witch healer."

~ ~ ~

Juliet watched Brannick settle Mary on what was essentially a hospital bed. Recovery from dark flame wouldn't be easy for her. Despite the fact that she'd only had the drug in her system for a short time, the volume of the drug that had kept her comatose over a period of days meant she'd have to go through a painful withdrawal.

A trained nurse would stay with her throughout and the healing efforts of a witch would help make the transition tolerable.

Agnes assured Juliet and Brannick that Mary would receive the best care, then led them out into the well-lit courtyard. Brannick took both bags from Juliet, a thoughtful gesture.

Several townhouses flanked either side of the lush central landscaping. Juliet counted three doors on each side. Agnes headed toward a cottage at the back of the property, past another green belt with tons of purple petunias and beds of white alyssum.

The small, charming house had the look of something well-tended by a woman who loved to garden. A massive spray of pink climbing roses formed an arch over strong metal supports. Brannick had to dip his head not to get caught by a few flowers that needed pruning.

"I used to live back here, when I was first consigned to Five Bridges and made the place my own. I probably should have torn the cottage down when I built the townhouses. But I liked the house a lot so I kept it as is.

"When I got your call, Juliet, I had one of my assistants bring over some essential groceries. Just let me know if you need anything else and I'll send one of the guards out."

She unlocked the door, then handed the key to Juliet. "You're both welcome to stay as long as you need to. Though I should warn you that we have guards on the rooftops and there is no levitating allowed above the second-story rooflines. My guards are trained to shoot on sight, to wound first, if possible. But if not, we've stopped caring who dies.

Do you understand? We're fighting to save lives here and we're under frequent attack, not unlike Vaughn and Emma at their safe house."

Juliet nodded. "I understand."

Brannick's warm, rich voice flowed over her shoulder. "We both do."

Agnes once more narrowed her gaze at Brannick. "Of course you do. You built a tunnel rescue set-up with support from the human part of Phoenix."

"That's right."

"And has all this happened recently because Roche found out?" She flipped her hand back-and-forth a couple of times.

"I don't think he knows about my tunnels," Brannick said. "But he did figure out that both Mary and Juliet were helping women escape from Revel. That's one of the reasons he took Mary. She drove for me."

"I see. Well, that explains a lot."

"There's something else." Juliet felt compelled to add the other component. "Roche was using Mary's abduction to try to force me to work for him in his specialty sex club, the one that features dreamgliding for his wealthy human clientele."

Agnes drew her lips tight together, compressing them and shaking her head. "There is so much beauty in being an *alter* fae, but Roche has made a travesty of our gifts."

She took a deep breath then clapped her hands together as though to clear her head. "All right then. Give me a shout if you need anything. Otherwise, I'll see you tomorrow night." She glanced up into the night sky. "Dawn won't be here for a couple more hours." She headed back down the walk.

Though Brannick shoved the door wide, he waited for her to walk through. She smiled up at him as she passed by.

The interior was much more modern than she'd anticipated. The wall separating the living area from the hall had been replaced with a couple of heavy wood supports and opened up all the way to a small kitchen and dining area in the back.

To the left was a small study that overlooked the front communal garden. Agnes had left a wall of books inside as well.

Moving toward the back, she put a hand to her stomach and turned to Brannick. "Suddenly, I'm starved. Are you hungry?"

"Yes, I am." He set both bags next to the stairs, then headed toward the fridge. A moment later she heard the soft suctioning sound of the door opening. "Agnes provided steaks and beer. Guess she was thinking of me. But there's some lettuce in here."

Juliet couldn't help but smile. "Hey, all of that sounds great right now, but I'm going upstairs to freshen up, if that's okay. It won't take me a minute, then I can help throw something together."

"Do what you need to do." He held up two beers.

"Yes," he said. "Absolutely. Must have a beer."

"I'll fire up the grill. We've got plenty of time before the sun starts easing over the horizon."

Juliet picked up her bag. The stairs faced the backyard so she had a view of Brannick as he stepped outside, beer in hand. She could see a gas grill as she started up the stairs.

The second floor turned out to be the sole bedroom with an attached bath. She removed a full-length lavender gauzy dress from her satchel and with her hastily put together cosmetic kit headed into the bathroom.

One look at her hair told her what she needed to know. She always had a sort of wind-tousled hairstyle going on, but right now she looked like she'd been in a tornado. Well, maybe not that bad, but she had work to do.

She got undressed except for her thong, then slid into the floor-length, halter gown. It was made of cotton, very comfortable and had a crumpled look. It felt good to be out of slacks.

Next, she tidied her make-up and for a moment even considered using cover-up to get rid of her freckles. But a sudden memory, of Brann kissing each one, led her back the other direction and she put the make-up away.

He called up to her from the bottom of the stairs. "Grill's getting hot."

"Wonderful. Be down in a sec."

She headed to the bathroom once more and using her curl-calming spray worked her tendrils into a less wild state.

She put on a pair of flat t-strap sandals with lavender flowers on the 't'. Lifting her skirt, she headed downstairs.

When she reached the bottom, she could see Brann through the open sliding door and for a moment, her heart stopped. He had the steaks on a nearby table ready to go and the gas grill closed to get good and hot. He held a beer in his hand.

The scene was so damn homey, tears stung her eyes. Nothing but pure affection poured from her in that moment, watching him, remembering how he'd made love to her on the desk in her small canal home, then in the shower. How he'd made love to her in the dreamglide all those months.

A thought occurred to her, a very wicked one. And Brannick would have enough essential power to pull it off as well, especially since they were sharing powers.

If they wanted they could combine real-time with the dreamglide while making love. This was the same kind of erotic experience Roche wanted her to do with his upscale clients.

There was a risk however, though it wasn't at all physical, but rather involved the possibility that Brannick would regain all his memories of their time together.

They'd already started filtering through to his conscious mind. She felt certain, however, that if she engaged in real-time sex while she employed the dreamglide, he might suddenly experience a complete recollection of all that had happened.

Then he'd learn what she'd done to start the process in the first place, that essentially she'd broken into his dreams and seduced him.

Her heart rate rose. She didn't want him to know.

She was pretty sure once he did, he'd end things with her.

He glanced in her direction. "Your beer's on the kitchen island." His gaze took her in head-to-toe, landing at least twice on her cleavage. He smiled. He appeared to approve of her summery gown. "You look great."

"Thanks. And I'll start the salad." She needed to buy herself a little time to calm down.

After she took a long slow swig of the dark ale, she forced herself to breathe. She honestly couldn't bear the thought of Brannick leaving, not now.

In the end, she decided she should stay away from mixing real-time sex with dreamgliding.

Tears bit her eyes. Why was she being so emotional? She'd always known her time with Brannick would come to end.

Except … dammit … she loved him.

A long slow gasp filled her throat.

Somewhere in all the sex, and the dozens of long conversations in the dreamglide, she really had fallen in love with a vampire. And it was time to face the truth of it.

As she stared out the window above the sink, she watched a breeze push the trees around.

Oh, God, what had she gotten herself into? She loved Brannick. Maybe she had from the moment she'd met him in the White Flame club.

"Hey," he called to her from across the dining area. "Are you okay?"

Glancing at him over her shoulder, she had to blink a couple of times to bring his face into focus. "Sure." She didn't say that she felt like her heart was being ripped from her chest. "I'm going to make a salad."

He nodded. "I just put the steaks on."

When she lifted her beer to him, he smiled then headed back outside.

The moment he was gone, she turned toward the window once more and let a sob escape her chest. Why had she let this happen?

She pulled red leaf lettuce, tomatoes and a cucumber from the crisper.

Fortunately, the sink placed her with her back to the rest of the room. As she washed the vegetables, she let a few tears fall into the stream of water. She didn't try to stop them. She knew what she'd done and even at the time she'd understood the consequences. But she'd told herself she was just getting her needs met so it was okay.

Yet how could she have known he'd open up to her in the dreamglide and be such a wonderful companion? In that sense, he'd seduced her right back, not just with his phenomenal body, but with everything he'd shared with her through the five months of their time together.

By the time she had everything sliced up and placed in a bowl, she was better composed. She gathered up plates and silverware at the same time, then set the table.

Afterward, she took her beer outside to join Brannick.

He opened his arm to her. It was such a tender gesture that her eyes burned once more. But she bit back the tears and instead slid her arm around his waist.

He held her close, a comfortable sideways embrace.

She didn't say anything. She didn't trust herself to open her mouth. She just sipped her beer and stared at the grill. He'd already turned the meat.

Finally, she was able to say, "The salad's ready."

"Just a couple minutes and we'll be good to go." Brannick remained silent as well.

During dinner, Juliet found it increasingly hard to make small talk. So much so, that Brannick finally asked, "Is anything wrong?"

She couldn't tell him the whole truth, but she had to say something. "I'm overwhelmed with what we've been through in such a short period of time. Three nights in all. I mean, you and I barely know each other—"

"Except for the conversations you said we had in the dreamglide."

"Yes, except for that. But this conscious side of yourself is still new to me and I can't be more than a stranger to you. Most of the time, I find myself wanting to say something, to make a comment or even a joke. But then I realize you won't get it, that it would be about one of our dreamglide conversations. I think that alone has taken a toll. I keep having to weigh my words."

He glanced away from her and sipped his beer, then set it back on the table. "The few, full-blown memories I have of you are amazing. So I have some insight into what we were like together, as well as who you are.

"But truthfully, I don't know what to make of this situation either. I mean, you must know how I feel about relationships in Five Bridges."

"I do know," she said. "And in that sense we're the same. Yet we've carried on a very close, intimate relationship all these months." She looked away as that feeling of impending loss returned.

He reached over and grabbed her hand. "Hey. I didn't mean to make you feel sad. Maybe we should both try not to think about it right now. Instead, how about we celebrate that we brought Mary out of hell tonight."

At that, Juliet relaxed. "You're right. I've been caught up in the wrong things."

She left the table and brought back two more beers.

He opened both, handing her one. He then held his bottle angled toward her. "To Mary."

She smiled once more as she tapped the neck of his bottle with hers. "To Mary."

Conversation fell to a pleasant recounting of the rescue and his gratitude that Agnes had a safe house for women like Mary where she could stay and begin her recovery.

After dinner, clean up was quick since Brannick helped. She liked that he'd brought dishes over, scraped them clean and washed while she dried. She was reminded of the few times he'd actually talked about his wife, Olivia, and their marriage. She'd heard the love in his voice and his great appreciation for her.

Now Olivia was gone, along with their two children, one of them unborn, and Brannick was a vampire living out his life in Five Bridges.

And she got to share beers with him, steaks, and even wash the dishes.

When she'd hung the damp towel on the oven door handle, she'd started to leave, but he caught her arm and pulled her back.

He searched her eyes. "I've been wanting to kiss you all through dinner. It's been hard not to reach for you. But you seem upset, so I'm not sure what to do here. I'll leave you alone, if that's what you want."

She gasped. "No, that's not what I want at all." The rest of the words got jammed up in her head.

Because she was afraid she would blurt out something terrible, like the truth, she leaned up and kissed him. And not a gentle kiss but one full of exactly what she wanted from him right now.

He responded with a heavy groan, encircling her with both arms and holding her tight against his chest.

The feel of him was what melted all restraint. She no longer cared exactly how the next hour or so progressed, or even whether or not they ended up having a combination of real-time and dreamglide sex.

She just wanted to be with him, nothing held back.

He deepened the kiss so that his tongue pulsed within her mouth, short erotic jabs that reminded her of other things he liked to do with his tongue.

She grabbed the back of his neck and pressed her lips harder against his.

When he drew back, his eyes were at half-mast. "How's the bed upstairs?"

She couldn't help it; she grinned. "Big."

His lips curved as well. "Good. But I need a shower."

"Sounds like the perfect place to start."

~ ~ ~

Brannick led Juliet upstairs, holding her hand the entire distance. He'd had a difficult time figuring out what was bothering her. She'd been upset about something from the time she'd changed her clothes. Though he thought he understood at least part of it. He was pretty sure she was looking too far into the future and not seeing him in her life.

He could relate because dammit this time with her, having hot sex on her desk in her home by the canal, sharing her fae abilities, watching her slam her feet into Roche's chest, all made him want something he was determined not to allow into his life.

He despised Five Bridges and from the time he'd signed up to serve as a border patrol officer, he'd been sure of an early death in this stinking long-lived world.

But being so close to Juliet and having a memory of their intimacy, if not all of it, had created a powerful longing for more than he could possible give.

When he reached the top of the stairs, he felt oddly grateful they were both in an unfamiliar place though he couldn't say why. From what he could remember of the dreamglide sex, they'd been in each other's bedrooms a lot, but never in this one.

She led him to the bathroom. "Want to share?"

"Hell, yeah," he said. "I'm remembering what happened last time."

She tilted her head and played with one of her long curls. "Actually, I have something else in mind." She turned on her heel and he followed on a quick trot like a begging dog.

The bathroom, in the same mode as the rest of the house, was small. The shower was part of the claw-foot bathtub. He took off his boots and socks, then stripped out of his leathers and tank top. The whole time he watched her as she very slowly lifted her arms and untied the halter of her clinging lavender gown.

He waited, as though struck dumb as men often were by the hope of getting to see a naked woman.

She played it well, easing the straps down very slowly. His arousal stiffened the slower she went. Seeing that her gaze was on his cock, he held his erection in his hand and stroked for her.

Her lips parted and her tongue made an appearance.

But the halter kept moving lower until the fabric dipped to reveal her peaked nipples. When she let the top go and took her breasts in her hands, his fist went faster.

It all seemed so familiar, yet not. She must have done this before, but he couldn't remember.

He watched as she lifted a finger to her lips and slid it inside then drew it out. It was wet as she circled the tip of one of her nipples.

He groaned and released his cock. He closed the short distance between them, then took her in his arms. He let go of her in almost the same move since he had to get her dress off.

She was laughing as he tugged it over her hips to pool around her feet. She kicked her sandals off.

When she was naked, he drew back just enough to get a good look, but couldn't bring himself to let go of her. He dipped down and took a breast in his mouth, or as much of it as he could manage. Juliet had beautiful breasts.

The sex earlier had been quick and very hot. But right now, he wanted to take his time. He didn't know what tomorrow would bring, or even the next few hours.

Her hands were on his head. She used her nails to push his hair back. "I love that you're doing this to me. I love it so much. You have no idea."

At that, he rose up and met her gaze. "What are you saying?"

Tears filled her eyes. "I've been so freaking lonely, Brann. I was married and I loved my husband. Life was going to be so good. We were trying for a baby."

He pulled her close and his own eyes burned something fierce. He squeezed his eyes shut not wanting to remember his family or what had happened to them, or even that in his recent delirium he'd spoken with his wife again.

"Maybe we could be together, or at least try." Had he actually said the words out loud? He drew back and caressed her face.

Her head moved slowly back-and-forth as though in disbelief. "You mean like a relationship? A real one?"

He shrugged. Damn these words were so hard to say. "Maybe we could date."

He was breaking his rule even speaking the words out loud.

CHAPTER EIGHT

Juliet gripped both of Brannick's arms. "You want to date me?" They were the words she'd longed to hear for months. But even in the dreamgliding, Brann had held to his non-relationship position.

"Is that something you'd like to do?" His brows were drawn together and a dart of concern flashed through his green eyes.

She reached up and kissed him on the lips. "Yes, so much. You have no idea. I mean, if you knew what you were like, I mean when we made love—"

"I caught a glimpse of it in the dreamglide. The last time I was there, I felt how close we'd become and that sensation hasn't left even though the memories are still spotty."

While holding his arms, she smoothed her thumbs over his arms. His skin was warm beneath her hands and so real. She was overcome again and leaned into him, settling her head against his shoulder.

She wanted this so much with him. At the very least she wanted to date.

It occurred to her she'd made the ultimate mistake in engaging with Brannick in the first place because now she craved him. "Remember when we first met? At the White Flame club after Mary recommended me to you?"

His arms tightened around her. "How I could ever forget? You were so sincere, so determined to help."

"I was. I am. Nothing else matters very much. But I loved your commitment as well. It got to me. I think that's why I found you in the dreamglide." Her breath caught. She'd almost told him the truth, but she doubted he had enough knowledge of fae things to fill in the blanks.

He drew back and took her shoulders gently in hands. "If I'd felt in any way free, I would have asked you out then and there. I kept biting my tongue to stop myself from asking for a second meeting. I kept trying to think up a reasonable excuse to see you again."

She smiled and caressed his face. "I was doing the same thing. I was so attracted to you. Maybe it was your intensity, I don't know." She slid her finger down the habitual pinch between his brows, smoothing out the skin. "This is always here, you know. I see it as your doggedness to do what you can in our world."

He inclined his head slowly. "That's not likely to change anytime soon, if ever."

"I know. But it's part of what I love about you and yes, that's me saying I'd love to date you, whatever that looks like in Crescent or here in Revel. Even if it's a stolen, brief, secret time, I don't care."

She knew when the last words left her mouth she'd just described the five months of their dreamglide sex: Stolen, brief and secret. So, secret that even Brann didn't fully know what had happened between them.

"Then it's settled. Once we figure out how to neutralize Roche's intentions toward you and Mary, we'll start going out."

She smiled, if a little. "We should revisit the White Flame since they honor all five species."

"We'll definitely do that."

"Then you can take me back to your place and we'll do some wrestling in your Alabama Crimson sheets."

He drew back and held her gaze. "We'll wrestle, and I'll use my tongue a lot, the way you like it."

She caught his face in her hand. "I love your tongue. Everywhere."

"I know you do. And I love your mouth surrounding my cock and taking me in as far as you can."

She nodded in three quick jerks of her head. Her lips had parted mostly because she was finding it hard to breathe. Her whole body trembled with anticipation.

He released her and turned to get the water flowing. "First, I'm going to clean you up really good."

~ ~ ~

Brannick used a lot of foamed up soap on his hands and took his time with her body. He'd never thought he'd be with Juliet like this, though his fantasies were often full of her, especially when he woke up first thing at night.

He massaged her breasts, taking his time. She had sensitive breasts, and he was pretty sure he could make her come easily with a couple of fingers buried inside her and his mouth tugging on a nipple. "Have I made you come like this in the dreamglide? With my mouth I mean?"

Her lips were parted and her nostrils flared. "Yes." The word came out hushed, almost hoarse.

"Thought so. How about you spread your legs and let me make it happen now."

She moaned as she sidestepped and gave him room. He rinsed off her chest, took her breast in his mouth and began to suckle. He slipped two fingers inside her sex and her back arched. "Oh, God that feels good. So real."

He chuckled, then licked her stiff nipple. He knew what she meant. He could sense the dreamglide sex had rocked, but this was his tongue on her breast, in real-time.

As he drove his fingers in and out, angling to catch the sensitive rim, her hips started to rock. He sustained a steady rhythm. *Is this how you like it?*

Her voice entered his mind. *I can hardly breathe. Suck harder.* She panted between gasping moans.

He obliged her, and the sensation of her breasts against his tongue and her stiff nipple had his cock twitching. Her hands were all over him, one of them rubbing up and down the arm that pistoned his fingers and the other across his back. She kept digging her nails into his muscles, and he loved it.

Brann, go faster. Just a little.

He increased his speed and sucked in strong pulls on her breast. He felt her go very still and quiet, which he knew meant she was close.

He sped up a bit more, then her body rolled and she cried out in a long anguished sound. "Oh, God!"

He kept up the movement of his hand and the pulls on her breast, savoring each cry and moan, then the shuddering of her breath as she began coming down.

He slowly came to a stop and released her breast then eased his fingers from her body. He loved how her sex held onto him as though not wanting to let him go.

He was blocking the flow of water in the small space, so he moved to the side to let the warm stream beat down on her. He caressed her abdomen and fondled her bottom. She turned her face into the water and let it run over her. She used the soap and took off the last bit of make-up.

When she shifted back to him, he supported her with his arm around her shoulder and leaned her back a little so he could look at her. A memory resurfaced of doing something similar. But mostly of looking at the freckles on her face and enjoying the sight of them. He took his time now, as he knew he had in the dreamglide memory, to kiss each of the prominent ones. "I love your freckles. You're so beautiful, yet somehow they anchor everything about you."

Had he also said something like that in the dreamglide? He wasn't sure. As he drew back from kissing a freckle on her left cheek. He met her gaze. "Have I said that before?"

"In a different way. I don't think you used the word anchor, more like earthy or something."

"I love that we're doing this."

She angled her head to expose her throat. "There's something I'm desperate for you to do again. I mentioned it earlier, you know, that I had something else in mind during shower time."

The slope of her neck was a strong, clear invitation and lit up his vampire needs. He licked a line from the base of her neck all the way to her jawline. *You want me to bite you?*

I do. So bad. You have no idea.

Have we done this in the dreamglide?

She moaned. *A lot, and you said it was very close to tasting my blood, though it wasn't completely real. But it's amazing when I know that I'm feeding you.*

He kept kissing her neck and tonguing the area above her vein where he wanted to strike. *So how do you want it? Because I can take your blood from more than one place.*

Her body arched once more. For such a contained woman, she really let loose when it came to sex.

She was breathing hard. *I'm feeling greedy right now. I want to feel your fangs on my neck then anywhere else you want to use them. Maybe you should pick.*

He couldn't help but smile. *This is going to be a tough decision, because I want to do it all.*

~ ~ ~

Juliet waited as he made up his mind. She'd already come once, but Brann was an amazing lover. He knew how to take her to the pinnacle, ease her back, then ride her to the top all over again.

He continued to lick her throat, then slowly descended down her right arm, licking and kissing the entire way.

He sank to his knees, not a small feat in such a narrow tub. The water beat on his back. She wanted to leap on him and bite his neck. That's when she realized her own mouth pulsed oddly as though she had fangs, though she didn't. She was definitely sharing all his vampire qualities.

When he reached her wrist, she gasped. She thought they'd done everything together, but apparently, his conscious mind had a few tricks left.

He took both her forearm and her hand in his grip, then turned her wrist, so that he could easily reach the collection of veins at the base of her palm. He began to lick in slow wet swipes.

Yes. Even her telepathic voice sounded hungry to her own ears.

He licked a few more times. She kept her gaze fixed on his bobbing head. He paused, drew his head back, then struck. She cried out and her sex clenched hard. When he began to drink, she leaned her head against the shower tile and closed her eyes. Her whole body trembled with pleasure.

You taste amazing, Juliet. Your blood is like nothing I've ever had before.

She couldn't remember that he'd said anything similar in the dreamglide even though the dream-blood would have had a flavor.

What's it like, Brann?

I'm trying to find the right description. His mouth had formed a seal over most of her wrist.

She settled her hand on the back of his head, enjoying the rise and fall as he suckled.

He continued, *It's like a kind of sweet grass with a wine flavor. I know that doesn't make sense, but it's amazing and I'm feeling pumped, stronger.*

Is that different for you, feeling stronger?

Yes. Completely. This is about you, Juliet. Can't explain it.

My mind is feeling very loose. Ah, your vampire thrall.

Yes. She loved his resonant voice, even during telepathy. *But didn't you experience it, or a version of it, when we were dreamgliding?*

Juliet thought for a moment. *Yes, but not like this. All I want to do is stay here forever.*

It'll be more intense when I take from your neck again.

Can't wait.

After a moment, and way too soon, he licked the wounds to seal them, then rose to his feet. He had blood on his mouth as he pulled her into his arms. He kissed her so that she tasted her own life force.

Because she was sharing his nature, she groaned heavily. *I want to taste your blood, Brann.*

He drew back and searched her eyes. "You do?"

"I can't explain it, but I'm like you now and I want your blood."

He kissed her again, harder this time. *That is such a turn on.*

He drew back, then shut the water off. "Let's get more comfortable and don't worry, I'll let you have all you need."

He stepped out of the tub and onto the rug, then turned back and offered his hand. She loved this about him, how careful he was with her, to keep her safe, to offer assistance.

As soon as both feet were planted on the mat, he took a towel from the rack behind him and started wiping her down. She grabbed another one and draped the white terry over his shoulders.

He kept drying her off, and she returned the favor. She moved the towel over every inch of his gorgeous body, letting her hands feel the sculpted shape of each muscle. She worked on memorizing him, not knowing what the next night or even hour would bring. Her wrist tingled where he'd taken from her.

When they were both dry, he picked up a couple of washcloths and took her by the hand. He led her to the bed, whipped the covers to the foot of the bed and told her to lie down on her back.

She had no problem taking orders from him. She could feel his excitement.

When he stretched out next to her, she took his erect cock gently in hand. She used her thumb to rim the head. He closed his eyes and drew in a stream of air through pursed lips. "Damn that feels good, but maybe you should stop."

She smiled and released him, but kept her hand on his thigh.

He looked down at her, meeting her gaze. "You sure you want to drink from me?"

She caressed his shoulder. "I do. You know how you've been taking on some of my fae skills? Well, the vampire in me needs this. I mean, even my gums throb like they're trying to produce fangs, but can't."

"Lean back down."

She dropped her head flat on the bed like before. He rose up on one elbow and laid the washcloth on her chest. "When I break the skin, it might not keep flowing for you. Vampires can release two chemicals, one that helps the blood flow and another that seals up the wounds."

"Understood."

He settled his wrist on the washcloth, then leaned down so that she had a perfect view of his fangs. The sight of them made her back arch. She didn't understand why, exactly, but the dangerous nature of what she was doing with him turned her on.

He made a quick strike with his fangs. "I've released a chemical, so hopefully I'll be able to feed you longer."

She slid her hands beneath the washcloth, then drew his wrist to her mouth. She closed her eyes as the vampire part of her, so newly formed, took over. She formed a seal around the wound and began to suck.

She groaned heavily as the first taste of him hit her tongue. She couldn't explain it, but it tasted like Brann, like a flavor she knew in the marrow of her bones.

You are exquisite.

And your body is beautiful. Jesus, Juliet, I'm feeling a thrall. You can tell me to do anything right now, and I'd do it.

She opened her eyes and met his gaze. She could see that she had control of him, and it excited her. *I ache between my legs. Think you can do something about that while I feed?*

His eyes rolled in his head. "Pull your knees up and pivot with me as I shift position."

She was right with him. She held onto his wrist, suckling as he moved.

"You'll have to switch to the other side of my wrist. I need to turn my arm in a different direction."

She did what he asked, which gave him just the right angle to kiss her abdomen and move lower.

As she settled her lips around his wound once more, his blood spilled into her mouth. She caught it and formed another seal.

By then he'd moved low, and when his tongue hit her sex, she released a heavy, muffled groan.

Brannick went to work on her. Juliet got lost in the dual sensations of the vampire need to gorge on his life force and the feel of his tongue and his lips as he played over all her tender heated folds.

She was breathing hard through her nose as pleasure began to soar. *Pierce me with your tongue, Brann. Now.*

He grunted as he slid his free hand under her hips and grabbed both cheeks. He lifted her up and drove his tongue deep into her well.

She kept suckling, kept tasting him as he penetrated her with his beautiful tongue.

He started to thrust faster. Ecstasy built inside her, like a rush of wind fast approaching. She didn't stop drinking, but let the wind come.

It poured through her sex, pleasure on pleasure, driving up her chest and funneling into her brain. She trembled head to foot. Brannick kept thrusting into her, and the pulsing pleasure continued until her whole body was in a powerful state of ecstasy.

On instinct, she swiped the wounds on his wrist and released him. Her back arched as her mouth opened and she cried out repeatedly, unable to believe the long string of pulses that kept breaking over her sex. Brannick was right; blood was empowering.

Finally, the last orgasm shook her body from her feet to the top of her head. Maybe she passed out or something, but she definitely saw stars and for a moment wondered if she was looking up into the night sky.

She lay panting as Brann moved to lie down next to her again. She rolled her head, struggling to bring in enough air. "I think I left the earth with that one."

He leaned over and kissed her, then touched the sides of her lips with his thumb. "You have my blood on you."

"It was so good, all of it, the way you worked my sex and the way you taste. Oh, Brann." Her emotions rose up like a wave, all her affection for him, how much she'd loved the past five months with him, everything.

For a moment, she was taken back to how it had all begun. She knew she'd done a bad thing, and given how close she felt to him, she almost told him the truth.

But she couldn't. She was afraid to lose this moment with him.

She cupped his face with her hands. "You've come to mean so much to me." Her throat was tight all over again.

He caught her hand, turning it to kiss her palm. "When I'm in the dreamglide, I remember everything. But the moment I fall out of it, my mind closes up. Yet the emotion remains and I feel the same way. I just wish I could remember more."

She wished it as well.

Then again, she didn't.

~ ~ ~

Brannick felt the fae part of him come alive as he kissed Juliet's palm over and over. He could feel what she was feeling, the profound way she had enjoyed her time with him.

Though his memories still lagged, he knew he felt the same way when he was with her, as though he wanted to devour her.

Full of such a demanding drive toward her, he slid his legs over hers, positioning himself between her thighs. "I need to be inside you."

He balanced himself on his forearms and leaned down to kiss her. He lowered himself onto her, loving the feel of her hands as she fondled the muscles of his back and his arms.

Placing his cock at her entrance, he pushed, then drew back, wanting to watch her as he made his way inside.

He rested on his forearms and curled his hips. He loved the way she held his gaze, lips parted. He kissed her freckles again, pushing in farther with each touch of his lips to her face.

What was newly fae within him felt connected to her, his awareness of her emotions heightened. "I've wanted to be here with you, just like this, from the moment you walked into that club."

"You have been." She dragged her fingers through his hair.

"In the dreamglide?"

"Uh-huh."

As he pushed, her body rolled. He loved that his cock brought her so much pleasure.

But he needed something more from her. Using his hand, he shoved her thick, brown curls away from her neck and licked up and down her throat.

She moaned heavily. "Yes, Brann, please. Take from me at my neck."

He stopped the movement of his hips, angled his head and struck quickly. The moment the blood flowed, he began thrusting steadily once more.

Her whole body jerked, and she moaned. "I feel dizzy from the thrall again and it feels so good."

What surprised him was that though he was drinking from her like a vampire, the rest of him was channeling his fae instincts. He reached for something he didn't at first understand. Yet he felt compelled to keep at it, to keep pressing into the unknown. It was like walking through a fog within his mind.

He pushed, the same way his hips kept pistoning inside Juliet, driving toward ecstasy.

He was after something.

Suddenly, he broke through. He saw the blurred edges of the room. He was in bed with Juliet, drinking from her, in more than one place.

Brann, what have you done?

I think I've created a dreamglide and pulled us both in.

She grew very still beneath him, but he didn't know why. His own need seemed to escalate. He'd heard about this, being in both places at once. Hell, Roche had built an entire sex club around just this experience.

He felt completely captured by his former experiences with Juliet as well. He became one with them in terms of emotions. He could remember them all.

He drove into her faster. But Juliet had grown so still, as though stunned. *Juliet, be with me. Please. Don't leave me now.* He kept drinking from her.

He felt her move once more, her arms snaking around his back. *I'm here. This is incredible. Every sensation feels twice as erotic and intense. But hold on tight, I'm feeling something.*

I am too, like it's going to pick us up.

Just like that, they were airborne, yet he remained joined to her. He groaned because his real-time-self continued plunging in and out of her and drinking from her throat.

The wave passed at least for the moment. He was now in real-time. Her blood was a fire down his throat, building him up.

Brann, this is amazing. The way this feels.

I know. It's extraordinary. Like gliding.

Here it comes again. I want to come like this with waves picking us up.

She cried out as the dreamglide wind catapulted them, rolling them over, yet keeping them entwined at the same time.

I'm close to coming, Juliet. How about you?

~ ~ ~

Juliet held tight to Brann. But she wanted to experience the gust-like sensations in a different way and stretched her arms out to each side.

Brann, go faster. Here comes another gust.

Brannick pistoned into her, going vampire fast. *I can feel it, but I can't hold back anymore.*

Me, neither.

When the gust came, they rolled and rolled. The orgasm swept over her just like the wind, flowing through every part of her.

Pleasure peaked, drifted away then with another roll through the dreamglide, peaked higher still.

She cried out in a loud constant cry. In the dreamglide the sound reverberated,

Brann released his hold on her neck, swiped the wounds, then drew back to shout his ecstasy. The wind didn't stop but kept rolling them over and over.

Juliet opened her eyes within the dreamglide and there in a beautiful panorama were all the times she'd been with him from the beginning. The erotic nature of it combined with the wind, and that Brann continued to drive into her, sent her soaring once more.

She held onto him this time, her body arching with his, slamming against his groin, feeling the push-pull of his beautiful cock as pleasure rose and fell.

Another wind came. He held her gaze in the dreamglide. "Can you come again?" He smiled at her, his green eyes lit with a glow.

"Yes. But it may be the death of me."

His smile broadened, the one she knew so well from all her dreamgliding time with Brann. She returned his smile and gripped his shoulders. He held her tight.

This time, when the gust came, she leaned up and kissed him as they rolled around and around. They were stationary yet moving, a miracle of the *alter* life.

He plunged his tongue as he continued to drive into her over and over. She could feel him come this time, his cock pulsing inside her.

Ecstasy took her on yet another ride, only this time, she must have fainted with the joy and pleasure of it.

When she opened her eyes, the dreamglide was gone. She was in bed in Agnes's small house and looking up at Brann.

His back was arched, his body very still, his eyes closed. His skin glowed with a silvery light as it had in her canal home, and he looked like he was caught in an out-of-body experience.

When he finally opened his eyes, they were still lit up. He glanced down at her, then around the room. "Everything seems so quiet like when a storm passes."

"It was a storm of wind, yet we were completely safe."

He began to relax as he lowered himself to his forearms. "So that's why Roche built an entire business for dreamgliding sex. It was incredible."

She stared at him, waiting, wondering. Had the dreamglide changed things for him? Prompted any memories?

She worked at staying as relaxed as possible, but how much did he remember now?

"What are you thinking about?" He stroked her curls, petting her head in a way she'd always loved. Did he know that?

"I'm wondering if the dreamglide changed anything for you." She searched his green eyes. He seemed content, something he'd allowed himself to experience in a dreamglide, and now he was clearly feeling it during real-time. Even the furrow between his brows had eased.

He smiled. "I feel like it changed everything, yet nothing really. And you've never done this before?"

"Participated in dreamglide sex combined with real-time? No, never." She smiled and caressed his face, tracing a finger over an eyebrow, down his cheek, then his lips.

He kissed her, a beautiful, warm, lingering kiss. He was still buried inside her, and because he was a big man, she could feel him even though he was no longer erect. "I feel wonderful when I'm with you, Brann." She shook her head. "I could so get used to this."

"Well, I did ask if you wanted to date."

"You did."

"I don't remember your answer."

She caressed his face, running her thumb slowly along his cheekbone. "You know damn well I'd love to."

He nodded several times in a row, his brow growing furrowed once more.

Her fae senses told her that his mind was shifting gears in a major way.

Oh, God, was he remembering?

He searched around and located the extra washcloth. He carefully slid it between them and as he pulled out, he placed it against her well. "Would you mind if I headed back to the shower?"

"Of course not. Is everything okay?"

"Sure, I mean, yes. Can't explain what's going on, but I need to think. About all of it."

Juliet's heartrate rose as he left the bed and she found it hard to breathe.

She knew his memories hadn't completely returned, but her fae instincts were screaming at her that she was in serious trouble.

~ ~ ~

Brannick felt uneasy as he got the water steaming hot, then climbed under the spray. His fae intuition had kicked in again, letting him know that something big was on the way. He needed to prepare for it, yet it didn't feel like Roche. This felt different, like it had to do with Juliet.

He had to bend to wash his hair. Most showers weren't built for men his size. He took his time, but fear jabbed at him. He was in trouble; he just didn't know what it would look like when it arrived.

As he finished rinsing off, something similar to the dreamglide suddenly rushed through his mind.

The he understood.

The memories were coming.

Yet, he resisted.

He planted a hand on the wall and stepped out of the tub.

A piercing headache followed.

He slid to the floor and put both hands over his eyes. What the hell was happening?

Images began flying at him erratically, one after the other, of his bedroom and Juliet, then her bedroom and him pulling back the comforter and dropping onto the bed. She leaped on him and laughed.

Another memory followed, the one on the bridge when she wore her red-flowered dress. He understood that all his prior experiences in the dreamglide were coming forward, one after the other and that his newly acquired faeness was telling him to let them come.

The moment he accepted the memories, the headache ceased and it was as though a movie began to play in his mind. He could now hear the conversations, all the ones Juliet had told him they'd had.

He saw himself completely relaxed with her and enjoying being her lover. The memories were sequential as well, though he was working through them backward, the most recent first. He also let them move swiftly through his head.

He smiled a lot and at times became so aroused that he almost called for Juliet, then another memory would take him on a different dreamglide. One time, he'd actually gotten into a canal paddle-boat with her, though it hadn't lasted long. His size had started sinking the small craft.

He'd levitated her out of it before it sank and they'd returned to her home laughing and shortly afterward made love.

Back the memories went. His affection for her grew more and more profound, until he was all the way at the beginning, asleep in his bed.

That's when he understood exactly what Juliet had done to initiate the affair.

And that's when he knew he'd never be able to be with her again.

CHAPTER NINE

Brannick stayed on the bathroom floor for a long time, his bare ass on the rug. He stared at the cupboard opposite and barely saw it. He kept running the last few images over and over in his mind of what Juliet had done to him in the dreamglide.

She'd broken a huge Revel Territory law to start the process. He saw everything now, every single memory he had of her, including the fact she'd used her dreamglide to break into his dreams without invitation or permission.

She'd essentially hijacked him in his dreams. In that sense, she was no better than Roche. Even the Tribunal prosecuted any fae caught doing so.

Dream boundaries were most often violated for the purpose of gathering information like security codes and passwords. The sale of the information following a dream hijacking became the evidence used in a trial. The cartels, being vulnerable to this kind of tampering, made sure the Trib took this crime seriously. At least twenty fae were serving time for dream violations.

Though Juliet hadn't stolen anything from him, she'd broken the law and infringed on his basic *alter* right.

Yet he was also appalled at how much of a willing partner he'd become right away, without hesitation, as though his unconscious mind didn't care about the rules. Instead, he should have turned her away and reported her then and there to the Board of Sages. Her own kind would have prosecuted her immediately.

Everything he believed about Juliet became tainted. She'd violated a sacred trust and shattered every reason he had to trust the woman.

He rose from the floor and slowly put on his leathers and tank. He hadn't meant to get dressed again. He'd planned on staying through the day with Juliet, making love to her, sleeping beside her, then doing it all over again.

He couldn't now, and given that dawn was close, he needed to get the hell out of Agnes's compound.

He worked on his socks and boots. When he finally stood up, he met his reflection in the mirror. He drew close, staring at the groove between his brows. Juliet was always trying to smooth it out. But she couldn't. He lived in Five Bridges. He'd lost his family to dark flame and his parents and sister to the bad choices he'd made.

From that point, when the cartels had taken their revenge, when his sister had been sacrificed by one of the dark covens, he'd promised himself he would take a different approach to his life here.

And he had.

He'd shut down his need for vengeance and had kept his road straight and narrow, no exceptions. He ran his tunnel rescue system in the same way. He'd set up specific guidelines. Because of it, he'd saved over three-hundred women, a few of them as young as thirteen. Without those rules, his organization would have collapsed a long time ago.

He served as a border patrol officer because he was committed to the rule of law. He'd thought Juliet held the same values.

He moved into the bedroom. She sat up in bed, but she'd never appeared more somber.

Yet, seeing her brought the most recent memories rushing forward, of making love to her, of experiencing a combination of real-time and dreamglide sex.

He'd kissed her freckles.

He'd felt something profound for her.

He'd asked to date her.

Now all of it seemed like the worst kind of manipulation. She'd essentially seduced him into a relationship with her.

"Juliet."

"You know everything, don't you? The memories have finally merged."

"They have. You seduced me into this relationship during a dream hijacking."

She sighed heavily. "I did."

"Which also means that you lied to me from the time the first memory surfaced in the garage."

"Only about how the whole thing started with you."

"Why didn't you tell me the truth?" He needed to know her rationale.

"It's very simple. I loved my time with you, and I didn't want the dreamgliding to end."

"So you deliberately misled me."

She seemed oddly relieved. "Yes. I should never have approached you in the dreamglide and for that I apologize, but not for the rest, not for what followed. Knowing you, being with you despite the questionable beginning, has been one of the finest experiences of my life."

"You don't sound remorseful at all. I'd think you'd at least give me that." He scowled at her, angry by her almost indifferent attitude. He had no idea what she was thinking or how she justified her actions.

~ ~ ~

Juliet's heart beat so hard in her chest she felt as though it would burst at any moment.

It was difficult to look at Brannick. Though she'd always known this moment would come, she'd hoped oh-so-foolishly that it wouldn't. Yet here it was, her terrible sin exposed.

Oddly, she remembered that old saying about chickens coming home to roost. And they had, by the thousands and each of them squawking at her for being so stupid and for breaking such a critical law in the first place.

His voice beat at her from across the room. "So you have nothing to say."

She glanced up at him once more. She could feel her heart tearing at each of its moorings. "Would you have asked me to date you, if you hadn't felt this kind of connection to me?"

He frowned even harder. "I don't know. But it's not the point. Or are you trying to justify your behavior, because this doesn't fly. The end doesn't justify the means. Ever.

Juliet reached under the comforter and began pulling the top sheet up around her. Once she was sufficiently covered, she slid her legs over the side of the bed and stood up. She moved toward him, though she kept her distance. She knew she had to fight for him. She could see his anger. But the fae part of her intuition told her he was using her wrongdoing as an excuse to end the relationship.

She had to fight, something she'd never had to do until she'd come to Five Bridges. She was weak in that way, and being fae didn't help. But she was done with trying to play by the old, human-based rules. She lived in this world, and she'd been lonely as hell until she'd met Brannick at the White Flame.

She reiterated her position. "Again, I'm sorry for what I did, but I don't regret I broke the law to put all this in motion."

He compressed his lips into a tight line. "You're seriously pissing me off. You have to take responsibility for this, so tell me why you did it? Why would you, who I'd come to believe was a woman of honor, break into my dreams like that?"

She released an odd sound from the back of her throat, something like a sigh combined with a grunt. "Because I fell hard for you at that stupid club the night I first met you. I couldn't get you out of my head. You were extraordinary, and that's something I don't think you understand about yourself—how amazing you are.

"But I also knew your tragic history and how hard you'd worked to pull your life together so that no one else would ever get hurt again. And I saw how you looked at me that night. The fae part of me could feel your longing and that your loneliness matched mine.

"I promise you, I didn't set about to do anything initially. In fact, I kept hoping that you'd reach out to me in your dreams. But after the first week, I knew you wouldn't. I'd felt your level of commitment, the strength you carry here." She pressed a hand to her chest.

He stared hard at her. He didn't even blink.

She continued, "I took a chance. I didn't even know if I could do it. Agnes had always told me I had above-average fae ability, but I'd never extended myself to become more than I was. It was my way of pretending I was still human.

"So, the night I first came to you, I was trying out my skills. I saw you through the blur of my dreamglide and I sensed you were dreaming about me."

"The hell I was."

"You were. And, I don't know, I lost myself in that moment. I didn't even think about what I was doing, or whether it was right or wrong. I was responding only to the depth of my need and your loneliness. Breaching your dreams was like stepping through a doorway, nothing more.

"Maybe if there'd been resistance I would have thought twice. Instead, I drew you into my dreamglide, pulled the red comforter back and saw your state of arousal." Heat flew up her cheeks at what had happened next. She couldn't speak the words aloud and decided to skip to the result. "You didn't repel me. I would have left, Brannick, if you'd told me to leave. Instead, you were completely welcoming. You told me you were so glad I'd come to you."

Brannick drew closer to the bed, his shoulders hunched as he glared at her. "I woke up with you straddling me in a dreamglide. What man in his right mind would refuse a beautiful woman, with his cock already driving inside her?"

Having her actions spelled out so blatantly, increased the heat on her face.

"Finally, you're exhibiting a normal reaction. You should be embarrassed. You should be ashamed. What you did was wrong. Don't you get it? I could have you prosecuted in one of the Tribunal courts. You know I could."

She thought about all the things they'd shared in the dreamglide, the level of intimacy they'd enjoyed both physically and in their conversations for the past five months.

She realized something important. "You know what, Brann, I don't give a fuck about that. What I care about is you. You've lived a shadow life in Crescent, holding to your rules and your ideals. And I get why.

"But it's time to let all that go. I'm here. I'm real. And I'm what you need and you know it. So you can leave if you want to or you can be with me, in the same way Vaughn is with Emma.

"It's your choice, but I'm not apologizing. I thought I would. I thought I'd fall to my knees and beg you to forgive me for this terrible thing I've done. But I'm not going to. We've shared something amazing and real despite that most of it occurred in the dreamglide."

He shook his head, his lips and cheeks drawn back in disgust. "You keep thinking that if you want, but I'm outta here."

She watched as he moved past her and started down the stairs. She knew better than to call him back. He'd have to spend some time thinking about everything that had happened between them. Only he could decide if she was worth having in his life despite her illegal seduction of him.

She did, however, need to remind him of Agnes's security system. With the sheet still wrapped around her, she moved to the top of the stairs. "Brannick, don't levitate out of the compound, even if you use your disguise. Agnes has a sensor field set up that would reveal your position."

He'd stopped at the bottom of the stairs to listen, but didn't look up. "Call me if you get into trouble. You might even have enough power to reach me telepathically. I'll be at my home in Crescent, but you should be okay here. Agnes knows what she's doing." He slapped the bottom post of the rail, then moved out of sight as he headed up the hall.

When she heard the front door slam shut, she hurried to the window overlooking the courtyard.

To her relief, he didn't try to levitate, but headed in the direction of the well-guarded entrance.

She placed her fingers on the cool glass. Her cheeks felt hot and her head dizzy. Was he really walking away? Would it be for good despite all that they'd shared?

When he disappeared from sight, she dropped to sit on the floor and leaned her head against the wall.

What she'd feared from the beginning swamped her; he'd learned the truth and left.

The tears flowed. Fortunately, she had the sheet to wipe her eyes and cheeks over and over.

She understood exactly what she was losing, all the conversations she'd never get to have again, the intimacy, the physical touch, everything that had been so real in her marriage, and almost real in the dreamglide with Brannick.

She sat on the floor for a long time, regretting what she'd done one moment, then not regretting it the next. If she never saw Brannick again, she honestly couldn't feel bad about having spent five months in his arms.

Over the next few nights, Juliet stayed in Agnes's compound for security reasons. She split her time between supporting Mary during her withdrawal and with Agnes. The sage fae had been an important part of Juliet's life from the time she'd entered Five Bridges, and she considered her a good friend.

As for Brannick, she'd spoken with him once on her cell. He'd been withdrawn to the point of being curt, though her faeness detected just how sad he was as well. Unfortunately, he was being damn stubborn, holding to his principles, and there was nothing she could do about it.

Though she'd confessed the truth to Agnes, the older woman had steadfastly refused to comment on Juliet's law-breaking seduction of Brannick. Juliet had hoped to be either chastised for her unworthy use of her gifts or supported for taking such a bold risk. But Agnes had merely shrugged her shoulders. "Interesting choice."

That was it. *Interesting choice.*

Her 'choice' didn't *feel* interesting at all. Losing her relationship with Brannick felt like she'd lost both her best friend and her lover.

Mary was recovering slowly. She had dark shadows beneath her eyes and no appetite. She was on two different kinds of intravenous fluids intended to heal her and to suppress some of the withdrawal symptoms.

Each of the *alter* species could self-heal. But an addiction to any of the flame drugs created a new set of problems that took time to counteract, especially given the quantity used on Mary. Her body had been saturated with dark flame to keep her unconscious. Juliet wasn't sure of everything that had happened to Mary during her captivity, but a loss of consciousness would have meant she hadn't been used sexually.

On the fifth night after Brannick's departure, Juliet sat in a chair chatting with Mary about nothing and everything. During their time together working in Brannick's rescue organization, she and Mary had become friends.

As she sat beside Mary's bed, Mary slid both hands prayer-like beneath her cheek. "A very faint memory of leaving my cell at Roche's sex club keeps circling back to me, even though I was unconscious. I have an impression of being held by powerful arms, but they don't feel vampire in nature. Did Brannick carry me out?"

Juliet shook her head slowly. She knew how Mary felt about the wolves of Savage. "Fergus was with us. He's the one who took charge of you and flew you back to my home."

Mary looked away, her lips turning down. "I suppose I should thank him at some point, but I hate owing anything to Fergus or any of his kind."

Juliet then recalled how Fergus had picked Mary up and released a potent howl. She told Mary about it.

"I don't understand. Why would he do that? He must have risked all our lives making such a primal sound."

"I honestly don't know what came over him. He was otherwise in supreme control. I hate to say this, but I think it might have been because of you."

"Me?" Her light blue eyes widened. "Why?"

Juliet was reluctant to speak the words, but she said them anyway. "He's reaching the peak of his mate-hunting cycle. I think he liked you."

Mary made a disgusted sound at the back of her throat. "Shifters. Ugh." She even shuddered. "Okay, let's not talk about Fergus anymore. Has Brannick called you back yet?"

A few days ago, Juliet had confessed everything to Mary. Her friend had been stunned, even appalled until Juliet confessed being very much in love with a vampire from Crescent.

"No, he hasn't reached out to me. Just the once to make sure I was still alive and kicking. He hung up pretty fast."

She forced herself to keep breathing, but the mere mention of him made her chest feel like it was being pulled in a dozen different directions all at the same time. She hurt though she tried hard not to let too much of it show. "I don't expect him to be calling anytime soon. He doesn't really have a reason to. I mean, getting you away from Roche was his biggest concern and now you're here and very safe."

"You really love him, don't you?"

Mary was a very direct sort of person, so the question didn't surprise Juliet.

Tears bloomed in her eyes. "I ... Oh, God … Yes, I do. More than I can possibly say."

~ ~ ~

Brannick yelled at the punk vampire, high on dark flame. "Use your levitation, asshole, or you're going to fall off that ledge and break your fucking neck."

He stood outside a supermarket in a fairly safe area of Crescent. An emaciated drug addict was walking the edge of the metal ramada that covered most of the parking lot. Dark flame tended to put its addicts into a dreamy state, much like the dreamglide he'd shared all that time with Juliet.

He got tired of watching the man weave back and forth. Besides, the audience was growing and in a situation like this, if the man fell, he could end up hurting one of the bystanders.

Brannick levitated up behind the addict and put him in a chokehold. He swung him quickly in the direction of his patrol SUV, then flew him straight to the vehicle. Once there, Brannick cuffed him and tossed him in the back. By then, the vampire had passed out.

He grumbled to himself as he put the SUV in motion, heading back to the station. "Exciting life of a peace officer. Taking care of drunks."

Great, now he was talking to himself.

Brannick's nights had been less than stellar since he left Agnes's compound. His boss, Easton, had been punishing his two night absence with shit jobs like pulling drugged-out vampires off ramadas. Other duties had been equally as meaningless. Three of the drug-runners he'd captured in west Crescent had been released on Easton's orders, despite having been caught with vests stuffed with a variety of flame drugs.

He had no patience these nights. He was irritable as hell and blamed Juliet for that. He had a lot of fae intuition mucking up his thoughts as well as his nightly patrols. Granted, he'd saved more than one life, because he sensed something else was going on in a given situation. His odd faeness had ferreted out the truth when otherwise he couldn't have done it.

Mostly, he was discontent in a way he hadn't been in a long time, not since he arrived in Five Bridges thirteen years ago. Every other thought belonged to Juliet, even though he'd never be able to forgive her for what she'd done. She'd violated his dreams and seduced him.

Did he have thoughts that maybe he shouldn't care so much? Sure he did. He was a man first and what he'd had with Juliet was nothing short of amazing. He'd be a fool not to want her in his life. But how could he trust a woman who'd lied to him, besides crossing that forbidden boundary?

He worked at building up his wall against her. He knew in time, the searing memories of being with her would fade. Although, it would help a lot if he had serious work to do, like taking out some bad guys in Rotten Row.

When a call came in regarding three prostitutes in a cat fight outside a dive bar near Sentinel Bridge, he rolled his eyes and turned his vehicle around.

But as he drove, his discontentment turned into something bigger, as in what the hell was he doing with his life?

~ ~ ~

A full week after Mary's rescue, Juliet woke up with a headache. And she never had headaches.

She tried to recall her dreams, but couldn't. Also unusual. She believed in keeping dream journals and had written in one up until about five months ago when her erotic relationship with Brannick had taken off.

She felt uneasy as she prepared for the day. She'd already decided to extend her stay in Agnes's compound for a few more weeks. Roche's abduction of Mary had changed things for her, even though she had no idea what his present intentions might be. It wasn't just that she wanted to be safe, either. But she also didn't want to put anyone else in harm's way because of Roche's fixation on her.

As she rubbed her temple, she wondered absently if Roche was trying to mess with her in the dreamglide. She didn't have a real concern, not after she'd built up her block as thoroughly as she had. Still, the headache bothered her.

She crossed to her closet, and pushed hanger after hanger aside, most bearing her usual gauzy loose clothes. Some were dressy club gear she hadn't worn in the four years she'd been in Five Bridges. She and her husband had enjoyed going out a lot. The black dress she'd worn at the White Flame was the first time she'd gotten dressed up since her *alter* transformation.

She was restless, something that had to do with Brannick, yet didn't, not really. This was more about her and how her time with Brann had changed her, made her want something different from her life in their tough *alter* world.

She missed Brannick like crazy, but he'd made no effort to contact her. She was pretty sure he'd moved on or was at least trying to. Her gaze dropped to the floor and she saw Brannick's duffel, the one he'd left here when he took off the last time. She missed him so much.

But he wasn't here anymore, and like him, she needed to get on with things.

She sat down on the edge of the bed and stared at her clothes. She'd always been on the artsy edge of things and part of that had been in an attempt to work around her curly hair. Loose clothes and her philosophical attitude toward life, seemed to jive with her, at least up until now.

She rose from the bed and started pacing. The cottage bedroom took up the entire distance, from one window on the north side back to the window near the bed at the opposite end.

Something else had to change, she just wasn't sure what.

~ ~ ~

Well over a week after he'd left Juliet for good, Brannick had another three vampire prostitutes in the back of his SUV. All of them had been drinking and one of them showed the red marks of blood flame on her throat and cheeks.

He was still on shit-job duty and getting sick of it.

The loose-tongued women started flirting with him, asking if he wanted one of them to blow him. They were a noisy bunch, which set his nerves on fire.

His temper had gotten worse, and his dreams had been full of Juliet. To her credit, she never once tried to snag him in her dreamglide.

When the woman addicted to blood flame asked him how many inches he had, something inside him snapped.

He was done.

He put on his siren and sped back to the Crescent station. He called on a couple of rookies to process the women, then went inside. He lifted a hand to Lily who called out a greeting, but he didn't stop to chat.

He wasn't in a chatty mood.

He went straight to Easton's office, but the corrupt chief wasn't there. Brannick thought for a moment, then unclipped his Glock and holster and placed them on the middle of the desk.

He was done being a border patrol officer, done cleaning up the sour mess of his messed up world, done taking orders from a man who took his from the three drug cartels that ran Five Bridges.

When he left the office, Lily met him in the hall, her eyes wide. "Did you just do what I think you did?"

"Yep. I quit."

"Just like that?"

He searched her eyes. "You ever have one of those moments when you know you can't keep going, or if you do your head will explode?"

Her lips quirked. "I did, right before I threw my second husband out of the house. It was either get rid of him, or kill him. Since I didn't want to go to prison, I kicked his lazy ass to the curb and never looked back."

Brannick's lips curved, then something caught his eye—light brown curls. He looked past several officers. The woman was staring at something on the wall.

It couldn't be …

"Lily, excuse me."

"Sure. I've got to get back to my desk anyway. I can hear the phone ringing."

He moved swiftly and had just pulled the door to the entrance open, when the light brown curls turned toward him.

Holy fuck, if he hadn't seen Juliet with his own eyes he wouldn't have believed it. "You came to Crescent? Here? To see me?"

"I did." Still the same soft warm voice, but she didn't seem like the same woman. His acquired fae abilities intuited something major was going on with her.

He looked her up and down. "You're wearing leather and suede." The purple suede vest, dangling with fringe, was snug at the waist and the black pants fit her like a glove. She had on boots as well. Where were the loose clothes?

There were too many people milling around, so he took her arm and led her out onto the sidewalk. "I don't get this. What are you doing here? And why are you wearing this get-up?"

Even her hair looked different. She wore it up off her neck with most of it pulled back. It still had a rough-and-tumble look but with an edge this time. Her lipstick was a darker shade as well, very striking.

She didn't smile either. There was a seriousness about her that hadn't been there a week ago.

She held his gaze. "I have a proposition for you and don't worry, it has nothing to do with you and me on a personal level."

He had no idea what she could possibly have in mind. "What kind of proposition?"

"Is there someplace we can go and talk or do you need to get back to patrolling?"

He knew his mouth was agape, and it took him a minute to bring his thoughts together. "I quit."

"What do you mean?"

"I resigned about three minutes ago."

She shook her head, her curls bobbing. "Why? You love your job."

"I do. I did. Things have gotten so fucked up over the past few years. The cartels …"

"I know. They run just about everything."

He dipped his chin. "But I don't want to have this conversation here."

Her lips curved. "I know a place in Elegance we could go."

He held her gaze for a long moment. "I hope you don't think I have any interest in a relationship."

"I don't. Like I said, this has nothing to do with you and me."

"Then the White Flame it is."

Without another word, she rose into the air, using her newly acquired levitation skills and headed southeast toward Elegance. He stayed right with her, passing over Sentinel Bridge that connected Elegance with Crescent, but slowing and making a descent a couple streets before the tall, stone Tribunal building.

The club was named for a mythical antidote that would reverse the genetic mutations of the various *alter* serums. There wasn't an *alter* person in Five Bridges who didn't wish the myth was true.

The marquis was a sophisticated black and silver with a flickering white flame at the right end towering twenty feet into the sky. Roof supports held it locked in place.

Once settled in a maroon leather booth, Brannick sat across from her as he had the night he first met her. He didn't want any misunderstandings about their relationship. He might like her in leather and he might be intrigued by the obvious shift in her personality. But she would always be the fae woman who had violated his dreams.

She ordered a rum drink. He order scotch neat.

She sat back, hands settled on her lap. She looked around at those dancing to the music, to others in the neighboring booths. "They look almost normal, don't they?" She was smiling, but even her smile seemed different.

"Okay, what gives? You're not the same woman I was with a week ago."

She held his gaze. "I'm not sure. I'm part vampire now and it's changed me. I feel purposeful, more than I was before. In fact I'm not sure without have acquired your skills that I would have risked flying into Crescent."

"Shit, I just realized you made this journey by yourself. Weren't you afraid of Roche? That he might be on the lookout for you?"

"I was careful. I held my cloak tight. I figured if he couldn't see me in his own place of business, he wouldn't be able to detect my presence in the dark of night."

He felt his desire for her rise, a tide within him that wanted to flood his entire being. But he held it in check. Besides, nothing about her demeanor spoke of her interest in him.

She was all business.

The drinks arrived and he brought the cool glass to his lips. Gulping a solid swig of scotch helped. Juliet sipped her mai-tai through a narrow red straw.

"So, what's this proposition?"

Her dark blue eyes lit up, and she leaned forward, but sent the words into his mind. *I want to take down Roche's empire.*

He frowned. *You're kidding.*

Nope. She wagged her head back and forth. *Not even a little. Listen, Brann, I've had time to think everything over during the past week. I know I've offended you badly because of what I did. But as I said before, I don't regret it. I can't.*

Her attitude wasn't warming him at all.

She continued, *I feel as though what I gained from being with you in terms of an increase and even shift in* alter *power has been worth it. Of course I didn't go into the relationship thinking I'd be gaining a vampire persona, or anything like that. I just wanted to be with you.*

But the result has astounded me. She set her drink on the table. *Until I met you, I thought I had to just keep my head down. But I know that's not true anymore. In fact, I think it's just the opposite, especially since Roche has been trying to mess with me in my dreams.*

His temper fired up. "You mean he's still after you?"

"Yep."

"Why didn't you call me?"

She lowered her chin. *We should stay in telepathy, don't you think?*

He agreed. *But why didn't you call me, Juliet? I told you I would protect you.*

I know. And actually, this is part of the reason I came to you tonight. Roche's recent attempt to gain control of me only recently happened over the last few days. When I was waking up, I couldn't remember a single dream and that's not like me at all. And I had a headache. In addition, the fae part of me knew he was hovering around my dreamglide, trying to find another way in.

He's still after me, and that won't change. But once I realized what he was doing, I knew it wasn't enough to play defense anymore. You know, Emma and Vaughn took that horrible wizard down. I don't remember his name.

Brannick did. He helped carry several frightened young teenage girls out of the bastard's underground labyrinth. *Loghry. His name was Loghry.*

That's right. She sipped her mai-tai again. *But it got me to thinking that maybe you and I coming together wasn't just an accident or a random lustful act on my part. Even if we can't be together romantically, maybe we can form a team. Maybe you and I can help fix what has gone so horribly wrong in Five Bridges.*

He thought for a moment. *A force for good.*

She nodded slowly. *And that's my proposition. A partnership, maybe even a very secret one that no one knows about, something just between you and me. And completely on the down-low, the way you run your tunnel rescue system.*

Brannick eased back in his seat and stared at Juliet. Now that he had all the memories from their time together in the dreamglide, he could look back at them whenever he wanted.

Juliet was right. She wasn't the same person that had broken into his dreams and taken him in her dreamglide. She might have come after him out of her loneliness, but she'd found something of far greater value, a strength of purpose that hadn't been there before.

The question was, should he engage in this kind of partnership with her?

~ ~ ~

Juliet felt the wall Brannick had built between them as though if she extended her hand, she'd hit cement. She felt nothing warm and affectionate coming from him at all.

However, she had no expectation of a relationship with him, and she'd meant every word she'd said. She wanted a working partnership, a duo of shared powers, for the purpose of re-shaping Five Bridges. Nothing more.

Brannick might not know it, but she wouldn't leave the White Flame without getting him on board. Besides, he'd quit his job. On a really basic level, they were in exactly the same place.

Why did you leave the force tonight? she asked.

Not sure, exactly. Easton has had me working real shit jobs for the past week. I was being punished for surviving Roche's attack on you and Mary.

Wait a minute. Do you honestly believe he knew what was going on?

There's not a doubt in my mind. He took a sip of scotch. *When I arrived at the station just now, I had three drunk vampire prostitutes in the back of my SUV. The most I could charge any of them with was for creating a public disturbance. They weren't engaged in committing a crime and Easton knew it.*

Juliet spun the straw in her mai-tai. *That still doesn't explain why you quit, because I'm sure this isn't the first time Easton has made your service feel like a waste of time.*

His brow grew tight in that way of his. He swirled what remained of his whisky. *I've been restless. Okay, more than restless.*

She smiled. *You want to do this with me, don't you?*

He lifted his gaze to her. Despite how careful she was being in holding her emotions in check, his eyes always got to her. They seemed to reach into her soul and grab on tight.

She forced herself to take a breath then another.

When he didn't answer, she laid out her thoughts carefully. *This will be a working relationship only. You have my word on that.*

He lifted a brow. *Your word? And what is that worth?*

She'd thought about this issue a lot. *Does one breach invalidate an entire life?*

In this case, I think it might.

Are you saying no to working with me, then, because you believe you wouldn't be able to trust me in the field?

~ ~ ~

Brannick wanted to refuse the arrangement for more than one reason. He wanted to stay in the right and lord it over her. That way, he wouldn't have to deal with how his gaze kept falling to her freckles. Jesus, he'd kissed them a lot during their shared time in the dreamglide. She'd make this soft cooing sound when he did it. Maybe it was the sound he wanted to hear more than anything else.

He looked away from her and drank once more, finishing his scotch.

Dammit, he was going to say yes. *All right, I'm in. And I do trust you in the field. You were amazing the whole time we worked to recover Mary. Just keep your dreamglide away from me.*

Don't worry, I will.

So, what do you have in mind?

He watched her chest rise and fall. He expected a swoosh of air to follow, but she held it in. She seemed so different, yet the same. *I think we should start with Roche, find a way to take him down. I'm even wondering if we might be able to do it in the dreamglide.*

Wouldn't he have to be asleep for that? Or unconscious?

She shook her head, her expression somber. *Not a fae of Roche's power. Think of it as similar to telepathy. You have enough telepathic ability to pierce anyone's mind, at any time, right?*

But I'd never do it.

I know that, she said. *My point is that you could. Remember how Roche once tried to hijack me in a waking dreamglide? That's when Agnes taught me to build a dreamglide block.*

Okay. I get where you're going. But are you suggesting we just enter his dreamglide and take him on?

Some of her grimness left her features. *Okay, here's what I thought we could do. What if you and I use my dreamglide to stalk him? We could learn all about his operation then choose when and where to attack.*

Brannick nodded. *I get it now and that's exactly what we should do. What do you suggest?*

I'm still living in the cottage in Agnes's compound. I've decided to stay there for my own safety. We could be in the cottage physically while we dreamglided back to the Fae Cathedral. How does that sound?

Like a solid plan.

So, how about we start now? She asked.

Now?

She smiled. *Why not?*

You're right. I said I was in and I am. I'm game if you are.

Brannick rose from the table, and laid a couple of twenties down to cover the drinks and extra for the tip.

When she headed toward the door, he followed and his hand automatically went to the small of her back, something he would have done had they been dating.

He immediately withdrew it, but not before he heard her gasp.

When she paused in her steps, he murmured over shoulder. "Sorry, Juliet. Force of habit. Won't happen again."

She didn't look at him, or even say anything to him in response, but continued on a path to the door.

The one, small physical connection was unfortunate, however, because at least a dozen images whipped through his head of the various times he'd touched her in just that way, a hand to the small of her back, in the dreamglide.

So, what exactly had he gotten himself into?

CHAPTER TEN

The moment Brannick had touched her back, a shiver raced up Juliet's spine. She could still feel the warm pressure even though he'd quickly taken his hand away.

As she passed by the couples dancing, a profound sensation of regret tightened her stomach.

The past week had been difficult because of a lost relationship with Brann, and his sudden touch had reminded her of what she'd been missing.

Despite the grief she felt on a personal level, the new business-like relationship she'd just established with the vampire gave her a feeling of hope, something that hadn't been part of her life since she'd arrived in Five Bridges. There would no doubt be more difficult moments ahead, but she was willing to endure them for the plan she'd set in motion.

Once outside, she levitated straight up into the air, wrapped herself up in her new vampire shield, then headed due west toward Revel Territory. Brannick flew beside her, on her left, but hadn't said anything more to her after his apology.

At the same time, she marveled how they could see each other. But this was one critical aspect of the vampire shielding ability, that vampires could see one another, even when shielded. Other species couldn't.

Within a few minutes, she reached Agnes's compound, landing at the checkpoint outside the main entrance.

The security detail moved swiftly into position, sidearms drawn, until the squad leader gave the order to stand down.

Juliet led Brannick immediately back to the cottage without stopping to talk to Agnes. The sage fae had already given her permission for Brannick to come and go as he pleased.

Since she'd be with Brannick in the dreamgliding world, their physical bodies would need to be secure. She thought about taking him upstairs to lie down on the bed, but she knew it would be a big mistake. She'd barely gotten used to being alone in that bed and didn't want to start the process all over again.

The past week hadn't softened her desire for Brannick. She felt locked into a connection that she doubted time could ever change.

No, her situation with him would never be about 'time healing all wounds' but about learning to adjust to being around Brannick as only a friend.

Therefore the bedroom was definitely off-limits which meant the small living room to the right of the entrance would have to do.

A cottage-like sofa in a light blue chenille sat against the far wall. Brannick was so big, he would almost take up the whole thing, which meant she'd be physically close to him throughout the dreamglide. Not a bad thing for a mission, but really hard on her heart.

She sat down first and patted the seat next to her.

Brannick frowned slightly, but didn't challenge her choice. She was glad for that. The less they talked about their relationship, the better.

Once seated, he said, "As I recall from last time, I focused on the dreamglide and followed you in."

She stared at him for a moment. "It's weird to have another species' abilities, isn't it?"

"Very. And they're fully formed, like the way you levitate as though you've been doing it since you were a kid."

"Exactly. Yet, there's something else at work as well, a sort of strengthening of the skill as time passes." She drew a deep breath. "You ready?"

He leaned into the sofa a little more, his hands on his thighs. He looked both relaxed, yet at the same time ready to launch, an odd juxtaposition.

She mirrored his position, settling herself against the couch, her hands in her lap. She closed her eyes and with little more than a thought moved into her dreamglide.

She was in the same room, sitting on the sofa only her eyes were open. The dreamglide tended to move a few feet away from the real-time location, but the edges were blurred, the biggest indication she was in a different reality

Brannick joined her immediately, then stood up from the sofa. "That was damn easy."

She rose to her feet as well. "Yeah, it was."

He turned to her, but his expression softened.

She gasped softly.

Oh, no. Somehow in all her planning, she'd forgotten that his less conscious self ruled him in the dreamglide.

She could see from the light in his eye he was thinking something he shouldn't. "Brannick, you're not the same in the dreamglide as you are in real-time, are you?"

He shook his head slowly. "I'm more like the man who made love to you for five months, if that's what you're wondering."

No, no, no.

He started to move toward her. She held up her hand to stop him and wagged her head, but he merely smiled.

Surrounding her with his arms, he pulled her close. "Guess I'll have to apologize right now for what I'm about to do."

Her protest got muffled as he slanted his lips over hers. When he pressed his tongue against her lips, begging for entrance, she resisted. This wasn't Brann, not really. Though it gave her something like hope to know he was so torn internally that he'd kiss her in the dreamglide.

When he didn't give up, however, but began fondling her backside with his big strong hands, she melted against him. She parted her lips, savoring the thrust of his tongue and the way his chest muscles tightened as he drew her closer still.

She'd forgotten for a moment how the dreamglide could feel as close to reality as anything could get.

But she couldn't give in, not all the way. This wasn't Brann, and she knew the moment they left the dreamglide, he'd be really upset with her.

He must have felt her shift in emotion, because he released her just enough to look down at her with a crooked smile. "Didn't you like the kiss?"

She planted her hands on his chest, her palms savoring the size and curve of his pecs. "What I don't like is that I know you don't want to be with me. Not really. And I want to respect your wishes here."

He lost his devilish smile and caressed her arms. "This is what I want, Juliet. Being this close to you." He pulled away, if slowly. "But the moment you and I are back in real-time, that's when my past shouts at me to be sensible, to weigh your actions against your words. You have to understand. I've kept my sanity in Five Bridges by holding to my commitments, to my values, and to the rule of law."

She pivoted away from him, forcing herself to quickly search for and find her internal balance. "I know." She patted her thighs twice with the palms of her hands.

Turning toward him again, she smiled. "How about we focus on what's important here."

"Finding Roche?"

She inclined her head.

"So, what's the best way to proceed?"

"I think you should surround us both with your vampire cloak, even within the dreamglide. And I'll engage as well. Maybe together, we'll create something unusually strong."

When he stepped toward her and began the process, she could feel heat coming off his body. She accessed the same ability that now lived so oddly within her own bones. The cloaking shield seemed to mingle, moving back and forth between them, then solidifying.

His green eyes widened. "Shit, that does feel powerful."

"I know," she said. "And we'll need it that way to be anywhere near Roche."

He narrowed his gaze. "The fae part of me knows we're on the right track and that we'll find him."

"How do you know that? Even I'm not feeling it, and I'm more fae than you."

"I think the vampire in me is more predatory than your wisdom-seeking faeness."

"That makes sense, sort of. Maybe you should do the hunting, then. I might get in the way, otherwise."

His lips curved slightly. "Oh, I don't know. You hunted me once before and were very successful at it."

At that, she lifted her chin. "You are so not allowed to joke about the one thing for which your conscious self refuses to forgive me."

"You're right. That's not fair to you."

She could see he was hardly remorseful at all. "And it would help me a lot if you'd let me go. This part of you that loved being with me in the dreamglide was half the problem. Because, if you'll recall, you engaged with me that first time without a moment's hesitation. Remember? I would have left in a heartbeat if you'd made a single protest. But you didn't."

He gripped her arms, his green eyes lit with sudden passion. "How could I do anything else, when you were riding me like a seductive Valkyrie, your hair and eyes wild? I loved it. I don't regret it. Not any of it."

"Just your conscious self."

He nodded slowly.

She saw the depth of his conflict and came to realize just how much their time together had truly meant to him. She wondered if there was something she could do about it, if there was some way she could help Brannick bring his two selves together.

For the moment, however, she had to let go. "All right, let's forget about our ongoing issue for now, Mr. Vampire-turned-Fae. Take the lead and see if you can find this bastard."

He released his hold on her arms. "Fine. But we're not done, Juliet."

At that, she slammed both her hands against his chest. "Don't put this on me. You have to figure this out for yourself. Both your *selves*."

"I know. Just, don't give up on me."

Those words hit her hard, and she wrapped her arms around his waist, pressing her head to his chest. "I won't and I can't. You mean so damn much to me, Brann."

He surrounded her with his arms. "Ditto, and I mean that. Sorry that I've been such a pain. God, I've missed you, but why didn't you come to me in the dreamglide this past week?"

At that, she could only laugh as she pulled away from him. "Are you kidding me? This is what got me into trouble in the first place."

His lips twisted into a funny grin. "My conscious self is an idiot."

She saw the look in his eye and knew that he'd keep this up if she let him. He'd obviously missed her, and she was pretty sure if she encouraged him a little, he'd make love to her right now.

"No." She held his gaze in a strong grip. "You listen to me, there will be no more fooling around until you figure this out. Do you understand? I'm not going to violate you again, even if you gave me permission a thousand times. Have you got it?"

~ ~ ~

Brannick thought it a strange thing to be so completely at odds with himself. But he'd always felt at peace with Juliet in the dreamglide, as though this was real-time and not the other way around.

His jaw flexed a couple of times. "You're right. It's not fair to you when it's my problem." He glanced around, then took his time walking the perimeter of the dreamglide. He pushed his hand at the blurry walls, testing the physical boundaries over and over.

He lifted his gaze to the top. More blur. But there was something else. He reached through and encountered what he could only describe as a strong metal meshwork made of something like reinforced steel bars.

"Hey, these are the blocks you've built, aren't they? The ones Agnes taught you to make."

"Yes. It took me a lot of practice, but I had to keep Roche out."

"So, it's kind of a cage that travels with you when you move to a new location?"

Her brows rose. "I think that's one of the best explanations I've ever heard. But, yes. It's exactly like that."

He kept exploring, checking for weaknesses. "You said you had a headache when you woke up, which was unusual, and that you knew Roche was coming after you again. So, is he tampering with your blocks, trying to find a way in?"

"I don't know what else it could be. Besides, it feels like Roche."

Brannick turned in a slow circle and let the space speak to him—very fae—as though his intuition meter had been switched on high. He focused on Roche, especially on the images of Roche in his sex shop just before Juliet slammed into him. He pictured the fae monster at the top of the double row of cells, his red hair, the teal flames on his cheeks, his small feral eyes.

Juliet drew close to him and slid her hand in his palm. He felt an odd electrical impulse flow up his arm and spread through his body. He'd felt something similar when he'd made love to her in a combination of real-time and the dreamglide.

Only this current situation wasn't sexual at all.

Her voice penetrated his mind. *Keep focusing on Roche.*

He turned to look at her. *You can feel me doing that?*

Yes, and it's more than a guess. I can sense that you're thinking about the moments just before we got Mary out.

You're right. I am.

Her lips curved. *How about we go there right now and have a look around?*

He loved her fighting spirit. She had the aura of a saint and maybe that was part of who she was, but she had no problem going to war. He shifted to face southeast, in the general direction of the underground world and Roche's sex shop.

When the dreamglide began to move, it was slow at first then whipped through the dream world like a battleship at full speed. He watched thousands of different images pass by the small living room. Yet as they neared the destination, the dreamglide began to change and the next thing he knew, he was standing on the cement floor of the prison, which was blurred around the edges.

The timing was very different. Women were being moved in and out of cells, but behind the blur of the dreamglide. *We're safe in this position, right?*

Juliet moved to stand next to him. *We are.*

With a thought, he piloted the dreamglide forward to the end of the row. He heard one of the guards call Roche's name. Brannick scrutinized the guard table, then turned to look in the other direction.

And there was Roche, kissing the neck of a blond who had teal flames on her cheeks and dull eyes. She wore one of the beige prison smocks.

Brannick watched Roche glance in the guards' direction, then stand upright. He shoved the woman away. She fell against the wall and slid to the floor.

Roche started looking around. He drew his gun from a back-waist holster. His movements set all the guards on alert and they hustled into formation, blocking the exit to the hall.

But Brannick was inside the dreamglide, unlike last time when he'd been in real-time but hidden within his vampire cloak.

He didn't move the dreamglide even an inch. *Juliet, I'm getting the sense that if we so much as breathe, he'll know what we're up to.*

Me, too. We'll sit tight.

Brannick loved how calm she was under pressure.

Roche slowly moved in their direction. Brannick's newly acquired fae sense told him that if they remained still, Roche wouldn't be able to detect them, not even if he passed through their dreamglide in the same physical space.

"Is that you, Juliet? Did you come to see me? Ready to trade up from the vampire who dumped you? We could have some fun, you and me, and earn a whole lot of money."

Roche drew close to the end of the dreamglide, the part where blur and rebar joined. Brannick held his breath.

Roche took another step, then another.

He heard the faintest intake of breath from Juliet.

Roche stepped forward and passed through what Brannick knew

was a substantial cage in the dream-world. But in real-time, Roche kept moving and gave no evidence he knew what was happening.

He was so close that Brannick wished he could deliver a solid punch and knock his ever-present smirk from his lips. Despite the impulse, Brannick restrained himself.

Roche walked all the way to the guards' table. Once there, he whipped around and retraced his steps, again passing through the dreamglide.

He stopped near the woman on the floor and took another look around. His shoulders lost their tension and he returned his weapon to its holster. He kicked the woman on the floor. "Back to your cell, you piece of shit."

The woman struggled to her feet, then fell down again. He summoned a couple of guards who also hurried through the dreamglide.

Roche turned on his heel and headed the other direction, pushing the door open that led into his club.

Brannick turned to Juliet and smiled. With Roche gone, he felt free to talk aloud again. "Not half bad."

Her lips curved as well. "Not half bad at all. So, how about we do some exploring. I've wanted to see his entire operation, including where he makes the dark flame. I've been told he keeps all of his business interests close to his home. In which case, we ought to head back out to the hall, then move south. We might just be in the middle of his nest."

"Let's go."

Brannick turned, preparing to pilot back out into the hall, but Juliet caught his arm. "I know this might seem like an odd request, but how about I take the lead for the next few minutes? I'd like to see whether or not I can direct this dreamglide since it seems to be emanating from you."

He narrowed his gaze at her, and took a moment to process her request. He was used to being in command, and didn't give it up lightly. In the end, he acquiesced. "I think it's a good idea. We should be equal partners, because who knows what's around the next bend."

~ ~ ~

Juliet used her mind to guide the dreamglide and within a few seconds they left the side hall and were flying down the central avenue, heading south. Each time an electric golf cart appeared, she rose up into the air, even though it wasn't necessary. Just habit, to get out of the way when something bigger was coming toward her.

But Brannick encouraged her to stay level with the people and vehicles, to let the dreamglide pass through everything.

"We might need the skills."

She couldn't have agreed more. The first few times were unnerving. But after a couple of minutes, she got the hang of it. She then offered for him to take a turn.

"You bet. I need the practice, too."

She relinquished the guidance process which seemed unnatural to her. Yet, she had a rapport with Brannick that was hard to deny, and he easily took over. The dreamglide barely slowed as he took the helm.

He laughed a few times as he, too, rose toward the ceiling when another person levitated toward them or a golf cart turned the corner.

Eventually, they each got used to the process of letting solid matter pass through their not-so-solid state. They traveled even faster because of it.

When Juliet held the reins again, she reached a prominent intersection which a number of fae traveled, most on foot and some levitating. Hundreds or maybe even a couple thousand people lived in this underground world. She paused, though high in the air this time, and let the traffic pass. She could have remained at street level, but all the movement was distracting, and she wanted to have a good look around.

Many who passed by were construction workers, and a billboard at the southwest corner had a picture of a new condo development in the works three miles west. She took a moment to process the distance and turned to Brannick, just as he turned to her.

He telepathed first. *That has to be below the border to the human part of Phoenix.*

She looked around. *I'm smelling a new kind of drug-running racket. Their tunnels wouldn't have to be very long, would they?*

No, they wouldn't. He frowned as he glanced west and down the avenue called oh-so-subtly 'Roche Lane', and then east.

Juliet did the same. She saw several hard-looking fae warriors, bulked up with muscle, levitate toward the intersection, then fly north in the direction of the massive food court. *They're probably on a barbecue run,* she said.

Maybe. Or back to Roche's sex shop.

Juliet glanced at him. *What do you think is down there? Or are you thinking what I'm thinking?*

Smell the air.

It always amazed Juliet that even in the dreamglide, she could catch odors and fragrances. In this case, the faint hint of dark flame floated all around them. *It has to be the factory.*

Let's go find out.

Juliet didn't wait for further encouragement. Instead, she piloted their dreamglide down the fairly broad avenue. More muscled types came at them, but she stayed steady and flew through them all.

Other, weaker types began to emerge looking hollow-eyed with teal flames on their cheeks. Many were emaciated and drifted down a variety of smaller streets.

I want to see what's going on here.

Go for it.

She turned north down one of the narrow streets. She heard music and saw that several flashing lights indicated bars. There were also a number of apartment buildings into which some of the laborers disappeared. A couple of men were passed out on the street and ignored.

The passageway narrowed and a darker smell emerged, full of urine, feces and death.

Brannick's voice hit her mind about the same time the odors did. *What the fuck is that?*

I think where fae workers go to die. She stayed put for a moment and became aware of a cloud of flies.

She turned the dreamglide around and sped back out, going a helluva lot faster than when she'd gone in. *We've seen the dregs. I wonder if each street is like this in Roche-land.*

Probably. Our friend doesn't seem like the type who would care. Only if it affects his business.

She moved back to the main street and headed east once more. *How many miles have we covered do you think?*

Probably two.

So, we're not quite below the Graveyard.

No, I don't think so, but getting closer.

Juliet saw the double doors of a gun-metal-gray building and knew this was the factory. Her life and Brannick's had been turned upside down because of what Roche and his kind manufactured in this place.

Three employees pushed the swinging doors wide, then walked out. Each was as thin as a rail with the usual flames on their necks and cheeks. The smell of the drug within the dreamglide had grown even stronger.

Once inside the factory, the first thing Juliet noticed was the shouting. Brutish fae males carried thin, reed-like sticks and whipped the legs of those working the numerous assembly lines.

The drugs were manufactured and packaged along at least thirty lines with ten times that number of laborers getting the dark flame ready for distribution.

She'd heard Roche was one of the main distributors for the entire U.S., but until she saw the size of the operation, she hadn't understood his level of influence.

Jesus. Brannick's reaction mirrored her own.

I want to tear this down, she said.

You and me both, sweetheart.

She smiled up at him. *This would be worth doing, wouldn't it?*

His green eyes had a flinty look. *Yes it would. You know what else, I'll bet if we looked around, we'd find another outlet above ground.*

You mean like the one at the sex shop?

Brannick dipped his chin. *That's exactly what I mean.*

She took in a slow breath. *Your turn, Brann. Lead the way.*

~ ~ ~

Brannick moved through a building that represented everything he hated about his world. Dark flame had stolen his life and killed his family and Roche had made a fortune out of the misery of masses of people, both human and *alter*.

He got the gist of what Juliet had in mind. They both wanted this production facility destroyed. It might take a few months, but with a lot of strategic planning and the use of several trustworthy vampires, he knew it could be done.

First, though, they needed to find another way out.

He already knew they would have to follow the pattern of the initial mission. They could easily sneak in through one of the front doors of the Fae Cathedral. But they wouldn't be able to leave the same way, not with the amount of security personnel Roche employed.

Another exit had to be found.

He flew toward the east end of the building and began drifting through door after door, each leading to the normal rooms found in a production facility; cafeteria, bathrooms, offices for management.

At the north end, close to the executive offices, Brannick found what they needed. A spacious elevator.

He took the dreamglide within the elevator and rose up and up. The doors opened onto a private space guarded by two powerful fae warriors, each wearing tight, black t-shirts, black leathers and bearing an assortment of tattoos.

He flew through them and entered what turned out to be Roche's private mansion. He stopped his forward movement, but rose to hover halfway to a tall twenty foot ceiling.

The bastard's living area looked like the hotel of a fancy Las Vegas lobby with marble pillars and massive plants. The lighting made it look like it was high noon.

Juliet took his hand. *This is what seems so unfair about what men like Roche do. They build their fortunes on something that brings so much pain and suffering to tens of thousands of people, then build palaces.* She shook her head.

I'm with you on that. Roche should live at the end of that alley with the corpses and flies. That's where he belongs.

You got that right.

Brannick didn't need to see the rest of the place. He flew the dreamglide toward the fairly long foyer and a set of heavy, wood-carved double doors.

Shall we go outside?

Juliet nodded. *I'd really like to see where we are in Revel and in relation to the Graveyard. His home is probably in a fancy neighborhood.*

As Brannick passed through the doors, the opposite of Juliet's prediction was true.

Juliet glanced around. "Oh, my God. Well, if he wanted to disguise his location, this would do it."

"This is unbelievable."

The street onto which Roche's house emptied used to be a strip-mall but now only showcased a long row of derelict storefronts. A Revel patrol SUV cruised by, then another.

Roche's men? Juliet asked.

Undoubtedly. In order to live in an area that would usually be overrun by homeless addicts by now, he'd need his security force patrolling constantly.

Brann, look to the south. The street is blocked with a lot of barbed wire.

I see it. And to the north, not fifty yards away is the Graveyard.

Juliet turned around. *You wouldn't know this was his home.*

Brannick dipped his chin. *Not in a million years.*

The abandoned row of storefronts had boarded up windows as though preparing for a hurricane. Colorful graffiti created an odd yet striking panorama across the entire face. Desert weeds and cactus had filled in the torn up asphalt of the parking lot.

Juliet shook her head. *I have to give him credit. He chose his location well, because who would want to live this close to the Graveyard?*

He glanced at her and saw that she'd wrinkled up her nose. That's when he smelled it as well. *Jesus, that has to be a decaying body. Well, Roche is nothing if not innovative. And I'll bet he makes sure when his addicted workers die, he lets a few rot out here to keep everyone else away*

Juliet pursed her lips. *So, how do we do this? How do we tear down the factory without killing hundreds of innocent people?*

Brannick thought for a moment. *I've been thinking about it this whole time. We won't be able to tear it down all at once. If we did, we'd have a war on our hands. But now that I've seen the layout, you and I and maybe some others could begin to strategize a long-term plan. If we do anything else, the cartels will get involved and that might do a helluva lot more harm than good.*

Juliet's large blue eyes glimmered with excitement. *Then this is how we'll start, you and me. If we take it slow and we're clever, if Roche doesn't find out what we're up to, we can chip away at every vile establishment in Revel.*

Brannick added, *We can operate in the same way I've run my tunnels. We'll choose our targets carefully, use the dreamglide to figure out how best to structure each mission, and eventually we can bring this organization down, one bad guy at a time. If we keep our identities a secret, there can be no retaliation.*

Juliet smiled. *So, we're partners.*

Yes, we are.

Then I suggest we return to the cottage and start putting a plan together.

He headed the dreamglide back to Agnes's compound, and because the formation of a thought created the destination, within seconds, they were back in the cottage living room.

But he didn't drop out of the dream state. Instead, he took Juliet in his arms. "Don't leave the dreamglide yet. Be with me. Right here."

"What? No, Brann, I already told you. I'm not doing that."

He kissed her. He knew what he was doing was wrong, but he wanted to be with her. And he knew she had a weakness for him. Hell, he was pretty sure the woman was in love with him.

Brann, no.

Yes. He dragged his tongue over her lips.

I can't do this.

She tried to pull away from him, but he held her fast. Being with her had ramped him up. He'd wanted to make love to her from the moment he'd entered the dreamglide, but her excitement about taking on Roche's empire had added gasoline to the fire.

Let me make love to you one last time.

It wouldn't be a last time, and you know it.

He drew back, but held her gaze. "I want to make love to you. Do you remember what it was like last time, the wind, the movement, the thrill?"

"Of course I do. It was amazing. But you don't want me in real-time."

His eyelids grew heavy. "Oh, I want you something fierce, just like I do now. Please, Juliet. Please." He didn't mind begging.

His gaze dropped to her swollen lips. He kissed her again and this time, her lips parted for him.

Then he knew he had her.

CHAPTER ELEVEN

Juliet loved the feel of Brannick's tongue in her mouth, pulsing as it always did. She loved his body, the way she could feel different muscles flex and release and how it took so little for his arousal to start pressing against her thigh or her abdomen.

She knew she shouldn't do this, but the time spent with Brann hunting through Roche's domain had excited her. They'd ended up with a solid commitment to build a secret resistance movement to the drug-related horrors that haunted all of Five Bridges. She could feel a powerful vampire electricity flowing from his body, and she wanted it, all of it, inside her, pushing hard.

Despite her good intentions, she was going to do this thing with Brann, though every cell in her body warned her against it.

She drew back and unbuttoned her vest. His eyes flared and he dipped quickly to kiss the mounds of her breasts. She was already breathing hard. This would be quick and amazing.

When he drew back and began to remove his shirt, that's when things turned sizzling hot. Real-time and the dreamglide merged suddenly and in real-time, Brann pulled her up from the couch and mirrored what he was doing in the dreamglide. She couldn't believe it.

She gave a cry and got herself out of her leathers as fast as she could before the real-time Brann changed his mind. Brannick lost the rest of his clothes as well.

As before, the wind-like element began to flow through the

dreamglide as though the passion each of them felt whipped the space into a fury of movement.

The couch was too damn small, so he drew her down to the floor. In real-time, she ran her fingers through his brown hair. He looked panicked, but she could tell he wasn't going to put a stop to things.

He pushed her legs part with his knees then settled in-between. He was fully erect, and she was streaming, so ready for him. As he pushed inside, she gave a cry. She was one with Brann on the floor of the cottage in real-time, yet experiencing the wind of the dreamglide.

Passion flowed so strong, but still she caught his face in her hands. "Tell me straight up that you know you started this."

"I know. I did. This is on me."

"Good." She had no illusions about Brann's conscious self. But it didn't matter, not when he possessed her body as he did with his cock drawing in and out and hitting her just right.

She arched her back and a long cry left her mouth of sheer pleasure. The wind whipped around her, as the dreamglide reflected how she felt and what Brann was doing.

Heat radiated from his body and the humming electrical field of his vampire nature tingled wherever his body met hers.

He nudged her neck, and she cried out again. "Yes, do it, Brann, I want to feed you."

A quick strike came next, which sent a thrill between her legs. More sizzle and heat.

He began to drink, grunting with each thrust of his cock and pull on her neck. She felt her life force leaving her and flowing down his throat.

She could feel his muscles bulking up as they'd done before each time she'd fed him. He drove deeper now, curling his hips. She glided her hands down his back and caressed his ass, loving the way it moved up and back and the way it arched, which gave her so much pleasure.

That's when she let everything go. She became one with him, feeling what he felt, savoring his body, the feeling of him drinking. Pleasure built like a bonfire. The dreamglide wind buffeted her, adding another layer of sensation.

On he drove. *I'm going to come, Juliet. I'm so hard for you. Are you ready for me, Baby? You ready to come?*

"I am. All you have to do is go a little faster or a lot, doing that vampire thing you do." She moaned at the thought of it.

He released her neck and swiped at the wounds. He was glowing as well, a silvery aura around his body. She probably was as well.

When he lifted up, he held her gaze. "Come with me, Baby. Come now."

He increased the rhythm of his hips, going faster and faster.

She stared into his intense green eyes. She breathed in heavy gulps as ecstasy bore down on her, the wind of the dreamglide sweeping over her body.

"Brann." She cried out his name as pleasure began to flow.

He kept looking at her, driving harder and faster.

He roared his passion, his eyes glowing, his body an electrical current that kept taking her to the heights, over and over. The wind carried her back and forth as well.

She cried out again and again, her chest expanding, her heart on fire.

When the wind began to die down, and his hips slowed then finally stopped, she lay with her arms stretched out to the sides, gasping for breath.

He kissed her neck, her cheeks, her forehead then lingered on her lips. She took his tongue inside and suckled gently, wanting him to know how much she loved doing this with him.

When her breathing had evened out and she looked up at him, he wore his serious expression once more. His brows were pinched tightly together. "What if in all this I lose you the way I lost my family or worse, the way my sister died? Do you understand?"

She knew what lay beneath his words. "Does it really matter how I die? Or when? I'm choosing to go down this path. In fact, I think I made this choice five months ago when I met you in the White Flame. Resistance fighters don't tend to survive the war, and I've already accepted my fate.

"Don't get me wrong. I plan to stay alive. But even if you ended our business arrangement, I'd find another way to battle men like Roche. Do you understand? I'm in this fight 'til the end."

"I don't think it's that simple," he said.

"I know you don't. But for me it is."

He looked around and grabbed his t-shirt, shoving it between her legs as he pulled out of her.

She could tell he was really upset as he rose. "I'll be back. I need to figure things out. But a shower sounds really good."

She let him go. As he'd done before, he was using the shower as an excuse to create distance. She'd said all she could say, and now that he was in full possession of their dreamglide conversations, he knew she spoke the truth. She'd held nothing back from him during the five months he'd been her lover.

She also knew his sister's death had terrorized him as nothing else could have, causing him to withdraw from all close relationships. She didn't blame him. She wasn't much different. She valued both Agnes and Mary, but she'd never truly confided in either. She'd kept her cards as close to the vest as Brann had, at least until she'd seduced him in the dreamglide and he'd opened up to her. Then she'd told him everything about herself, her fears and hopes, even about her marriage.

Maybe time would resolve the issue between them, maybe it wouldn't. But for now, she knew enough to give Brann plenty of space.

She stood up, gathered her clothes and headed to the small, downstairs bathroom. She cleaned up as best she could in the half-bath then got dressed again.

She loved sex. She wondered if she was even normal for how much she enjoyed being with a man she loved.

When her choice of words hit her mind, she mentally repeated themselves over and over: *The man she loved.*

The man she loved.

She loved Brannick so much. On some level, of course she had from the first. But it was a hard thing to accept she was in love with someone who might never be able to return that love.

She left the bathroom, and had just reached the dining area near the bottom of the stairs, when a loud explosion rocked the space all around her. Yet there was no debris. She turned in a circle, but she didn't see any real damage.

It didn't make sense.

She started to feel dizzy and very strange. Her dreamglide called to her, pulling her toward it.

Brann. It had to be Brann. He'd made a decision about her, about them.

Joy rushed through her so fast she cried out.

She gave herself to the dreamglide and in a blink was inside. At first she didn't understand, because the space was hazy with black smoke. And the smell was bad.

She didn't get it at first, except that it appeared the explosion had occurred within her dreamglide.

That's when she understood exactly what had happened. Roche had finally broken through and her reckless entrance into the dreamglide made it too late to do anything to protect herself.

He emerged from the black smoke, the teal flames on his cheeks pulsing, his red hair flowing away from his face. He looked demonic. "Did you honestly think, Juliet, that I didn't know you'd found my home? But I don't let anyone cross into my territory without retaliation. And now, at long last, I have you."

She tried to back away but he moved like lightning. He surrounded her with a tight powerful grip then pulled her out of her dreamglide and into his.

He'd finally succeeded in hijacking her. The moment she left her own secure space, she became as docile as a lamb.

He whispered into her ear. "And now, I want you to leave Agnes's compound in real-time and come to my home. You know the way."

It was a simple thing to direct her real-time self to head down the hall, open the front door and levitate to the compound's entrance.

The guards barely acknowledged her as she rose into the air and headed southeast, toward the southern end of the Graveyard. She arrived at Roche's home in less than half-a-minute.

He stood with the doors wide, and opened his arms to her.

She went to him, as one completely hypnotized, and gave herself into the hands of the monster.

~ ~ ~

Brannick stepped out of the shower no more resolved on the path he should take than when he'd decided to get cleaned up. He dried off and headed into the bedroom. The last time he'd been here, he'd left without his duffel so he knew he had a couple of clean shirts ready to wear.

He found the bag in Juliet's closet. He opened it and pulled out a black tank.

When he was completely dressed, boots and all, he realized something didn't feel right. In fact, the house felt empty, which made no sense at all.

He moved slowly downstairs and smelled something very peculiar, something like smoke.

"Juliet?"

But she didn't respond.

Had she lit up the barbecue? Yet the smoke didn't have the smell of charred meat. If anything, the odor was more chemical in nature. It also seemed familiar in a way he couldn't put his finger on.

He called for Juliet again. When there wasn't a response, he went outside and walked the entire perimeter of the cottage. Where the hell was she? Had she gone to talk to Agnes? If so, why hadn't she told him?

He headed up to the main part of the facility, but couldn't find Juliet. He located Agnes, however, but she said she hadn't spoken to Juliet recently.

A terrible dread filled him.

When he finally opened the compound entrance door and questioned the guards, he got the answer he feared. Juliet had levitated and headed southeast while he'd been in the shower.

The sensation of dread increased, pouring over him like a flow of sludge, weighing him down. He'd felt like this once before, when he'd learned his sister had been delivered up to a dark witch coven.

He felt compelled to return to the cottage. Juliet might have left by the front door of the compound, but that's not where the damage had been done.

When he went back into the house, he walked straight for the dining area near the foot of the stairs. He could smell the smoke again.

As he examined the nature of it, his fears intensified, because this wasn't ordinary smoke but the kind he'd smelled once before many years ago and had hoped to never experience again. When the witches had killed his sister, this was the same odor in the air. They'd used a spell to control her, to have her say aloud she was a willing sacrifice and she would die in their service.

His first thought was that one of the dark covens had gotten to Juliet. But the fae part of him knew it wasn't that easy. The stench in the air told him the witches were connected, but he intuited that Roche had gone to them and purchased a spell. He'd wanted control of Juliet for years, and he'd finally found a way to get the job done.

Brannick worked hard to remain calm, especially since, as he focused on the situation, he sensed the other part of what had happened. The smoky smell was the key, because it carried a metallic quality. Roche had finally broken through Juliet's powerful dreamglide block, then hijacked her as he'd been trying to do for a long time.

Part of him wanted to fly straight up into the air and find her now, go straight to Roche's house and tear the damn thing apart until he found her.

But a wiser part that aligned with his acquired fae abilities, forced him to grow very quiet. He needed to think the whole situation through, including what he and Juliet had just done.

He'd made love to her, but immediately afterward he'd been filled with remorse. Only this time, he knew he was the one who'd crossed the line. He'd seduced Juliet when he shouldn't have. When real-time merged with the dreamglide, he should have stopped the whole thing.

But he hadn't.

Yes, he'd been caught up in the passion of being with her, especially the erotic combination of the dreamglide with real-time. But there had been a moment when he'd actually made the choice to make love to her.

Maybe it had been the passionate depths of her dark blue eyes, or how much she enjoyed being with him, or perhaps her purpose in becoming as she'd said, a resistance fighter. All of it had gotten to him.

But he'd also recalled how she'd refused his initial overtures when they'd first entered the dreamglide. She'd made her position clear and he'd loved her for that.

Now Roche had her, and he'd used a dark witch's spell to finally break through Juliet's blocks.

Roche had been there from the beginning, the main supplier of dark flame throughout Five Bridges, Arizona and in more recent years the entire U.S. Maybe he even manufactured the *alter* fae serum that corrupted the human genetic base and made long-lived fae out of regular humans.

Roche had been there the night his sister had died as well.

He'd been the one constant all this time.

Something shifted at the base of Brannick's soul, something so extraordinary it felt like tectonic plates moving around. His view of the world rumbled with a dozen earthquakes.

He finally confessed the truth to himself that he'd allowed Juliet to seduce him in the initial dreamglide because he'd fallen hard for her at the White Flame. And every damn time he'd made love to her in the dreamglide, as well as every conversation he'd shared with her, had deepened that love.

He'd been pretending all these months that he didn't love her, that it would be too dangerous for him to love anyone.

What he hadn't realized until this very moment was the terrible truth of what Juliet had said to him recently. Five Bridges was a death sentence to every *alter* human being who chose to make a difference in their world. He could no more control Juliet's ultimate fate than he could his own.

He felt a soft drift of fingers down his face, and he knew without having to explore the sensation very long that his wife, in her ghostly form, was with him again.

She appeared, smiling, barely more than a soft mist. *I love you, Brann. And I can see you've finally made the leap. I've had permission from the powers who serve paradise to say good-bye, all three of us.*

Brannick's chest swelled as three beings appeared before him: His wife, his child and the baby born in another realm. He tried to reach for them, but they weren't real, yet each approached him, even the babe, and ran fingers down his face. He could feel their beautiful spiritual energy touching him, loving him and wishing him well.

Good-bye, Brann. Remember, all is forgiven. Now tend to Juliet. You'll do tremendous things together. You'll see.

Both his children smiled and continued to smile as his original family disappeared. He wiped at the tears on his cheeks. His soul felt free at last. Free to live and to love. Free to battle for the woman who meant everything to him and for the life he wanted for them both, as well as for all decent citizens in Five Bridges.

He let the sensation roll through him as he considered the desperate situation before him. He could have accessed his own dreamglide, but instead wondered if he could take over Juliet's without her permission. The moment the thought entered his head, he knew he could. He might have developed a few fae abilities, but he was still a vampire and with that came a strength of will that he'd always valued. So, yeah, he could be inside the woman's dreamglide.

He remained standing because he knew in his gut this experience would be very different. He'd have a conscious awareness of exactly what was going on in both realities.

With a brief thought, and his mind fixed on Juliet, he moved straight into her dreamglide. The stench of the spell infused the space. He saw the blown out blurred wall, with the twisted steel rebar bent toward him like a flower that had blossomed.

Because the dreamglide belonged to her, it was with her, inhabiting her current location.

He looked down through the blurred floor of the dreamglide and saw Juliet below him. She lay on her back on a sofa that looked familiar. Remaining very still, he glanced around. Sure enough, she was in Roche's home.

Fortunately, the fae bastard was nowhere to be seen. Good.

His fae senses also told him that however unguarded Roche's home appeared, there were powerful fae warriors in the house, lined up and ready to attack.

Roche had set a trap for him.

He drew out of Juliet's dreamglide and was back in real-time at the foot of the stairs in the cottage.

He had to think and to plan.

He felt certain Roche didn't know just how much of a fae Brannick had become during his time with Juliet. His solitary vampire nature at one time might have sent him storming to the house alone, ready to be slaughtered. But the fae part of him had added a strong level of wariness.

He felt the need to take a team in and considered his options. He knew Vaughn had to stick close to the safe house, because it was under a constant threat of attack. He turned therefore in a different direction, toward Savage Territory.

He contacted Fergus telepathically. In a few brief sentences, he told him about Juliet's abduction, how he knew where Roche lived and that Roche was using Juliet to draw him into a trap.

Fergus didn't even pose a question but simply stated the exact response Brannick needed. *I'm in. Tell me when and where.*

Brannick pictured the entire operation in his head. *I want a heavy diversion at the entrance to the Fae Cathedral. Contact Keelen and tell him all that's going on. The more of Roche's security force that I can draw away from his home, the better.*

Then I'll need a small group of your best fighters to enter with me through Roche's front door, which is from the strip-center side. But come well-armed. Roche has men in there ready to fight.

He explained the layout in detail as well as the elevator they could use as needed to get to the factory level. *And I've got Juliet's ability with dreamgliding, so I can scout every location first.*

Fergus detached his telepathy for a few minutes to get his end set up. He returned a moment later. *I reached Keelen. He and five other squad cars are heading to the Fae Cathedral to make some noise like last time. Each is prepared to battle and die, just like you, so don't give me any shit about withdrawing if things get tough.*

Brannick smiled, then wondered why he'd ever thought he was alone in this world. Here was a whole group of men ready to take up arms, and none of them were vampires.

He talked timing over with Fergus, then set his internal clock. In three minutes, he'd meet Fergus and six of his men at the strip-center.

With his plan in place, he left the cottage and headed toward the compound's entrance. He took a moment to speak with Agnes. He explained the situation to her in detail, then asked if she could repair Juliet's dreamglide. Otherwise, Roche could get to her all over again. He knew the sage fae had tremendous power.

Agnes grew very serious. "I'll get in there right away and start taking care of the damage."

Her willingness to jump in and help reminded Brannick once more he was part of a team now.

He went outside to let the guards know he was heading out and hoped to be back soon. He shielded himself with his vampire cloak, then rose into the air and began a slow drift to the southeast. He wouldn't enter Roche's home until Fergus's team was with him.

Once he arrived at Roche's home, he found he could remain upright for a limited amount of time, while moving back and forth into Juliet's dreamglide to check on her. As long as he made it a quick trip, his real-time self remained conscious. He could feel Agnes working her magic as she continued to repair the dreamglide.

Juliet still lay quietly on the couch, but teal flames had appeared on her cheeks. Roche had drugged her.

Brannick had to work hard again to keep his temper in check. Otherwise, he could inadvertently let Roche know he was on his way.

But the knowledge Roche had shot her up with drugs made his blood boil, and it took some doing to suppress his rage.

Hopping back out of Juliet's dreamglide, he levitated above the strip-center, his gaze fixed to the southwest. A few seconds later, Fergus appeared in the distance, flying with six of his warriors. Only the more powerful wolves could take to the air, a real advantage when traveling from one territory to the next, otherwise they could be turned back at any of the five major bridges they intended to cross.

Brannick removed his vampire shield, so that he'd be visible to the wolves.

When they arrived, he led the way to the front walkway of Roche's home until they stood as a group in front of the door. He glanced at each man, then engaged in group telepathy. *Speak mind-to-mind only. We've got sharp ears on us and all kinds of surveillance. Our primary objective is to get Juliet out of there, and once I have her, I'll fly her back to Agnes's compound. But I'll return as fast as I can.*

Right now, I'm going into my dreamglide to find out what's happening inside and where Roche has positioned his men.

All seven warriors nodded, chins lowered, shoulders tense, AR-15s in hand. They were a fierce, tattooed bunch, most with long, wild-looking hair. They moved as a unit, a pack, and were ready to make war.

Brannick let them know he would make a rapid sweep of the house with his dreamglide. Fergus asked if he'd be unconscious, but Brannick assured him he'd recently discovered that if he moved fast, he could remain upright and aware for a limited time.

Fergus lifted his brows. *Shit, that sounds like some power. And very fae.*

Brannick understood his astonishment, that a vampire was holding so much essential fae ability. *I know. Weird for me, too.*

He then entered his dreamglide and moved through Roche's home. Except for Juliet on the couch, the room was empty. But a look into the two main exit points, other than the front door, showed fae security lined up and waiting, about ten in all, just as Brannick had sensed.

When he couldn't locate Roche, he focused on him and the dreamglide sped to his location. He was below in his factory and sending his workers out. Those that left passed a number of security men moving into the factory. Roche was protecting his product first.

Brannick headed back to the house and saw that the security detail hadn't changed position. Brannick went outside and merged with his real-time self. *Six on the left, four will come from the hallway on the right where the elevator is. But be careful, Juliet is in the middle of the room, lying unconscious on a sofa. Ready?*

Fergus smiled. *Hell, yeah.*

Brannick jogged up the front path, opened the door, took three steps inside then crouched. As Fergus and his men moved in behind him, Roche's men appeared, well-armed and ready to fire. But Fergus's team let loose with their automatic rifles, which sent Roche's detail leaping for cover.

As soon as the men disappeared down both halls, Brannick moved swiftly forward and gathered Juliet up in his arms.

The wolves continued to fire at the walls, tearing up the drywall and giving Brannick cover.

Brannick levitated and took Juliet back out into the street and up into the air. She was limp in his arms, but safe, for now.

He flew her back to Agnes at the compound who took charge of her.

Agnes said not to worry, she'd rebuilt Juliet's dreamglide blocks and she'd start her on the blood cleanse right away to get the drug out of her system. She also said that by the appearance of the teal flame markings on her cheeks, Roche hadn't given her anywhere near the same potency he'd used on Mary. Agnes expected Juliet's recovery to be fairly quick.

Brannick let Agnes know what was going on at Roche's house, then headed once more into the air.

~ ~ ~

Juliet came to consciousness and sat up, then put a hand to her head. Oh, God, the pain. "Wow, that's bad."

Agnes rose from a nearby chair. "Your head will hurt for a while. Brannick brought you in about five minutes ago, and I've got you on a drip that will remove the drug from your blood pretty fast."

Juliet's gaze shifted back and forth over her lap as she mentally started piecing together what had happened. "The last thing I remember was Roche blasting through my dreamglide barrier. It smelled so bad."

"He used a dark witch spell. He must have paid a huge price for it, because nothing else could have taken down your dreamglide block. It was as though he'd set explosives to it."

"That's exactly what it looked like." She recalled standing in the cottage near the stairs and feeling the explosion. "You said Brannick brought me here? Because I don't remember anything from the time Roche hijacked me from my dreamglide."

"You were in his home, laid out on the sofa with teal flames on your cheeks."

She put a hand to her face. "Are the markings gone yet?"

"Almost."

She forced herself to think. "I just flew out of your compound, didn't I?"

"That's what my guards tell me."

She leaned back and settled her head against the pillow. Her mind was still swirling because of the drug, and it was hard to focus.

She thought back to standing in the cottage dining area. She'd just gotten dressed in the small downstairs powder room.

She'd been thinking about Brannick of course. They'd had another round of phenomenal sex, and he'd admitted to being at fault.

Yet he'd still abandoned her, even going upstairs to shower.

Then Roche had found her. Was it because she'd been distracted by Brannick?

Or maybe it was the other way around. Perhaps Roche had found her and seized the opportunity to break through her carefully constructed blocks because Brannick was momentarily elsewhere.

Though her mind kept spinning, her intuition seemed to be operating in high gear. She kept her attention focused on Brannick and on their relationship. She loved him, no question about that.

Her next thought frightened her. She knew they'd both been resistant to a relationship in real-time, but what if her own reluctance had created a blind-spot? What if Brannick's resistance had created a similar one?

She opened her eyes and glanced at Agnes. The sage fae stood near the bed, attentive but waiting. Juliet asked, "Are Brannick and his forces attacking Roche's home right now?"

"Yes, but Brannick said he has Fergus and his wolves with him as well as Officer Keelen and some of the Revel Border Patrol at the front of the Fae Cathedral. He's not alone."

Juliet wasn't convinced the size of the support force would matter because her instincts told her Roche wouldn't do most of his damage in real-time.

He'd use his dreamglide.

Juliet squeezed her eyes shut and let the drip continue to work its healing magic on her drug-loaded blood. She needed a clear head right now badly.

She added what healing power she could summon to the mix, which helped forge pathways in her mind, burning off the fog.

But something nagged at her.

Brannick would need her. She wasn't sure why except that he might be over-estimating his new fae abilities or even relying too much on his vampire power and drive.

Alter fae tended to have a lot of back doors, especially in their thinking. They were a tricky species. Devious, even. Roche was a good example of the worst parts of fae ability and behavior.

Juliet looked at Agnes. "Roche isn't done. In fact, I think he's targeted Brannick. It was the reason Roche wanted me unconscious. I need to get over there."

Agnes tilted her head and looked at Juliet's cheeks and neck. "The markings are almost gone. If you give this just a few more minutes, the drug will be out of your system."

Juliet debated for a moment. Her fae instincts told her she was pushing it, but she decided to wait. "As soon as the markings have disappeared, I'll be heading back to Roche's home."

Each territory had medical professionals, though they served in a limited way. Most healing was done through the natural ability of each species. On occasion, however, the assistance of medical support was necessary. In Juliet's case, it definitely speeded up the process for her.

Barely three minutes later, Agnes said the flame marks were gone. She removed the IV, and Juliet slid her legs over the side of the bed and stood up.

Agnes held her gaze. "Is there anything else you need me to do?"

Juliet shook her head. "Nothing. You've taught me well. And now I need to go see about a vampire."

CHAPTER TWELVE

Brannick stayed by the front door and watched Fergus and his wolves battle Roche's men. The walls on either side of the living room were chewed up from gunfire.

He held his vampire cloak secure and drifted yet again into the dreamglide. He circled through the rooms of Roche's home, then dipped down into the factory.

When he returned to real-time, he spoke telepathically to Fergus. *I've done another run of the house. You have three dead in the hall to the left and one to the right, so stay with it.*

Let me tell my men.

Brannick waited while Fergus communicated with the wolves. He and Fergus had already decided not to use group telepathy, which could get confusing in a gun fight.

Fergus took up his position once more, one knee on the floor as he held his AR-15 to his shoulder. He spoke to Brannick. *Did you check out the factory? Will we be able to get in there tonight?*

Negative. Roche has brought in about two dozen of his men. They're crawling through the place, all armed, all prepared to die to protect dark flame.

Fergus's nostrils flared. His nose elongated slightly then returned to normal, evidence of how quickly the shifters could transform. He made a chuffing sound, like a snort but held at the back of the throat. *Not sure I can hold my men back. Do you know how many dead shifter females have been found in the Graveyard, each lit up with flame markings on their bodies? Countless over the years and all because of men like Roche.*

Brannick felt Fergus's frustration. The alpha was a careful leader but passionate, like most wolves, including in battle. He wouldn't want to back down from a chance to destroy Roche's factory. He wasn't sure what he was going to do to prevent him, but he'd think of something. Forming a resistance was the way to go. He felt it in his vampire bones.

He started to address Fergus, but the air around him changed. He blinked because he could see the edges of a dreamglide but from the position of real-time.

What the hell?

And something more.

A dark, familiar chemical odor.

Like witch smoke.

Shit.

Roche was making his move.

He felt his vampire shield disintegrate.

The wolves began another round of automatic gunfire, aiming at both sides of the room. He had to lead Roche away from Fergus and his men. He levitated out of the foyer and into the living room, but was suddenly knocked flat from behind.

He lay on the carpet near the couch, struggling to get up.

Fergus called out. "Brannick, what the fuck are you doing?"

He started to answer, but was suddenly swept into a dreamglide, and not his own. In real-time, he could tell he'd passed out. A dense black smoke with a chemical stench like the one at the cottage surrounded him. With difficulty, he rolled onto his back. He found it hard to breathe.

The smoke began to peel away until Roche was visible, with his red hair and small, feral eyes.

"Having fun, Brannick?"

"Sure. And you?" Brannick tried to sit up, but the spell pinned him to the floor. "I see you're in thick with the dark witches."

Roche crossed his arms over his chest. "Did you really think you had the fae chops to take me on? You're a vampire and what brute strength you possess isn't any good in my domain." He spread his arm through the air, indicating the space around him. His smile was cruel.

Brannick looked around as best he could. He took stock of the situation, but it wasn't good. He was definitely in Roche's dreamglide.

"The moment you and Juliet stole Mary from me, I headed over to Elegance and paid a lot of money for both spells.

"The first one worked brilliantly until you got involved. Fortunately, I had this one as a back-up and it'll keep you right where I want you. There's no escape now, Officer Brannick, and yes, I intend to kill you in the dreamglide and you will be dead in real-time. It doesn't always work that way, but it will by my hands."

The dreamglide began to move.

~ ~ ~

Before Juliet even entered Roche's home, she knew something was wrong. She could feel it.

She tried to contact Brannick telepathically but got no response. The vampire was in trouble.

She tried Fergus next. *I can't reach Brannick.*

Juliet?

I'm here, outside the front door. What's going on?

We've got trouble, he said.

Okay to come in?

Yes. The gun battle is almost over, but something happened to Brannick. He took several steps into the living room, then collapsed. I can see that he's breathing, but I'm pretty sure Roche has him, maybe in a dreamglide. I'm not familiar enough with your fae world to be sure.

Okay. She warned Fergus that she was shielded, then opened the door. *I'm coming in.*

The moment she stepped into the large foyer, she felt the battle fury that circled through the air and kept the Savage warriors revved up.

Fergus, I'm behind you about three feet.

Keep your head down. A couple of Roche's men are still fighting. Don't want you to get hit by a stray bullet.

Juliet dropped into a crouch. From her proximity to the door, she couldn't see Brannick. But she knew she had to get to him.

Her senses told her he was unconscious and lying not far from where Roche had originally shot her up with dark flame.

Roche had him. No question about it.

Sitting on the floor, she slipped into her dreamglide. Before she began her hunt for Brannick, she circled the perimeter of the dream-space. Agnes had completely rebuilt her block, though even stronger than before.

Still, she felt the need to be as quiet as possible. She didn't want anything fae to leak her presence to Roche.

She very carefully attempted to contact Brannick again telepathically. For the moment, she would wait to move her dreamglide.

Brann, I'm here, in Roche's house. Can you hear me?

She listened.

But nothing returned.

Brann?

It was such a complete silence.

Yet, at a vast distance, as though from the earth to the moon, she could feel Brannick in Roche's dreamglide. Despite the faintness of the sensation, she knew he was still somewhere in Roche's home.

Roche hadn't taken Brannick far away at all, though she suspected he'd done it for a reason, possibly using Brannick as bait.

Juliet thought for a moment. Brannick's life was in danger, but she knew her faeness wouldn't be enough to get to him. Rather than call on her fae abilities, she accessed what was direct, bold and very vampire.

She glanced down at her black leathers, made in Brannick's mold. She wasn't just fae anymore, but something else, something more.

She was done thinking the situation through. Action was required.

She contacted Fergus again. *I'm going after Brannick in the dream-world and I'm going in shielded. When you've secured the halls, I'll need you to guard both of us in real-time in case Roche sends more of his men up from the factory. I'll be stretched out beside Brannick near the couch off to the right. You won't be able to see me until I release my shield, but I'll be there. Do you understand?*

Got it.

Can you guard us?

Hell, yeah, we can. Go get our brother.

It was such a bizarre thing to hear a wolf refer to a vampire as his brother. *I will.*

With the gunfire stalled out, Juliet raced across the room and dropped down next to Brannick. All she had to do now was steal her way into Roche's dreamglide without being detected.

Given Roche's level of power, as well as the fact he'd been able to abduct Brannick, she wondered if she had a chance in hell of coming out of this alive.

~ ~ ~

Brannick had heard Juliet call to him telepathically, though her voice had sounded as though she was using a tin can and a string. He knew something else as well, that if he'd responded, Roche would have known that Juliet was in the vicinity. He thanked his fae abilities for the wisdom to keep silent.

But he also knew he was done for and Juliet needed to keep her distance.

Roche had moved the dreamglide out of the living room and took Brannick down the hall to his study. Most of Roche's fae warriors lay dead, the two remaining on this side of the house were hunched over and waiting for Fergus and his men to attack.

Once within the study, Roche had demanded that Brannick contact Juliet to draw her into his web, but Brannick had refused.

Roche had never stopped moving from the time he'd brought Brannick into his dreamglide. He walked in a slow circle around Brannick. He could feel the witch's spell tightening the invisible binds on him. Roche murmured something incomprehensible, probably part of the be-spelling process. The stench around Roche's dreamglide had become thick and nauseating.

When Roche arrived back at his starting point, Brannick could no longer even move his head. He was frozen in place.

"So here we are." Roche smiled. "Tell me, Officer, how long have you been screwing Juliet in the dreamglide?"

"None of your fucking business." He could move his lips but just barely. He felt as though he had steel cables around different parts of his body, including his head, anchoring him to the floor of the dreamglide.

Roche moved to a side table and pulled open a draw. The long dagger he took out told Brannick exactly what Roche intended his fate to be.

His life didn't flash before his eyes, but his time with Juliet did. In a swift movie-like flow, he saw her from the beginning at the White Flame club then in all the conversations they'd shared in the dreamglide as well as each time they'd made love. He thought the collected images poetic because of Juliet and her style, the flow of her dresses and skirts, the wild nature of her hair and the way her dark blue eyes glimmered when he was with her.

He loved the woman and wished more than anything his time with her wouldn't end. He felt like he'd just gotten started.

Suddenly, her voice was in his head again. *I'm here Brann, inside Roche's dreamglide, cloaked like a vampire. But don't look around and try to find me. Roche is focused completely on you and on holding the spell.*

The sound of Juliet's voice within his mind invaded his chest, warming him as it always had. *You're saying Roche doesn't know you're here?*

Not even a little.

Fear rushed at him at what Roche would do to her if he caught her in his dreamglide. *Juliet, you should leave now, before he kills you as well.*

Not going anywhere, vampire, so get used to it. We're partners, remember?

Roche moved to stand next to him. He flipped the dagger, catching it in his hand. "I'll give you one last chance to bring Juliet to me or tonight you breathe your last."

Brannick smiled, one of the few movements he could make given the spell. "Fuck you, Roche. You and all your kind."

Roche's red brows rose. "You mean fae?" he asked sarcastically. "But I thought you had a thing for Juliet?"

"I wasn't referring to fae, but to you and your scum-sucking, drugged out cronies. May you all rot in hell."

"You first." Roche slowly lifted the dagger high overhead, his lips pulled back in a vicious grin, teeth bared.

Brannick had no idea what Juliet planned to do, but he wasn't surprised when she shot at Roche from the side, stretched out in a horizontal levitation just like at the sex club.

When she struck, Roche flew sideways through the air. He lost control of the dagger, hit the blurred wall and fell to the floor.

Brannick felt the spell give way a little. He could move his legs sideways and lift his head and neck. But his chest was still bound tight. If she continued battling Roche, he might be able to work himself free.

He kept his gaze anywhere but on Juliet, hoping to keep Roche from figuring out where she was.

But Roche took a moment, waved his hand, then smiled. He'd removed her vampire shield and could see her now.

She went after him again, feet first, speeding toward him.

But Roche stood upright and with a flip of his hands sent her spiraling.

Brannick thought she was done for, but to his amazement, she caught and righted herself midair. She had a fervor in her eyes he'd never seen before. She looked almost wild. Her hair had come undone so that as she moved, her long curls flew about in a torrential mass.

She came after Roche, feigning a punch with her right fist. He ducked, but she brought her leg up in a hard kick. Roche was unprepared and flew against the desk.

She chased him down, feet first again and punched him in the back. Brannick heard a solid crack, ribs or spine, maybe.

Roche groaned heavily and slid to the floor.

Brannick felt the band on his chest loosen a little and his legs were now completely free as was his right arm. The dagger wasn't far but he still couldn't reach it. If he could get to it, one careful throw and Roche would be finished for good.

He watched Juliet prepare for another attack. She moved to the far corner to gain distance in order to pick up speed. She catapulted herself in his direction.

But at the last moment, Roche whipped out of the way. Her momentum caused her to flip over as she righted herself. Roche levitated and caught her from behind in a chokehold.

Brannick's muscles flexed in his arms and legs. He needed to get to her, to help her.

But Juliet wasn't done. She held onto Roche's arms, using the leverage to kick backwards at him. Unfortunately, she couldn't connect. Roche was bigger and stronger. He simply held her upright, off her feet and let her flail.

Roche stared at Brannick smiling.

Brannick had to do something.

Fergus.

Of course. Brannick wasn't sure if he could pull it off, but he would sure as hell try. He focused on the wolf and contacted him telepathically. *Fergus, we need help in Roche's dreamglide. Now.*

Two seconds passed, then Fergus's sawdust voice broke through. *Beam me up.*

His choice of words almost made Brannick smile.

The next moment, Fergus arrived, gun in hand. But Roche saw him. "I'll snap her neck, wolf."

Brannick knew there was one more thing he could do. *Fergus, listen to me. I'm going to use my vampire shield and wrap you up. The moment you determine that Roche has lost track of you, take him out. And remember, what he wants most from this situation is Juliet. He won't kill her unless he has to. He also has the power to remove the cloak, so it won't protect you long, but it may give you just enough time to get the job done.*

Got it. Aloud, Fergus addressed Roche. "Don't hurt her. I'll do whatever you say. Just please don't hurt Juliet." For effect, he lowered his gun to the floor.

His placating tone didn't fool Brannick, but Roche's shoulders started to ease down. Good. They had a chance.

To Fergus, he said, *Here it comes.* He then used his vampire cloak and covered Fergus.

"Where the fuck did you go?" Roche added a whole string of obscenities. He waved his hand, but nothing happened to the cloak this time.

At first, Brannick didn't understand why until he realized the witch's spell was already breaking up, which meant Fergus could take him down.

Brannick watched Fergus pick the dagger up from the floor, then race toward Roche. He carved a long groove down Roche's forearm.

Roche screamed. The pain forced him to release Juliet. She lurched sideways, holding her throat, struggling for air.

Roche fell to the floor, grabbing his arm. Fergus didn't hold back. He kicked Roche's jaw. Roche flew backward, his head hitting the edge of a cupboard. He sank to the floor.

With Roche unconscious, the spell dissipated and Brannick was finally free. Even the stench had left the space.

He rose to his feet, intending to go to Juliet, but suddenly, Roche leaped onto his back. Brannick knew he needed to be all vampire right now. He threw his elbow back and heard the crunch of a couple of Roche's ribs.

When Roche staggered backward, but remained upright, Brannick turned toward him and summoned his physical strength. He sent every bit of energy he had into his right fist, closed the distance between himself and Roche, then plowed into Roche's chin.

His head snapped back and Brannick heard another crunch of bone. A broken neck this time. Roche fell backward and landed on the floor. His eyes were open, but the pupils were fully dilated. Blood trickled from his nose.

At almost the same moment, the dreamglide vanished and Brannick came back to himself on the living room floor.

The dissipation of the dreamglide was a sure sign Roche was dead.

In real-time, Brannick remained on the floor with Juliet next to him. He made sure she stayed prone. He listened for more gunfire, but the battle appeared to be over.

Fergus wasn't far. He gained his feet first. "My wolves are scouring each room. Looks like Roche's men are all dead."

Brannick rose, then turned in a slow circle, giving the space a careful visual check.

Fergus moved in the direction of the hall. "I'll check out the study. I want to make sure that bastard really is gone."

When Fergus disappeared through the doorway, Juliet gained her feet as well. "There's no question. Roche is dead."

"I know." Brannick marveled at what he could intuit. He felt Roche's death as though it had been imprinted on his mind.

Fergus returned a minute later. "He's not breathing, no heartbeat, nothing. He's gone."

Brannick took Juliet's hand. She squeezed his in return. They'd done it. Together, and with Fergus's help, they'd taken the monster down.

Fergus glanced around. "So how do you want this to go?"

But it was Juliet who said, "We're done here. Put all the bodies in the elevator with Roche on top, then send it down to the factory floor. That'll be enough of a message for tonight."

Fergus scowled. "Wait a minute. We can't stop now. We could take the factory. Bring Keelen and his troops over here. I know we could do it. I'll call in my pack from Savage."

Brannick turned to him. "And declare war against the cartels? Because that's what we'd be doing."

Fergus met his gaze. "Isn't that what we're already doing, by taking out Roche and his men?"

Brannick shook his head slowly. "Roche was always a wild card with the cartels. They won't mind changing him out for a factory manager they can better control and they'll get to keep his hefty percentage. We can leak the story about Roche's obsession with Juliet, that her kidnapping was the only reason for the attack in his home. Once she was safe, the battle ended."

Fergus ground his jaw a couple of times and made a wolfish grunting sound only the shifters could do. After a few minutes, his nostrils flared. "You're right. Because if we destroyed the drug supply, which is where the cartels make their money, it would mean a bloodbath afterward unlike anything Five Bridges has ever seen."

Brannick met and held his gaze. "We're alive, brother. We've survived and we will fight another day."

"Damn straight." He shifted his gaze to Juliet. "We'll do as you've said." He then ordered his wolves to haul Roche and his men to the elevator.

But when they brought the first body through, Brannick leaned down to Juliet. "We should leave. You don't need to see this."

Juliet held his gaze firmly, and he saw her determination. "I know what's coming, Brann, and I need to get used to this. We might not be at war tonight, but at some point, it will happen."

~ ~ ~

As Juliet reverted her attention to the bodies being taken to the elevator, she spoke quiet prayers within her mind. Roche was last, his red hair dragging on the floor, face white, eyes open and blank. He'd caused so much pain and terrible suffering, but now he was dead. She wanted to rejoice, but that's not what she felt.

Instead, she saw a man who had once been someone's infant child, a spirit to be loved and shaped. Yet somehow that life had gone horribly wrong. Maybe he'd been born with the inability to feel remorse about anything. Or perhaps he'd been tortured and abused as a child. She would never know. But the *alter* experience had turned him into a monster, adding enormous power to his already twisted mind.

And now the monster was dead.

Brannick squeezed her waist and spoke quietly. "Just heard from Keelen. The Revel Border Patrol chief showed up and sent Keelen and his men away. He also ordered several units out here onto the street."

Juliet's brows rose. "You mean in front of the strip center?"

He nodded.

"Okay. Then we'd better get out of here."

When Brannick heard the elevator begin its descent, he summoned Fergus and his men and explained the situation.

Juliet looked up at him. "Let me check to see what we're facing."

"I'll hold you tight 'til you get back."

With Brannick's arms around her, Juliet slipped into the dreamglide, drifted to the front walk, then hurried back. "There are three Revel Border Patrol SUVs out front in the parking lot but a good thirty yards away. Several officers have weapons drawn, but they're staying behind the open doors of their vehicles."

Brannick addressed the group. "We'll go out together and I'll shield us. Agreed?"

The wolves assented.

When Juliet knew that Brannick had wrapped everyone up in his vampire shield, her heartrate began to climb. If this didn't work, they could all get killed.

They moved together to the front entry. Brannick had everyone line up off to the side just in case the moment he opened the door, the officers started firing.

When they were all in position, she nodded to Brannick. He moved to the door, gave it a shove, then levitated back in place out of harm's way.

As she waited, her heart pounded in her ears. But no gunfire returned. Instead, she heard an officer call out, "Steady. Wait 'til we see who comes out. We don't want Roche killed."

She could barely breathe.

Brannick once more invoked group telepathy. *Levitate just above the floor so we don't make a sound, and stick close.*

Glancing at the wolves, she saw that each one had a determined look in his eye. Brannick led the way outside. She followed, careful to levitate but not so high as to hit the upper doorframe.

Surveying the border patrol, she realized none of the officers saw them.

The lead officer called out again. "Steady, men. Hold your fire."

Brannick's voice hit the group telepathy once more. *We'll rise slowly together on three. Again, I've got you all shielded, but stay close. We'll fly straight up about thirty feet, I'll call a halt, then we'll turn to the northeast and head out over the Graveyard. On three … two … one …*

Juliet levitated alongside Brannick as did the wolves. Once high in the air, he drew everyone to a stop well above the strip center. Glancing below, she saw that the Revel Border Patrol remained in position, still waiting for someone to come out of the house.

Brannick had done his job.

He lifted his arm and let it fall in the direction he wanted the group to move. As soon as he took off, Juliet stuck right with him as did Fergus and his men.

When they were at least two miles away from the front of Roche's home and well over the Graveyard, Brannick called another halt. "I'm going to remove my shield now."

As Brannick released it, Juliet once again felt his vampire cloak slide away from her.

Silence reigned for a few moments. Everyone exchanged glances. She felt the shifters' energy rise, which seemed to ignite her own. Smiles emerged and eyes glittered.

The first whoop hit the air, then another and another. Though levitating, the men lifted their fists and kept shouting. They'd all made it out alive and Roche, that bastard, was dead.

Juliet joined in, adding her very female voice to the mix.

Brannick, however, soon tamped down the celebration, but he was smiling. "You know someone will hear us. How about we take this to the White Flame and finish our celebration there. I for one could use a Goddamn righteous drink."

Wolves, being gregarious by nature, expressed their approval with more raised fists and another round of shouts.

To Brannick's credit. He didn't try to stop them. He merely set the example and flew east toward the club.

Fergus settled the most important matter with his men as he called out. *I'm buying the first round.*

The White Flame had a back room Brannick reserved for the impromptu celebration. Of course, it was near dawn, so the club had emptied of most of its night-loving creatures, especially those who couldn't speed home with a quick levitating dash to avoid the sunrise.

Standing beside Brannick, Juliet almost took his hand, then decided not to. They'd been through an awful lot over the past few hours and had survived an impossible situation. But she needed to remind herself that though he'd made love to her, he'd also done his usual and left her abruptly. He might have owned up to his part in initiating the lovemaking, but he was still conflicted.

Besides, more than anything, she needed to respect their partnership and not to do anything that would put it in jeopardy. Working toward a better world was far more important than anything else right now.

~ ~ ~

Brannick held a mug of beer in his hand, as did the entire team. He'd loved working with Fergus and his men as well as with Juliet. Everything felt new to him, and his spirit was lighter than it had been since he'd come to Five Bridges.

He slid his arm around Juliet, but he felt her stiffen next to him. She didn't exactly pull away, but he could feel how uneasy she was.

As the server passed around another tray of beers, Brannick leaned close to her and whispered, "Is everything okay?" His fae senses told him she had her guard up, and not without reason.

She turned into him, avoiding eye contact. "Of course."

He had a lot he wanted to say to her, but now was not the time. "We need to talk."

She lifted her chin slightly and this time met his gaze. "I'm always willing to engage in conversation with you. You're my partner."

He couldn't help but smile as he held her gaze. "Talking is good." He felt devilish. "So is something else I can think of."

A startled expression flashed in her eyes. "Brannick, I can't do this." He saw the flush on her cheeks, and he felt the depth of her fear.

He got it. How many times had he made love to her in real-time then left her alone? The last time he'd made his escape, Roche had hijacked her from her dreamglide. She had reason to be wary of him.

He also knew how she felt about him, which prompted him to drop down and kiss her on the lips. *I'm not at all satisfied with our partnership. We have a few details to hammer out.*

This time, she frowned. *What do you mean?*

He feigned innocence. *Just as I said, we need to talk.*

Brannick, what are you saying?

Sensing her exasperation, he turned toward her more fully. *Let me be more direct, when we get back to the cottage, we're going to talk about everything and get things settled between us once and for all.*

She blinked several times. *What things?*

He smiled again, and took a swig of his beer. *Just things.*

Okay, now you're getting on my nerves.

I plan to get on a lot more than that.

He didn't wait for her to respond, but turned his attention to the wolves. He lifted his mug. "To Fergus and the brave warriors of Savage. We got the bastard!"

The cheer that went up was a roar no doubt heard several streets over in every direction. A couple of the wolves even howled.

When Brannick had taken his revenge during the first few weeks of his arrival in Five Bridges, he'd been alone. More than that, he'd been warned repeatedly by some of his fellow officers that he couldn't kill off high level cartel members without repercussion.

He hadn't listened to them. He'd been wild with grief and uncontrolled.

And … alone.

What had happened tonight, however, had been different in every possible respect, even down to letting the corrupt chief of the Revel Border Patrol take possession of Roche's factory. If Brannick had let Fergus have his way and they'd destroyed the dark flame factory, the cartels would have retaliated.

But now Brannick and Juliet could move forward in secret and begin a slow, progressive assault on the fae underworld. The first order of business would be shutting down Roche's club. Of course it was possible with Roche gone, the club might lose its clientele all on its own. Either way, Brannick would do everything he could to rescue the women involved.

He would include Fergus, if the wolf wanted to join in. But Fergus had already mentioned that there were a few heinous institutions in Savage that needed a correction or two. Brannick thought it likely Fergus intended to start cleaning house as well.

After the last beer was consumed, Fergus sent his men home, since wolves were nocturnal as well and dawn was coming. He didn't go with them, however. Instead, he asked to accompany Brannick and Juliet back to Agnes's compound.

Brannick wasn't certain why the wolf had insisted on coming with them. But he wasn't about to refuse the man who had not only helped to bring Roche down, but who had saved his ass in Roche's dreamglide.

As soon as Brannick touched down in front of Agnes's compound, he turned to bid Fergus goodnight. One look at the flaring of Fergus' nostrils, told him something else was going on. He just didn't know what.

Juliet, however, had more of a clue. She drew Fergus apart from the guards at the front entrance and spoke in a low voice. "Do you want to know about Mary?"

Fergus's lips drew into a tight line as he nodded.

Brannick should have guessed, but it still seemed unusual.

Juliet smiled softly. "Mary is recovering extremely well, though given the amount of dark flame in her system, it put her into a tough recovery process. Otherwise, she's in very good spirits."

When Fergus glanced at the guards at the exterior of the building, Juliet added, "For my sake and Mary's, Agnes has doubled security on the roof and around the entire exterior of the compound. She also added several snipers to the tops of the surrounding buildings. Mary couldn't be safer."

"Good. That's good. I've been concerned. Roche isn't a threat anymore, but there are a lot of forces at work."

"You're absolutely right."

Brannick caught a strong scent of wolf musk, a reminder Fergus was entering his annual mate-hunting cycle. It was also clear that whatever was going on with the shifter, it wasn't simple.

Fergus planted his hands on his hips and kept nodding long after Juliet stopped talking. He glanced in the direction of the front door to the compound, his brow heavily furrowed. "Please tell Mary that I asked about her."

He nodded a couple more times and after meeting Juliet's gaze, then Brannick's, he said, "I'll bid goodnight to you both." With that, he turned on his heel, took a few steps, then shot into the air.

Two weeks ago, Brannick would have thought the man crazy for sniffing around a fae woman. But not tonight. Not anymore.

When he entered the compound, he saw Mary had come to the front entrance area. She was thinner than before the abduction. "Was that Officer Fergus?"

Juliet went to her and took her arm. "Yes, and he was asking about your recovery."

"I wanted to thank him for getting me out of Roche's prison."

Brannick remained where he was and let Juliet walk Mary back to her room by herself. He heard Juliet's soft, melodious voice as she no doubt shared the events at Roche's home and the part Fergus played.

He was glad she'd gone with Mary, since he needed to think about what he should say to her once she returned. He hadn't shared his heart with anyone since his arrival in Five Bridges, not in thirteen years.

It was about damn time.

After a few minutes, Juliet appeared at the end of the hall. She moved toward him slowly but his faeness could once again tell how guarded she was. He didn't blame her.

When she drew close, he smiled then took her hand. He'd half expected her to pull away, but she didn't. As he walked her to the cottage, she looked up at him once or twice. He squeezed her hand each time, but didn't say anything. He wanted privacy for what he was about to say.

Once inside the cottage, he closed the door and before a word was spoken, he drew her into his arms and kissed her. He could feel her hesitation and that she held back, but he kept on kissing her, savoring her the way he'd done for five months in her dreamglide, only now it was in real-time.

Brann, you seem different or am I imagining it?

He drew back, but didn't let her go. His heart kicked up a couple of heavy beats. How could he have thought, for even a moment, that he could live without this woman?

"Brann, you've got me really worried. What's going on?" She laid her hands on his chest, her brow as furrowed as his normally was.

He thought for a moment, because he wanted to get this right. He decided to speak his heart straight out. "I'm in love with you, Juliet."

Her lips parted and a soft gasp emerged. "What?"

He smiled. "I love you. I think I have from the time you sat across from me at the White Flame. You were so earnest and so damn beautiful, with your wild hair and dark blue eyes."

"You love me." It was a statement, but a shaky breath followed.

"I do." He petted her hair, enjoying the feel of her soft, out-of-control curls. "And I'm done blaming you for the dreamglide. Because you broke the law, I can stand here now and be with you. I wouldn't have otherwise. I would never have asked you out and I would have ensured that I kept my distance.

"Leaving you last week, however, became a death I knew I'd have to endure over and over for the rest of my life. I thought I was prepared to return to my solitary existence, until you showed up wearing a purple fringe and black leather. You took my soul by storm." He slid his hand beneath her chin and kissed her. "I love you, Juliet, with all my heart."

~ ~ ~

Juliet stared into Brann's beautiful, green eyes. Even the line between his brows had eased. The fae part of her kept absorbing the phenomenal change in Brann. This was not the man who'd left her after they'd made love earlier in the cottage living room. He was no longer conflicted. In fact, what she felt most was that the man in front of her was exactly like the man she'd made love to in the dreamglide.

They were one-in-the same now.

And she was free to love him as much as she wanted.

She smiled. She caressed his face and kissed him in return. Her heart felt swollen with an abundance of affection. "I love you, too. So much." Tears brimmed in her eyes. "You mean everything to me. And like you, I'd never expected to have love in my life again. I didn't think it was possible here in Five Bridges.

"When you responded to me the way you did the very first time I took you into my dreamglide, I was hooked. You were the man for me, even though I lived in denial all that time."

He searched her eyes. "So, we'll be together, you and me?"

"From this night forward."

An odd light entered his eye. "Will you marry me, Juliet, despite the fact that I'm a stubborn vampire?"

"Oh, yes." The kiss that followed led Brann to pick her up and take her upstairs. He spent the next several hours, well past dawn, making love to her, speaking his love in his wonderful, deep voice, and promising to make every night special for her.

Several times, she enjoyed him in a combination of dreamglide and real-time that had her crying out over and over again with pleasure.

She didn't know when they'd be able to return to her canal home. Maybe never. They were marked now, on the various cartels' radar. But she knew how methodical Brannick could be and how his rescue tunnel system had operated for years with no one the wiser.

He held her in his arms and talked about the future, about each of the cartels and the various men and a few women who aided the drug organizations. She knew they would have to be extremely careful and in many ways disappear from the world in order to forge a resistance operation that could eventually overthrow the ruling evil of their world.

But time was the one thing each of them had in their long-lived *alter* world. What had been stripped from her when she'd unknowingly taken the fae *alter* serum, hidden inside a dark flame potion, had been given back in just how long their lives could be.

She fell asleep cradled in his arms, held secure in her dreams. More than once she felt him pull her close, awakening her enough to savor the warmth of his embrace. Her heart swelled each time, at the comfort of his touch, his presence in her bed, and the way he professed his love against her ear, whispering to her in his half-sleep.

There was work to be done in Five Bridges, of renewing a land lost to its darkest elements. But now Brann was with her and what had seemed so impossible, became filled with light, hope and the promise of a future full of love.

EMBRACE THE POWER is coming in the Spring of 2016!

THANK YOU!

Thank you for reading DARK FLAME! Authors rely on readers more than ever to share the word. Here are some things you can do to help!

Stay connected through my newsletter! You'll always have the latest releases and coolest contests! Sign up here: http://www.carisroane.com/contact-2/

Leave a review! Reviews help your favorite authors to become visible to the digital reader. So, anytime you feel moved by a story, leave a short review at your favorite online retailer. And you don't have to be a blogger to do this, just a reader who loves books!

Enter my latest contest! I run contests all the time so be sure to check out my contest page today! Enter here: http://www.carisroane.com/contests/

Do you love cocktails!?! Caris has been working with the awesome paranormal romance writing duo, Trim and Julka, who have developed a series of Flame Drinks that correspond to each of the Flame books. You can find these specialty cocktails and their recipes at: http://www.trimandjulka.com/flame-drinks/ Please remember: Don't drink and drive and don't light these drinks on fire! Enjoy!

LIST OF BOOKS

To read more about each one, check out my books page: http://www.carisroane.com/books/

The Flame Series...

BLOOD FLAME
AMETHYST FLAME

The Blood Rose Series...

BLOOD ROSE SERIES BOX SET, featuring Book #1 EMBRACE THE DARK, Book #2 EMBRACE THE MAGIC, and Book #3 EMBRACE THE MYSTERY
EMBRACE THE DARK #1
EMBRACE THE MAGIC #2
EMBRACE THE MYSTERY #3
EMBRACE THE PASSION #4
EMBRACE THE NIGHT #5
EMBRACE THE WILD #6
EMBRACE THE WIND #7
EMBRACE THE HUNT #8
LOVE IN THE FORTRESS #8.1 (A companion book to EMBRACE THE HUNT)
BLOOD ROSE TALES BOX SET

Guardians of Ascension Series...

VAMPIRE COLLECTION (Includes BRINK OF ETERNITY)
THE DARKENING
RAPTURE'S EDGE – 1 – AWAKENING
RAPTURE'S EDGE – 2 – VEILED

Amulet Series...

WICKED NIGHT/DARK NIGHT

Now Available: Book 4 of the Flame Series – AMBER FLAME – featuring Officer Fergus, the first of three wolf heroes from Savage Territory! http://www.carisroane.com/amber-flame-4/

Also, now Available: EMBRACE THE HUNT, Book 8 of the Blood Rose Series

A powerful vampire warrior. A beautiful fae of great ability. A war that threatens to destroy their love for the second time…

Find out more about EMBRACE THE HUNT: http://www.carisroane.com/8-embrace-the-hunt/

Coming Soon/Fall of 2015: EMBRACE THE POWER, the final installment of the Blood Rose Series! Find out more about EMBRACE THE POWER! http://www.carisroane.com/9-embrace-the-power/

ABOUT THE AUTHOR

Caris Roane is the New York Times bestselling author of thirty-two paranormal romance books. Writing as Valerie King, she has published fifty novels and novellas in Regency Romance. Caris lives in Phoenix, Arizona, loves gardening, enjoys the birds and lizards in her yard, but really doesn't like scorpions!

Find out more about Caris on her website!

http://www.carisroane.com/

CPSIA information can be obtained
at www.ICGtesting.com
Printed in the USA
FSOW02n1301101116
27232FS

9 781530 231553